MW00790791

"A tightly [ ] procedure and a vivi[ ] background make *End of the Line* superior entertainment."
—Bill Pronzini

"For those readers who enjoy police procedurals and others who just enjoy good books ... the combined Hitchens is recommended."
—William F. Deeck, *Mystery*File*

"[The Hitchens] wrote entertaining police procedurals that were also good mysteries and above all entertaining reads."
—David Vineyard

"Before McBain's first 87th Precinct novel, the Hitchenses anticipated his concept of a series of cop novels featuring a 'corporate hero.' And, in fact, they brought it to fuller fruition."
—Jim Doherty, *Rara-avis*

End of the Line
Bert & Dolores Hitchens

Black Gat Books • Eureka California

END OF THE LINE

Published by Black Gat Books
A division of Stark House Press
1315 H Street
Eureka, CA 95501, USA
griffinskye3@sbcglobal.net
www.starkhousepress.com

END OF THE LINE
Originally published 1957 by Doubleday & Co., New
York, and copyright © 1957 by Hubert and Dolores
Hitchens; reprinted in paperback by Pocket Books,
1958. Copyright renewed January 4, 1985, by Patricia
Johnson & Michael J. Hitchens.

ISBN-13: 978-1-944520-57-1

Book design by Mark Shepard, SHEPGRAPHICS.COM
Cover art by Barye Phillips from *Die Gelbe Flagge* as
published by Ullstein Bücher

First Stark House Press/Black Gat Edition:
November 2018

FIRST EDITION

Like a silver eel the streamliner rose from the flats of the dusky desert, skirting the toes of the wrinkled hills, sweeping upward into the clear green twilight in the pass. Thunder followed it under the ground and a wind rushed outward at its passing. Lizards and cactus owls and a few jackrabbits froze at the vast vibration and waited for catastrophe to follow. In the cab the engineer looked at his watch. In less than two hours they should be in Los Angeles.

Ahead lay Lobo Tunnel.

At this moment in the life of the train a porter carrying a wet towel was running in one of the corridors. A conductor stood biting his lips, knuckles lifted to rap at a compartment door. Against a window a man crouched peering at his hands, horror-stricken, as if his world had just gone mad. For these Lobo Tunnel was to mean reprieve, and oblivion, and opportunity.

At the last instant, as the train swept into the tunnel entrance, the engineer stiffened, his lips parted, and he reached for the brakes. It was too late.

On sixty-four wheels Death roared into Lobo Tunnel, and made a noise that men would hear for years.

1.

John Farrel rolled over in bed and opened his eyes. For a moment or so his gaze was blank and confused, with a quality of unwilling inward searching, as if perhaps he evaluated his ability to face unpleasant news. Then his glance settled on a pair of dark blue socks hung on the arm of a rocking chair not more than five feet from the bed. The socks had at some previous hour been washed,

wrung out and laid to dry; and still held the wrinkles left
from laundering. With these as anchor, Farrel's gaze skir-
mished other parts of the room, seeking familiar things.
The dresser with its ticking clock, the sparse array of toilet
things; the open closet, his three suits, shirts tossed on
hangers, shoes on the floor. The table by the window,
piled with books and magazines. As these sights sunk in
the look of confusion and dread drained away. Farrel
swung his big, heavily built body erect and put his feet on
the floor, sucked in a breath, rubbed his palms across his
thinning hair.

A new day. Get hold of it, he told himself. Face it. What's
the matter with you? You're acting like a bum. Downstairs he could hear Mrs. Bellows in the kitchen getting
breakfast. Pretty soon she'd be rapping on the wall. The
morning sun was bright behind the blinds.

He stood up, forced himself to stretch, to breathe deeply.
There was a split in the knee of his pajamas and half the
buttons were missing from the jacket. He shucked the
garments, kicked them towards the closet and went into
the small, dim, adjoining bathroom. Mrs. Bellows rapped
on the wall downstairs but by now Farrel had the shower
running. He came back toweling himself, scooped shaving
stuff from the dresser, returned to squint at his graying
whiskers in the spotty mirror over the basin. Someone
rattled the door in the opposite wall, and Farrel growled,
"Hold your horses. I'll be out in a minute." He proceeded
to shave.

The occupant of the room which adjoined the other
side of the bathroom was a ministerial student named
Haines. He was young and quite earnest. His presence
among the other roomers at Mrs. Bellows's place puzzled
Farrel considerably. Mrs. Bellows was a shrewd, practical
and hardheaded little woman, the widow of a railroad
brakeman. Her boarders, until now, had all been railroad

men, some of them pretty easygoing. Farrel had almost come to the conclusion that she expected Haines to exert a refining influence, which would of course be an indication of softening of the brain.

When Farrel finished shaving he released the latch on the door to Haines's room and, giving the other door a big slam to let Haines know he was leaving, went to the closet to dress. Knotting his tie before the mirror, he thought sourly that his suit and his twice-worn shirt looked tired; and a feeling of let-down seeped through him, followed by a spurt of rebellion. To hell with it. If Ryerson needed male fashion plates for investigators, let him hire a bunch of chorus boys.

He took the snub-nosed Colt detective .38 special from the top drawer, slid it without inspection into the holster on his hip, flattened his coat over it. He listened to the shower running, walked towards the hall door, then paused. He came back, opened the bottom dresser drawer. In a nest formed by clothes and miscellaneous papers lay two whiskey bottles. One was much fuller than the other. Farrel took them both out and set them on the dresser. He emptied one into the other, screwed on both caps, returned the full bottle to the drawer and jammed the drawer shut with his shoe. Again he paused to listen to the shower, then went out quickly to the hall, walked to Haines's door and tested it. The door was not locked. Farrel stepped in over the sill, the empty fifth swinging in his fingers, and glanced around. The ministerial student had made no changes except to hang a couple of religious mottoes on the wall and tack a towel rack beside the dresser. The room was as tidy and barren as it had been when Mrs. Bellows had cleaned it up from its last tenant, a young patrolman who had left to get married. To Farrel there was something monastic in its neatness.

Farrel squatted beside the bed, thrust the empty bottle

along the floor against the headboard. Mrs. Bellows was a fanatical dust-hunter.

Five minutes later, at the table in a nook off the kitchen, Mrs. Bellows served a bit of hopeful praise for Haines along with the flapjacks. Two others who were eating, men younger than Farrel, nodded in indifferent agreement. Farrel merely looked wise.

She caught it, though, and considered it an argument. She leaned towards him from the stove, the pancake turner wagging in her hand. "You'll see, Mr. Farrel. He's next to you up there. You'll find out what a nice boy he is. The day will come when you'll change your mind."

"Now that'll be something," Farrel said, spreading butter.

Across town on the sixth floor of a modern apartment house, in a tiny kitchenette, a young man named Calvin Saunders was peering into a percolator, trying to judge its contents against the needs of breakfast. He was tall and well built. He had serious, attentive eyes. He wore a terry-cloth dressing gown over blue silk pajamas; both of these had been his mother's choice. His mother would have known to a drop how much coffee remained in the percolator, but she would have dumped this concoction of last night and made a new batch for breakfast. There was both a trace of unaccustomed freedom and of stubbornness in Saunders's appraisal of the inside of the pot. In the end he carefully measured the contents in a cup, decided the amount would suffice with a little dilution, put the coffee back into the pot and added a shot of water from the sink, and set it on the stove to heat.

He debated over the eggs; then with an air of accomplishing a novelty, scrambled them with cream; made toast; sat down to eat. In the middle of the meal he jumped up and headed for a cupboard, took down a pottery jug, very small, and brought it to the table. The label indicated a tropical fruit mixture. Saunders prized up the lid with a knife and spread the compote on his toast. The jug had sat in the cupboard for more than a year, waiting some special day, his mother had never said which. But this was it.

When he had finished he added the dishes to others already in the sink, wiped his hands on the tea towel and went into the bedroom. He contemplated his wardrobe. There had been almost two dozen white shirts in the lower drawers of the chest, fresh from the laundry. Now most were wadded into the hamper in the bathroom, and the drawers were practically empty. He inspected the few remaining, shook his head over them, and still with the air of guarding some new freedom, chose a colored sport shirt from the closet.

Before he put on his coat he slid the Smith & Wesson .38 police positive into his belt holster and put an extra clip in his pocket. All dressed, he looked around for his hat. His mother had always stood at the door for his departure, his hat in her hand. He missed her in this moment, a funny pang.

In the hall, his neighbor from the next apartment had just pressed a gloved finger on the elevator button. She was a slim, well-made kind of girl, Saunders thought. Brown hair of which he approved because there was nothing fuzzy or done-up about it. Good smile, good teeth, good legs. Her name was Betsy Halloran. Now she was looking Saunders over as if in some mysterious way she had taken charge of him. "Apricot," she decided.

"Hmmm?" he said blankly.

"On your chin."

He took out his handkerchief and got rid of the compote.

"What are you doing these days?" she asked next.

"Same as usual."

"Cops and robbers?"

He smiled slightly. "How are the cadavers?" He put away the handkerchief. "Tagging any stray arms or legs?"

"You know I don't do that."

"Medical librarian. You must file things. Like parts of people."

"Where are you eating now?" she demanded abruptly. "What I mean—well—speaking of legs, I have a leg of lamb. Mamie, that's my sister in Pasadena, she's coming by around three o'clock and she's promised to put it in the oven for me. If you like lamb—"

"I always keep my distance with the neighbors," he decided. "It prevents gossip and other unpleasantness."

"Your mother likes me."

"You took poor Mother in."

A frosty look crossed her face. The elevator swooshed into place on the other side of the double doors; the doors automatically opened to show the neat, empty interior. Betsy stepped in.

Her eyes were kind of greenish, Saunders thought, a point he hadn't exactly noticed before. "On second thought, well, since you insist—"

"I thought so." She gave him a stare as the elevator started to drop. "If you come, you may furnish the martinis. At seven."

"Nothing doing. Wait'll you taste my popskull."

"Martinis!"

"Popskull. Makes everything go *z-z-z-z-z-z-z!*"

"No wonder your mother went away for a vacation!" Head up, she marched off through the lobby, knowing she'd won. Saunders hopped down the short flight of stairs to the lower-level garage, took out his keys, jockeyed the green Chevvie convertible from its stall and drove out into the street. The sun was golden. A swell day, he thought; a dandy day if you didn't have to work. He thought of the fun to be had at the beach, and had a sudden vivid idea of how Betsy might look in a bathing suit, jumping around in the surf.

He waved to Betsy in passing. She was on the corner, waiting for the bus to Beverly Hills, where she worked for a bunch of doctors. She didn't wave back. Her attractively shaped mouth formed the word *martinis* at him. He widened his eyes, pretending not to get it. Then he was past the corner, headed for downtown L.A., for the big building on the fringe of skid row where the railroad had its offices.

The office of the Special Agent on the eighth floor gave a first impression of inhospitable bareness in spite of an adequate number of furnishings. There were seven desks against the walls, including the one used exclusively by Pete, the office man, an equal number of chairs, a dictating machine, filing cabinets, a hat-and-coat rack, a washbasin and drinking fountain, not to mention the bulletin boards. At eye level above the desks had been pinned a great array of FBI and local police bulletins, snapshots of some of the recent crooks caught by the railroad cops, a row of pigeonholes, calendars, and—off by itself—a large portrait of the gentleman who had been president of the railroad about 1910. How he'd got there was a puzzle; but he stayed simply because nobody bothered to take him down. Pete thought the picture probably covered a hole in the plaster.

Part of the barren effect was physical in origin, Pete thought, and emerged from the room itself, the large area of stark gray composition floor and the excessive height of the ceiling. High ceilings were usual in old buildings but this one seemed to dwarf the other dimensions of the room. It was dim up there, far away. The only time the upper gloom seemed fully dispelled was at high noon in mid-summer, when the sun shone straight down the big air well which opened up the center of the building. The rest of the year the shaded, low-hanging bulbs didn't touch it. Pete felt it hanging over his head all the time.

The second cause was psychic, in Pete's opinion, a miasma created by trouble and crime. It was in the atmosphere, this stew of theft and fire, breaking into boxcars, trespassing, switch-tamperings, lost and stolen luggage, disappearing people, on down to the not insignificant damages inflicted by juveniles with bee-bee guns and slingshots and stones. Add to this the impersonal comings and goings all day, traffic like that of a waiting room or a café—the only people who remained in the place continuously were Ryerson, the Chief, and Pete. And Pete had the outer office almost always to himself.

Ryerson's inner sanctum was walled off in one corner, a partition made of plywood paneling, stained dark, with glass above so that Ryerson could keep an eye on the whole place when he wanted to.

On this particular morning Pete was taking the cover off his typewriter when Ryerson went through on his way to his desk. "Hello, Pete."

"Morning, Mr. Ryerson." Pete unlocked the bottom drawer of his desk and took out the stenotype machine. He was a slim, sandy man with the build of a runner and long, nervous hands. Ryerson went into the inner office, put his hat on the rack, walked to his desk and stood there a couple of minutes as if thinking, then came back to the inner doorway. A couple of investigators came in and flopped down at desks; Ryerson nodded to them but his gaze was for Pete.

Ryerson was a bear of a man, over six feet; and if build and muscle were an indication of his fitness for a job he should have been swinging a sledge hammer in the repair shops on Alameda. "Will you bring me the file on the

Lobo Tunnel wreck?" he said to Pete. One of the investigators lifted his eyes from the pad of report blanks and gave Ryerson a curious glance. Ryerson half turned to go back to his desk, then added: "And I want to see Farrel and Saunders when they get here."

"Now, that's a pair," Pete said. Ryerson shut his door. Pete went to the files and squatted on his heels, opened a low drawer, flipped through the folders, selected three fat ones. They were kind of dusty. When he had them out he blew on them. There were newspaper clippings among other things inside, and these were yellowed and crackling.

He took them in to Ryerson, laid them on Ryerson's desk. "Thanks," the Chief said.

"What's new on this thing?"

"Parmenter."

"What'd he do? Swim ashore?"

"They let him go."

Pete made a ticking noise between his teeth and went out. In the outer office he met Farrel, just tossing his hat on a desk, and sent him in to Ryerson. Saunders followed in a couple of minutes. There was something new about Saunders Pete couldn't put his finger on. He looked somehow like a kid who has just set fire to the schoolhouse.

When Farrel and Saunders were seated, Ryerson pulled the Lobo Tunnel folders towards him, flipped up the cover of the top one, said, "Farrel, do you remember the name of the conductor on the Western Shores Limited?" There was, under the casual tone, the hint that he was testing Farrel, looking for some slackness, some diminution of powers.

Farrel's glance seemed idly speculative. "The Lobo Tunnel wreck? Wasn't that Parmenter?"

Saunders glanced from Farrel to Ryerson. He was much younger than these other two. He was like a youngster trying to catch the conversation of old folks talking over his head.

Farrel went on, "What's new with him? I thought the Mexicans had him salted away in Islas Marías prison."

"He was. Apparently he's been released." Ryerson leaned back in his chair and the swivel protested. He looked at Saunders somewhat measuringly. "Last night Parmenter telephoned an old friend of his, a retired conductor named Wall. Wall lives in Chula Vista now, raises lemons and chickens. Wall knows the background, knew we'd wanted to talk to Parmenter for a long time. He called in here. Burns took it."

Saunders found a trace of familiar ground; he knew who Burns was. Burns was the night sergeant in charge of the place from four-thirty to midnight. The rest of it didn't register.

Farrel said, "Maybe Parmenter had just crossed the border. That's where Chula Vista is, practically on the line."

"Might be," Ryerson agreed. "Wall says that Parmenter sounded old and sick."

"Islas Marías is no picnic, from what I've heard."

"They chewed the fat for a couple of minutes, and then Wall began to insist that Parmenter stop in and see him. Parmenter put him off, but he finally agreed to come to Wall's house tonight."

A suddenly knowledgeable light flickered in Farrel's eyes; he moved a little in his chair as though already his body protested the long cramping ride to Chula Vista and back. "What can we do? We can't pick him up, not unless there's more on him than what we used to have."

"That's all there is," Ryerson said flatly. "Just what you know. I want you and Saunders to go down there and try to get him to talk."

Farrel didn't seem to think this needed any answer from him. He ticked a thumbnail against the arm of the chair, turned his gaze from Ryerson out the window. Across the air well in another office a slim girl in a red dress was standing on a stool and stretching to reach something high on a cabinet. She was showing a lot of leg and Farrel looked it over.

Saunders cleared his throat. "Excuse me, Mr. Ryerson, but when did this wreck happen?"

Farrel switched a glance at him. Ryerson said, "Six years ago. Six years, two months and some-odd days."

Saunders smiled, a little blankly. "Isn't it a hell of a long time—" Under their attention he felt the smile dying on his face. But Ryerson seemed patient, Farrel's glance was almost kindly. "I mean, with the press of all the new stuff, and everything ..." What he meant was that the office was perpetually understaffed for the amount of work to be done. Ryerson was always howling for more investigators.

Farrel shifted his legs, put an elbow on the desk, facing Saunders. He spoke without emphasis. "To a cinder bull no train wreck's ever too old until he knows who or what caused it. There's no closed file to drop it into, no key to lock it up with. It's always right up there with the freshest crap in the hopper."

"I see," Saunders said uncertainly.

Ryerson shuffled the papers in the folder. He wasn't looking at Farrel but he seemed to be thinking about him, reserving some judgment, some decision on which he'd formerly made up his mind.

2.

Ryerson jotted something down on a slip of paper, tossed it over to Farrel. "Here's Wall's address in Chula Vista. It's out of town a way, you might have to ask directions. I'd try to get there before dark. Wall told Burns he thinks Parmenter will show late, if at all. But it won't hurt to be on the safe side, in case he comes early."

Farrel tucked the paper into his wallet. His fingers were a little unsteady, fumbling over the worn leather. "What line should we take? I gave this bird everything I had six years ago and it didn't get me anywhere."

"Maybe Islas Marías softened him up," Ryerson said. "Maybe by now his conscience is bothering him."

"What did he *do?*" Saunders put in.

"We don't know." Ryerson shuffled the papers in the folder, not thinking about them; he was obviously searching for some line to take with Parmenter. "Here's an idea. Parmenter's wife and kid. Now of course it's possible he's been in touch with them all this time. Or even that they followed when he skipped to Mexico. But again—maybe not. There's an address in there somewhere, a house Parmenter was buying, living in, at the time of the wreck." He looked across at Farrel. "Go out and check the place this morning. See if Parmenter still owns it. Talk to his wife if she's there. If she and the kid have gone, try to find out where they are now, try to get some news of them secondhand—something Parmenter might not know, might be glad to hear."

Farrel nodded slowly, reaching for the folders. "Will do."

"We're not going to stop with Parmenter," Ryerson went on. "Now we're starting, we're going to give it the full treatment. Thirteen people died in that wreck. I want to know what their survivors are doing, the families and relatives who collected all those claims. I want to know how those permanent cripples are getting along. Maybe some of them have made miraculous recoveries."

Farrel stood, reached for the files, sat down and began to shuffle through them for Parmenter's old address. Saunders was surprised that he seemed oblivious to Ryerson's angry sarcasm. He decided that Farrel had been all through this before; he was like an old horse who bows to a familiar yoke. Hell, Saunders thought suddenly, he's stale. He's plodding in a rut. He'll never find anything new in this thing; why can't the Chief see it? Saunders threw Ryerson a quick look, surmising all at once why Ryerson had put him on it with Farrel. Farrel knew the ropes but it was up to him to see it with a fresh viewpoint.

Ryerson answered Saunders's glance with a cool and unreadable glance of his own. Apparently he decided it was time to explain a few things. "Parmenter was on the train when it hit the obstruction in the tunnel. As far as we know, he did everything he could; he kept his head, gave the proper orders, organized help for the injured, prevented panic. At the hearings he gave testimony, and it all seemed perfectly on the level. We would never have given him a second thought except that as soon as some of the claims were settled he skipped off to Mexico."

"A case of nerves?" Saunders hazarded, thinking Ryerson expected something original from him.

"A case of money. A lot of it," Ryerson snapped back. "He lived high, wide and handsome down there. We were trying to get a line on his whereabouts when it broke in the papers, a shooting scrape with a Mexican over the Mexican's wife. We woke up then to the class of people he'd been traveling with. This was the son and the daughter-in-law of one of the Mexican governors. Millionaires."

Saunders was getting the hang of it. "The Mexicans put Parmenter in jail for the shooting?"

"Islas Marías. Off the coast. Mexico's version of Devil's Island, you might say. He served about five years. Might as well have been buried, we didn't expect to see him again. But now he's back in the States and we want him. We want to know where he got that money."

Farrel was copying Parmenter's old address into a shabby pocket memo. When he was through, Ryerson reached for the folders, stacked them, put them on the corner of the desk in front of Saunders. "Take these. What we know about Parmenter is in here, along with all the evidence given at the investigation, photos of the wreck, and other stuff. I want you to go through it this morning while Farrel's out checking on the wife and kid. Take your time, absorb it. If anything puzzles you, talk to Pete about it."

Saunders stood up, picked up the folders. "Yes, sir." He felt a surge of confidence in himself, in his ability to find something new and significant in the mass of material on the old wreck. "It's obvious that Parmenter received a payoff for keeping his mouth shut about something."

"That's what we'd like to know."

Saunders headed for the outer office. Farrel followed more slowly. He seemed a little tired for this early in the day.

Saunders put the folders on his desk and stepped over to the water cooler, drew a paper cup out of the slot, had a drink. When he turned he saw that Farrel had paused by the desk and was looking at the folders.

Saunders went back to the desk.

Farrel said, "Sixteen people died at Lobo Tunnel. Not thirteen."

Saunders started to say something. Farrel went on, "The Chief never includes the engineer or the fireman. Or the porter. I always figured it was the porter's dying gave Parmenter his chance to cover up."

Saunders had a sudden inspiration. "Look, in a wreck like that there must have been a lot of confusion, people dead and dying or running around half off their rockers, luggage scattered and broken open—maybe Parmenter just helped himself to something valuable."

Farrel seemed unimpressed with this simple but brilliant deduction. "Anything that valuable would have had a claim attached to it."

"Maybe not. Maybe there were reasons a claim couldn't be filed. Such as ... oh, not really belonging to the person who had it with him. Or the owner killed outright, no one else knowing he'd carried it along." The rush of conjecture filled Saunders with excitement and self-assurance.

"Parmenter took off after some of the death and injury claims were paid. Six months after the wreck."

"Wouldn't he do that, just exactly that, if he wanted to cover a theft?"

There was no reaction from Farrel; he just went on looking at the closed folders in a tired, thoughtful fashion. He seemed so damned shabby, Saunders thought in irritation; unalert, worn-out. Old. His clothes needed attention. His shirt collar was soiled. Good God, didn't he even keep track of his laundry? At this moment Saunders remembered with a start of guilt the shirts he had stuffed into the hamper at home. That night, so help him Hannah, he'd remember to leave them with the landlady for the laundryman.

Saunders argued, "We can't just settle on one idea, close our minds to everything else. Maybe the answer's been here all the time—" He tapped the folders. "—if anyone had seen it."

A funny look drifted over Farrel's face, as if he wanted to smile but was too tired to make the effort. "Now, that'd be something." He nodded good-bye and went on out into the hall.

Saunders sat down and opened the folders, and as a
means of orienting himself, getting an over-all conception
of the thing, he searched out the photos. These shocked
him horribly.

At first you didn't get it, it was just a jumble of great
garish lumps, odd scraps, against the background of the
tilted passenger cars; and then details sprang into focus
and you realized what you were looking at. The mangled
body of a woman hanging half out of a coach window,
for instance. The screaming face of a child. A man staring
at the stump of his own arm. A girl of about twenty—
maybe younger—*literally* tearing out her hair. Her left
foot was pinned under something. Saunders felt sweat
come out across his face.

The scenes seemed to occur at about twilight; there was
a good deal of light but none of it was direct, and everything seemed gray in the distance, insubstantial.

He wondered again why he couldn't remember anything
about it. He'd been in school then, of course, the second
year of City College; his last year; and he'd been pretty
mixed up about Marion Hulett and Marion's plans for
getting married and going to New York to study acting.
A nut; he saw it now. He wondered why she'd had him
running in circles. God knew he couldn't act; he couldn't
even recite *Invictus* without getting it all backwards. *I am
my captain of the soul....*

He forced himself back to the pictures. Well, these
horrifying ones weren't the official photos at all, it seemed.
There were others, bigger and better, without any people
in them. Some of these had been taken from up high,
from the sides of the cut, probably, or the entrance to the
tunnel. The passenger coaches were crazily tilted still, but
now night had fallen, the people had been taken away,

flares had been set out, and off in the dark there were the engine of the wrecker and a row of trucks and cars.

In the margin he read the name of a commercial photo studio.

He took all of the pictures and went over to Pete, who was pounding his typewriter. Pete glanced at the pictures, letting his fingers drift from the keys. "Fellow on the train took those early ones. Had a camera with him, big one, flash attachment, he'd been to a convention or some such thing. He brought us those copies a couple of weeks after the wreck. Nobody had even noticed him taking them, which gives you an idea." Pete reached for one, put it down on his desk, tapped it with a finger. "Now notice this. See him, here?"

At the fringe of the twilight, in the shadows, stood a small man. His figure, in light-colored shirt, dark trousers, wasn't too distinct, and distance made his face small; but the features were surprisingly clear. He had a small mustache and heavy brows, his hair grew in a peak low on his forehead, very thick black hair, and his eyes seemed colorless. What gave the face its odd character were the mouth and chin. The mouth was like a slash, practically lipless; the chin jutting and square, divided by an exaggerated cleft, something cruel here in the lower part of the face, something ruthless, destructive.

"Who's he?" Saunders said.

"The little man who shouldn't be there," Pete answered. "You'll find it mentioned in the transcript of the investigation. He was seen by quite a few people. He wasn't a passenger. We think he's a discharged section hand by the name of Emil Versprelle. Present whereabouts unknown."

"You mean he—he showed up when the wreck happened?"

"Oh, we had the idea Emil might have been there right along."

Saunders was aware of a sense of outraged betrayal. Why, Ryerson and Farrel had known all the time—a discharged section hand. Motive and all. What was this fiddling around over Parmenter? He said thickly, "Then this creep in the picture caused the wreck."

"That's jumping to a conclusion," Pete pointed out. "Let's say it seems likely that Emil liked excitement and arranged to be on hand when some occurred. And then cleared out to keep from being involved."

Saunders's face felt stiff. He wondered if Pete could be laughing at him somehow. "I see."

"We're still looking for him," Pete said, as if suspecting Saunders might not believe it.

"I see," Saunders repeated, not knowing what else to say. He went back to the desk, sat down, started a mechanical reading of the transcript. It had been a long investigation and the transcript was a thick one. He waded through some of the preliminary testimony and then found himself reading about the death of the porter, Stanley Cream.

Stanley Cream had been forty-two, married, had lived in Chicago until a year before the wreck, when he had moved his family to Los Angeles. He had been employed by the railroad for almost fifteen years and his record was exemplary. At the time of the wreck he had been caught in a vestibule, crushed there when the train jackknifed on hitting the obstruction in the tunnel.

Farrel had said he guessed Cream's death had given Parmenter the go sign on his way to sudden riches, but there was no clue to Cream's part in the affair here.

The obstruction in the tunnel ... Saunders searched out the part about that.

The obstruction had consisted of two handcars loaded with ties and rock, run into the tunnel far enough to be out of sight. When the engine had hit the barrier the handcars had leaped off the tracks and the rubble had spilled. The engineer had died in the cab. The fireman had died three hours later at a hospital.

A little further along ... Saunders turned pages ... a section foreman named Feretti testified that the two hand-cars were part of the equipment of Gang Number Ten, and had been taken from a siding about one mile from the entrance to the tunnel, where this gang had been working during the day. The person who had appropriated the handcars must have had a switch key to open the switch to the main line. Both handcars had motors. Except for the trouble of stealing the switch key, the loading and moving of the barrier into the tunnel must have been quite simple and easy.

There was the matter of the timetable, too, of course, providing someone really wanted especially to wreck the Western Shores Limited, and not just raise hell in general for the railroad. Foreman Feretti had carried a timetable and had also checked by telephone with the dispatcher at regular intervals.

No decision had apparently been reached as to whether the target had been the Western Shores Limited or not.

Asked about the man named Emil Versprelle, Feretti said that he had been discharged three days previously, by instruction of the railroad cops, because he was suspected of peddling marijuana cigarettes to the other section hands.

No connection could be brought out between Versprelle and any member of the crew of the Western Shores Limited. Hell, Saunders said to himself, no connection had existed. Here was a hophead with a grievance, knew the timetable, had a stolen switch key, hung around at the time of the wreck, vanished afterwards. What the hell more did they want?

What did they expect of Parmenter, of the trip to Chula Vista, or of the interviews with the survivors who had collected claims for injuries or deaths? He found that his eyes had strayed over to the glass-enclosed inner sanctum, to Ryerson's mammoth figure bent over the desk there. He was shaken by the memory of his impression that Ryerson must expect a fresh viewpoint, a new look at old facts, from him; and a funny mixture of anger and laughter boiled in his mind. What fresh viewpoint was possible?

But then that tired sloppiness of Farrel's came to mind, Farrel in his dull rut, and Saunders's determination stiffened.

He got up, went back to Pete's desk. Pete, always good-natured, ready to listen, stopped the rattledy-bang on the typewriter.

"I've been reading the transcript," Saunders began. "What could Parmenter have had to do with the wreck? He got on at San Simon—"

"They've changed the division point since then," Pete corrected. "He got on at Fernwood."

"Three hundred miles if it's an inch. He was on the train, almost into L.A.—not out beside the tracks at Lobo Tunnel."

Pete looked at him thoughtfully through the horn-rimmed specs. "He made one hell of a big grab somehow."

"If we'd been sent to look for Versprelle, I could understand it."

"Work on Versprelle if you want to," Pete said, as if surprised Saunders hadn't thought of it. "Ask the Sheriff's Office to get out an APB. His hobby is growing marijuana and making his own smokes. Maybe he's in some nearby hoosegow right now."

"He grew marijuana at home?"

"Oh, hell, no, he was too smart for that." Pete was chuckling. "Know where he had his patch? There's an old water tower this side of Lobo and six years ago there was still water in the pipes, and Versprelle planted his little garden right there under the noses of everybody, and on railroad property too—well, of course in the end that's how the cinder dicks spotted it. But he was doing fine for a while." Pete shook his head over it. "A gutty little devil. As gutty as they come."

Saunders went over to the glass-paned door, rapped, and stuck his head in. Ryerson looked up. Saunders said, "How about an APB on Versprelle?"

Ryerson said, "It's okay, go ahead," without any expression in his voice that Saunders could figure out. Saunders went back to his own desk to dig up the material for the APB, Versprelle's description, and so on, and then fell to wondering how many all-points bulletins had been sent out on this hophead, like paper boats set on a tide never to return.

Farrel had gone down to the company garage in the basement, checked out a car, driven out Alameda Avenue through the lumbering trucks, past the S.P. freight yards, turned east finally to the foothills beyond Glendale. He remembered coming here more than five years ago, right after they'd learned about Parmenter's skipping to Mexico; but he drove past the house without recognizing it, had to check street numbers and turn back. The place was shabbier, older, and the shrubbery much grown up, so that it seemed quite different.

A woman with a red, blotched face answered his ring at the door. He knew this wasn't Mrs. Parmenter, this faded blonde. But he showed his identification and asked if she knew where Parmenter's wife and child had gone.

She gazed at him through the screen. He saw all at once that the red blotchiness was the result of tears; and a funny hunch came to him that she was going to tell him something he needed to know.

3.

"You want my sister?" she said, and the tone told him this was unusual, not many people came asking for Mrs. Parmenter anymore. "I guess you hadn't heard what happened to her."

"No, I hadn't heard." The screen still separated them, she peering hazily at him through it. "I'd like to know, though."

"You're a police officer?"

Farrel nodded. "With the railroad."

"Do you want to come in?" She unhooked the door, stepped back.

"Thank you." He looked around, holding his hat, while she walked across the room and indicated a chair for him. There was something familiar about it all, the furniture, the size of the room, the way the windows looked out upon the shrubbery; but somehow the place seemed much more aged than the passing of five years and a few odd months would make reasonable. Farrel thought, Someone's lived here mighty poor. He walked over to the faded chair Mrs. Parmenter's sister had placed for him.

"Do you mind giving me your name, ma'am?"

"No, not a bit." She smoothed her gingham skirt, sitting down opposite. "I'm Libby Walker. Miss Walker."

Farrel got the idea that she felt a kind of relief at meeting him; that at the same time she'd rather he hadn't seen the signs of tears. "And you're Mrs. Parmenter's sister."

She hesitated briefly. "Half-sister. Our mother married twice. My sister's name was Suydell, Marie Suydell, before she married *him*." A twinge of dislike crossed her face.

"Where is your sister now?"

"In the nut house."

The tone was bristling; he decided that she had meant to shock him. Farrel studied her, crouched there on her chair, a small pale woman full of malice. "Camarillo?"

"That's right. Been there more'n a year now. First she was in the County Hospital with tuberculosis. When that kind of cleared up, her heart went bad on her. And then finally her mind went. The doctors gave me some chitchat, she cracked up over money worries. Well, nobody can tell me any different, it was worrying over *him*. Him in that Mexican jail, where he richly deserved to be."

"Was she in contact with him?"

"Tried to be. Wanted to be. Got sick, though. Isn't that what you came to talk about? *Him?*" She drew a long hoarse breath and pinched her lips up and for a moment Farrel thought she meant to spit.

"Have you had any word from him?"

She made the same face again. "Not likely."

"What about Parmenter's little girl? Let's see ... she was ten or twelve...."

"She's eighteen." Now the sudden, bitter tears stood in her pale eyes. "I came here from Detroit when Marie wrote me she was sick. I've kept the house, I've worked out to get money for us to eat—just ... just any kind of hard dirty work you might mention, that's what I've done."

"Could I see her?"

It was scarcely more than a whisper. "She's run away."

Farrel felt his legs stiffen against the shabby chair. "How long ago?"

"Yesterday."

"Do you know where she is?" Farrel asked.

"Would I be talking to you, wanting your help, if I did?" she snapped back. "Why do you think I let you in? To hash over my sister's troubles? To talk about that man?"

"What did your niece tell you before she left?"

"Nothing."

"Did she leave a note?"

Libby Walker nodded slowly, reluctantly. She fished a piece of tablet paper from her skirt pocket and held it out wordlessly. Farrel spread it against his knee. The handwriting was well formed, neat and adult; and he had the distinct impression that Parmenter's daughter was quite grown-up for eighteen.

> Dear Aunt Lib:
>
> I'm going away on a short trip and will be back soon. Don't let Mama know. I'll be perfectly safe, so don't worry. I'll write you in a few days if I can't return just when I expect.
>
> I'll be with friends. Again, don't worry about me!
>
> Love,
Peg

Farrel gave her the note again, she tucked it away into the same pocket. "How much did she take with her in the way of clothes?"

"A little zipper bag, with a few underthings, cosmetics … All of her dresses, her skirts and blouses are still here."

"It would seem then that she didn't mean to be gone long."

"A lot of bad things can happen in a short while," Libby Walker muttered.

Farrel said, "You think this might have something to do with her father?"

The puzzle was there, all right; but she said promptly, "How could it be? He's on some devil's island down there."

What had Ryerson suggested? Find out some news,

something Parmenter might be glad to know? Farrel's mouth twisted in a slight smile. Here was someone who really needed information. He said, "He's been released from Islas Marías. He's back in this country."

She threw up her hands in an outraged, broken gesture and then sat frozen, staring into his eyes; but he saw that she hadn't really assimilated it yet; the fact was working its way in and being attached here and there to other facts already stored in her mind. "I can't ... can't seem to—" Then she looked around suddenly at the room, and Farrel thought, She's thinking now that it belongs to him, to the man she hates and whose place—in a way—she has taken here these last few years. Her gaze swung back to him. "How long ago? When?"

"We don't know yet. We do know that he has crossed the border and has contacted an old friend living below San Diego."

She put her hands together, clenching them on her lap. "Of course. She's gone to be with him."

"You think your niece is loyal to Parmenter?"

"I couldn't change her." Under the words were grief and disgust.

"How could he have gotten in touch with her?"

She looked down at her clenched hands. "Telephoned. Written. Anything. I'm gone during the day. She's been looking for a job since school let out. But she'd be here during the afternoon." A dry sob shook her throat, and then as if the feelings bottled up inside her had become unendurable, Libby Walker jumped off the chair. "Will you excuse me? I'm going to get my hat and coat."

Farrel rose, moved away from the chair. She paused on the other side of the room and looked back. "What was this place? This friend's house?"

Her quivering impatience was like a flare, sparkling between them, and Farrel knew what she meant to do; but they couldn't have this stormy character interfering tonight in the delicate business in Chula Vista. "Parmenter isn't staying with this friend of his. He merely phoned, then the friend called us."

A spasm of anger shook her. "You don't know where Parmenter is now?"

"No, we don't."

Again it took a little while to sink in, and then she came back to the chair, with a broken drag-leg sort of stumble, and sat down, and Farrel braced himself for some bitter weeping. But she sat dry-eyed, knotted with tension. After a while of thinking it over she said, "I'm going to file a missing-person report. I'll put the police on it." She lifted glittering eyes. "I'll need to know the name of Parmenter's friend, and where he lives."

Farrel had sensed that this was coming; had already decided what he must say. He felt sincerely sorry for this distracted creature, and more than that, he might need her co-operation badly in the future. Besides this, he had no illusions about how speedily the Missing Persons Bureau would act in such a case, over a girl eighteen, who had left a sensible and reassuring note, and had most likely gone to join her father. "I think you've got a good idea there," he told Libby Walker. "Call the Missing Persons Bureau about your niece. The man's name is Wall, he's a retired conductor, and he lives near Chula Vista."

She nodded over the information, filing it away, Farrel thought; and then got up and moved away to a little table holding a telephone. She sat down, then looked over her shoulder at him. "Is that all you want, Mr. Farrel?"

He nodded. "Just about. I wondered if I might ask a favor, that you'll call me at the railroad office if anything new turns up. About your niece or her father." He took a card from his wallet and put it on the arm of the chair. There was a rip in the faded fabric, some of the cotton stuffing showed, and no attempt had been made to mend it.

"Certainly I'll call you." Her nose twitched; she was obviously pleased, thinking that somehow in the future she might hinder or embarrass Parmenter. Then a sudden curious glint showed in her pale eyes. "Did you come here to talk to my sister? Or didn't you really know where she was?"

"I really didn't know," Farrel answered. He moved over to the door.

"You thought then, that she might know where he is."

"Just hoping."

"She doesn't know a thing about him anymore," she said in a voice which was high-pitched again. "I don't think she even knows she was married. She's in a dream world. It isn't always unhappy, being nuts, you know. You miss all kinds of grief that way." She looked around her, as if the house represented some intolerable burden, something she'd taken over from the woman now in Camarillo Hospital, along with the missing girl and the work necessary for their survival.

Farrel let himself out into the sunny, overgrown yard. He drew a deep breath and headed for the car at the curb. A brown dog came down the street, looking from side to side, and when he saw Farrel he gave him the look he reserved for strangers.

Farrel got behind the wheel. He thought about Libby Walker. By now she was talking to the Missing Persons Bureau, and if she was anything like the usual run of customers she was wondering why they weren't as excited as she was. Farrel started the motor.

He knew that there was a question he should have asked her, perhaps should even go back to ask now. But he wanted to think about it a little longer. It was an odd, minor item.

Why had she shown no surprise, no curiosity, on learning that the railroad dicks were looking for Parmenter?

He thought it over as he drove back towards town. She could be filled with wishful thinking of course, wanting Parmenter to be in trouble again because she didn't like him, didn't want him hanging around her niece or the home she had supported in his absence. But in such case there should have been at least a moment of happy triumph.

Farrel thought, It's just as if she knows all about it, knows he's a crook and how he's a crook and takes for granted that I share that knowledge.

On his way back from the Sheriff's Office, Saunders stepped into a drugstore, to a pay phone, and called Betsy at the medical building in Beverly Hills. She sounded starched and professional. He apologized for having to break the dinner date for that evening.

"I'll be back late," he added. "If there's a light under your door—"

"I'm sorry, sir," she said. "I'm afraid that cannot be arranged."

He felt rebuffed. "What kind of double talk is that? You sore?"

"Oh, no, sir."

"Good-bye, then."

"Good-bye."

After he hung up, he decided that Betsy had had some peculiar reason for the starchy voice. Probably some old dragon, her superior, had made a rule against personal calls on the job. Or some four-star surgeon had been demanding that she look up the case history on somebody's gall bladder. Or then again maybe ... just maybe ... she'd been really put out because his job was spoiling their date.

And he had, he realized, fully intended to take martinis.

As she had wanted.

He ran into Farrel in the corridor outside the office on the eighth floor. Farrel stopped at once when he saw Saunders coming, waited against the wall as if he somehow hoped Saunders wouldn't come too close. And Saunders thought with ready suspicion, Hell, he's had a drink! He thought this and then forced himself to dismiss the idea. There was no odor of liquor about Farrel. And you didn't drink on a railroad job; you didn't buck Rule G.

Farrel looked braced up, more alert, that was all.

Farrel said, "I guess we might as well start driving right after lunch. It's a long drag down there."

Saunders nodded. "Okay."

"I'm going to Personnel now and ask them to dig out the old folder on Parmenter. Want to come along?"

Saunders felt a touch of disappointment that he hadn't thought of it first, but he said readily enough, "Sure. Good idea."

In the big busy Personnel offices, they waited under a bright light while a girl clerk went to the Records Room. Saunders glanced at Farrel a couple of times; the overhead lights were cruel to the old boy, he thought, noting the lines in Farrel's face, the streaks of silver in his hair.

When the girl handed them Parmenter's old folder, Farrel leafed through it quickly and rather indifferently, as if merely refreshing his memory on certain points. Saunders took his time, did mental arithmetic. Parmenter must be in his fifties by now. Not a frisky age, nor a good age to be emerging after five years in prison. His background, as summarized by the items in the folder, seemed very ordinary. He had been born in Duluth, Minnesota, had gone to school in Chicago and St. Louis, Missouri, and had been employed by the railroad approximately twelve years before the wreck at Lobo Tunnel. He had served in the Seabees in World War II, his only interruption of railroad service.

Saunders glanced up from the collection of papers. "Nothing out of the way here—" He broke off. Farrel had gone.

He didn't see Farrel until almost two, when Farrel called from the basement, asked him to come down. He found Farrel waiting there in a company car. Saunders had, somehow, expected to drive. It was a long trip, over freeways spinning with fast traffic, and he had taken for granted that Farrel would have been glad to turn the driving over to someone younger.

Saunders was beginning to sense, rather slowly, that Farrel was not a man you could take for granted; he kept surprising you.

The trip down to Chula Vista was boring. Farrel didn't talk much. He didn't seem interested in the scenery. They paused in San Diego for something to eat; but before the waitress brought the food Farrel stepped out for something or other, and when he came back he seemed to have no appetite; and again Saunders had to thrust away the thought that Farrel was drinking on the job.

In Chula Vista, Farrel parked near a bar and went into it to ask directions to Wall's address, and Saunders's suspicions became certainty. Farrel was tippling his way through the afternoon. When Farrel came back, Saunders was noticeably cool, and Farrel sensed it and looked at him with a sharp close look. It made Saunders feel like a prig and a fool.

Farrel was aware only of a weary amusement. In the bar he'd had a quick—too quick, his stomach was burning—double gin in orange juice. Now this young squirt was giving him a pinpoint stare. He turned the car into the street the bartender had indicated. Almost at once they left the town behind them and entered an area of truck-vegetable fields and citrus groves. Something was in bloom, making the late breeze fragrant. It wasn't dusk yet, but there was a sort of yellow somnolence in the air. It reminded Farrel of some afternoons in the country long ago, and the memory of the stunned pain which had ended those days rose in his mind and the feeling of weariness, minus any amusement, crept all the way to his toes and his finger tips. He wasn't aware of the motions, they were mechanical, but Saunders saw him yawn and rub his hand across the back of his neck and thought that he must be feeling the drink he'd had back at the bar.

Wall's house sat in a cluster of lemon trees. To the left were some wire enclosures with some very white chickens scratching around looking for a last bite before going to roost. Out by the road were patches of ivy geraniums, pink and lavender, and trellises full of climbing roses.

Farrel looked it over as they turned into the driveway. "He really did it, just like he said he would. Even to the damned ragged robins."

Saunders looked around for some birds and then decided that Farrel was talking about the red roses in bloom. "They aren't ragged robins," he pointed out. "A wild rose blooms just once a year, in the spring. These must be something else." He was thinking of the roses his mother tended, in Santa Barbara, before they'd moved to the apartment in L.A. "I think they're red Talismans. There's another name, I can't recall it."

Farrel gave him such an ironic look that Saunders flushed and said hastily, "Hell, I'm not trying to show you up."

"Now, that'd be something," Farrel growled, stepping on the brake.

4.

Wall, the retired conductor, was a roly-poly man with a fringe of white hair around a bald spot. He had gold-capped teeth which he showed in a wide grin, and he shook Saunders's hand with a firm calloused grip. He wore dungarees, rather tight around the middle, some old huaraches, a faded shirt. His wife made Saunders think of a nervous mouse. She sort of kept to the background, letting her husband do the greeting. She was small, gray, with quick eyes and hands tiny and clawlike. The Walls were obviously happy in this place with their lemon trees, their chickens and roses. They were courteous to Saunders and Mrs. Wall offered him some lemonade; but he sensed in them a much greater interest and curiosity about Farrel.

They all got seated in the small living room, and the conversation was on the point of getting around to Parmenter when Mrs. Wall burst forth with an astonishing query. Saunders had meanwhile decided that at some time in the past Farrel and the Walls had known each other fairly well, and this remark convinced him of it.

Her tone was apologetic, almost squeaky with embarrassment. "Mr. Farrel, I can't help asking—did you ever have any word of your ... of your *family?*"

There was a very awkward moment then. Farrel's glance dropped and he said, without looking at anybody, "No. I never did hear from them."

She made a distracted gesture. "Forgive me for asking. I just had to know. I hope I haven't raised any unhappy memories."

"It's all right." Farrel looked at her and smiled.

"Amy ..." Her husband also smiled, echoing her own

embarrassment. "Curiosity'll kill Amy someday, just like it did that mythical cat."

"My God," Farrel said in a tone of real surprise, "if a woman's not curious she must be dead!"

The others laughed at this, more at the conviction in Farrel's tone than at his words. In the midst of laughter, Saunders thought suddenly, the old boy was married ... sometime. Oddly, it didn't jibe with anything he had observed or figured out about Farrel.

Farrel interrupted the laughter. "Now ... about Parmenter. You're pretty sure he'll show up here?" He was looking at Wall, who sobered quickly.

"I'm pretty sure," Wall said. "He sounded tired, pooped-out, and I thought there was a kind of lonesomeness about him. I had to argue with him to get him to say he'd come; but I think he really wanted to all along. I think he's kind of anxious to see some old friends after five years in that Mex prison."

Mrs. Wall smoothed her gingham apron across her knees. "We thought, too, that maybe he was embarrassed about the prison sentence ... wondering if we'd want to see him, considering that."

Farrel said, "You thought he might come around rather late."

Wall nodded. "He said that. He said, 'I might be around after your bedtime,' and I said, 'Any time, just bang on the door.'" Wall glanced from Farrel over to Saunders. "Are you both going to talk to him?"

Actually, Saunders had expected Farrel to do the talking, that he himself would absorb things: Parmenter's manner, any appearance of guilt, any hint of a trail to be followed further. But Farrel said, "No, I'm going to keep out of sight. Somewhere where I can hear what goes on. Saunders will carry the ball."

Saunders started to open his mouth to ask what the

devil he was expected to base his queries on, when Farrel shot him a glance.

"We want to know if Parmenter has met his daughter and if they're together," Farrel went on. "I guess that's the best angle to work on. It's a legitimate query, she's missing at home and her aunt is worried. If the girl is with him we can ask politely what his plans are for the future. On account of the daughter, you see."

Saunders nodded as if it had been planned on the way down here but inwardly he seethed with anger and disgust. Why the hell should Farrel pull this off the hook at the last minute? What was he trying to do? A chilling idea crossed Saunders's mind, that Farrel was going to make him look like a fool.

"Parmenter doesn't know Saunders. He knows me from 'way back," Farrel finished, a note of weariness creeping into his voice.

Wall took a carved pipe off a little table beside his chair, began to fill it from a humidor. "I think you've got a good idea there. Now there's this. Instead of letting Parmenter know that I called you fellers, why not act as if the original query came from the aunt?"

"Yes, that's important," Farrel agreed.

"I don't even know the woman's name," Saunders said.

"Libby Walker. Miss Walker," Farrel said, almost indifferently. "I have a hunch Parmenter won't quiz you on these points. If he did coax the girl away from home, he'll be on the defensive about it, he'll be making excuses, not asking questions."

Mrs. Wall was leaning forward from her rocker. It was dim over in the corner, and Saunders thought of a mouse peering forth from shadows. "The important thing, then, is what Mr. Parmenter means to do next."

"The important thing," Farrel said, "is how much money Mr. Parmenter expects to have in his future. His plans will depend on it."

"I see," she said, though her tone expressed her incomprehension. Wall was placidly smoking the pipe. Farrel seemed to have nothing more to say. He sat with his hands locked between his knees, bent forward, looking at the rug. Dusk was creeping thickly into the room.

The eucalyptus trees were tall, rustling, a little ghostly in the gray light and under them, between the huge boles, the slender girl looked small and lonely. She wore a plain blue coat over a skirt and blouse, brown oxfords, brown gloves; her hair was tied with an orange scarf and this bit of color was bright in the midst of twilight. She carried a patent leather handbag and a small overnight case. Some ten feet beyond the group of trees was the bus stop, the bench, the sign on its metal standard, where she had alighted. As soon as the bus had pulled away, she had gone to stand among the trees. She looked about at her surroundings, not as if recognizing them but as if comparing them with some previously learned description.

She had bright, attentive blue eyes, framed in black lashes. Her face was quite pretty. She had a stubborn mouth, though, puckered now with the tension of waiting.

She moved a little, nervously, her feet crushing the fallen eucalyptus leaves, releasing the pungent oil into the still, damp air. Behind the trees was a wide canal, filled with irrigation water. Frogs and crickets among the reeds were beginning their night songs. The girl glanced that way, studying the metallic reflection on the water, the dying colors of sunset. It was cool. She was glad that she had worn the coat. Soon it was going to be dark. She tucked the coat higher against her throat, moved out a little from the trees as if seeking the light.

There were no houses near. This was country. One of

the roads which formed the intersection at the bus stop wasn't even paved, was merely a graveled track. The other, the one on which the bus had brought her, stretched into the shadowy distance between fields of beans, tomatoes, lettuce. Nothing moved in that panorama; it seemed a cultivated waste, deserted, barren of life. Suddenly off in the sky a plane droned. The girl moved quickly to a point where she could see its small black shape, and her eyes followed it as if clinging to this sign of humanity.

She waited. The sky darkened. Some birds chirped and rattled in the trees overhead. A soft wind came up, spread the smell of the canal water and the pungent odor of the trees. A frog plopped with a wet splash.

She leaned against one of the trees. There was nothing to see now. The dark had smothered the land.

A pair of headlights came into view far down the road. They bobbed and wavered as the car advanced. Their glow seemed especially golden and brilliant, she thought; and then added to herself, It's because everything else is so black. There isn't even a moon. She stepped forward expectantly.

The car bobbled on past without stopping. She had a brief glimpse into the cab; it was an old pickup, the man inside seemed totally engrossed in driving. Perhaps he was attentive and apprehensive because of the rackety noise of the motor. With a scratch of tires against the gravel he turned at the intersection, took off with increased speed on the dirt track. He went over a bump and she heard the clatter of boxes and crates from the back of the truck. There was a weak backfire, then silence.

She put the small case on the ground behind one of the tree boles and sat down on it, tucking her heels under her. Something rattled and scraped around in the tree over-head—a bird, most likely—and she looked up as if expecting to see; but there was nothing but the night.

She sighed deeply, put her head back, letting the pony tail of hair rest against the bark, and shut her eyes. She wished the waiting were over. She was not particularly tired, though, in spite of the trip from L.A. and the delay at the transfer point. She was young and vigorous. But by resting, relaxing, she was saving her energies; she wanted to be fresh and sparkling when the time came.

She had no watch, no way of telling time. It was possible, she thought afterward, that she might have dozed a little. Not through any need of sleep, but because of the dark, the hypnotic pulse of cricket song, the warmth of the coat against the breeze. She found herself suddenly wide awake, feeling a little cramped and chilled, and wondering what had roused her. Then the silence sank in and she knew. The crickets had quit.

The sudden stillness had a quality of listening in it, of alarm. She crouched on the case, hugging her knees. She expected the noise of an approaching car, a footstep, a voice. Then she wondered if some animal, a stray dog, a coyote or some other wild thing, had crept close to test her scent and so alarmed the crickets. She stood up slowly, bracing a hand against the tree. She seemed to sense another presence. She said cheerfully, clearly, "Hello! Who's there?" After a moment she added, "*Dad?*"

Her voice brought no rustling retreat, so it hadn't been an exploring animal. The crickets didn't start up again; no human speech answered her. The silence went on and on; it seemed to hold her in a vacuum. She turned slowly. The breeze was steady and unchanged. The whisper of leaves overhead stirred briefly, then died.

"I'm over here," she said, but now her tone was uncertain; she spoke not to another person but to a shape concealed by the dark. Some goose pimples came out on her arms.

There was no reply, though she seemed to catch a sound

like an expelled breath. An undefined sense of danger seized her. She shrank back, trying to be small and still, bending, her fingers searching below her knee for the handle of the overnight case. When she lifted the case, stood straight, she thought: I ought to run. This can't be Dad.

She moved silently and then, at the next instant, there was a snap of fire, the echo of a shot, and something thrummed into one of the trees and set its branches vibrating. The girl slid around to the other side of the bole, then crouched and scurried away. She tried to move without sound but a second shot came searching for her and she flung herself flat beside the water.

Slide in....

She slid into the canal feet first, trying to leave as narrow a track as possible. The water was cold; she bit her lips to keep down a sudden gasp, the chatter of her teeth. Then she reached above, to the bank, and pushed the grasses, the slimy reeds, together, working by touch alone in the blackness. The water stole through her clothing to wet her flesh. The little case wanted to float; she held it under until it filled. Then she lay motionless, the top of her head out of the water, and waited and listened. The current swept on to its destined source and she had to brace herself against it.

She had never before had to run and to hide for her life, and a kind of astonishment possessed her that she had been able to do it so quickly and so surely. It was as if danger had its own quarter of the mind, its own nerves, its own automatic reflexes.

It did not occur to her at first to examine what had happened. The fright was too enveloping. Lying in the water, she did not wonder why the errand to meet her father had brought her instead to death.

After a while a few crickets began to make tentative chirps, and when nothing happened to these pioneers, the rest of the chorus slowly picked up the beat. A frog flipped. The night had returned to normal. The girl waited a long time, however, before dragging herself back upon the bank. She was wet, chilled to the bone, expecting at any moment a shape to loom above her in the dark. The contents of her purse and of the overnight case would be thoroughly soaked. She remembered the return bus ticket to Los Angeles and wondered if it might be dried and used.

She thought incredulously of her father. Someone had meant to meet him here, she decided, someone other than herself. Had he made enemies in Mexico? Was he followed by one of them who wanted vengeance?

It was impossible, of course, that the bullets had really been meant for her.

Mrs. Wall turned on the lights, drew the window blinds and closed the door to the porch. She turned to look at the three men. "I'm going to get us a bite to eat."

Farrel said politely, "Thanks, ma'am, but we had a meal in San Diego."

"Wouldn't you like something home-cooked for a change?" She looked at Farrel steadily, as if reminding him of something he'd had once and might have missed. "Some cold fried chicken? Some ham?"

It sounded good to Saunders. For some reason he thought of the meals his mother had fixed. He said, "If you've got some rye bread and mustard and horse-radish, that ham's right up my alley."

She smiled, something motherly coming out in her, and said, "I'll only be a minute." She hurried out to the kitchen.

A look passed between Farrel and old Mr. Wall. Mr. Wall seemed to catch something from this that Saunders missed. He promptly knocked out his pipe into the ash tray and laid it aside. "Well. It'll be nice outdoors now.

How about a short hike to stretch our legs?"

Farrel nodded and rose from the chair. He hitched up his belt, tapped his hip automatically, checking the gun. They went towards the door to the porch. Saunders looked Farrel over. He decided that Farrel was the kind of guy who got sloppy just sitting around. His coat got wrinkles in it, his tie loosened itself, his shirttails worked up. And then, he added dryly to himself, there was the original slovenliness to begin with. He wondered suddenly then how long this Lobo Tunnel affair might take, and how well he and Farrel would be getting along at the end of it. Going through the door to the dark porch, Farrel looked stooped. The silver shone in his hair. Saunders thought about Ryerson. Did the Chief really expect Farrel to get anything done on this six-year-old case? Or was the assignment a kind of exile, getting Farrel out of the office and out of the Chief's hair? And with Saunders expected to carry the ball and dig up whatever actually came to light about Parmenter and the actual cause of the wreck? In this moment Saunders felt burdened with responsibility.

Farrel and Wall weren't gone long, and when they reentered the room they came from the kitchen. Wall was actually wiping his mouth. They both smelled strongly of whiskey. Saunders told himself it was just what he had expected. Farrel was on the booze, needed a refill now and then. He decided that Farrel had a bottle in the car somewhere, that he and Wall had taken it into the kitchen. Either that or Wall had recognized Farrel's distress signal, had taken him around the house to a bottle in a kitchen cupboard. Did it matter?

Mrs. Wall carried in a trayful of food and coffee. Ham sandwiches, a plate of cold chicken, potato salad, pickled eggs. She put the tray on a low table. Saunders hitched his chair forward. "Wow, am I hungry!"

She giggled. "Help yourself, young man! We raised most of it. Chickens, eggs, bought the ham off a neighbor who smoked it himself. Wait a minute. I forgot the cold tomatoes and the beer."

"I'll have a beer with the ham sandwich, if you don't mind," Saunders said. "To hell with Rule G." He looked ironically at Farrel, but Farrel didn't look back. He was picking up a boiled egg and a chicken wing.

"Rule G." Wall was smiling thoughtfully. "Long time since I'd thought about that. Long time since I had to, in fact. You can say this for being retired, it's nobody's doggone business whether—"

He stopped speaking. Mrs. Wall put the bottles of beer on the low table and faced the door. It was opening slowly to show the dark.

5.

The door drifted in, the hinges squeaking softly, and then stopped. They all waited for some sign of life on the porch, a footstep, a spoken word; but there was nothing. After a minute Wall rose and, speaking to his wife, said, "I forgot to latch it."

Farrel said, "Wait a minute."

Saunders remembered the plan, that Farrel would stay out of sight while he talked to Parmenter. He tensed. Perhaps it was too late for that.

Farrel stood up and went over to the door, opened the screen, went outside and shut the door behind him. He was gone about five minutes. When he came back he made sure that the door was closed completely.

Wall said, "See anybody?"

Farrel answered, "Wind's coming up. It must have pushed the door in."

Wall said, "I didn't expect him this early, anyway."

Somehow the mood of friendly cheer was broken, Saunders thought. Everyone was thinking about Parmenter now, about the errand which had brought them down here.

Farrel, chewing the chicken, suddenly motioned toward a door in the far wall. "Bedroom there?"

Wall nodded. "Is that where you want to sit? Shall I put a chair by the door for you?"

"Good idea."

Saunders had figured out the part he was meant to play, the responsibility the Chief had placed in him, but now he felt a strange sense of abandonment. After all, Farrel was the one who knew the ropes. He said tentatively, "Are you sure it wouldn't be better for you to talk to Parmenter?"

Farrel shook his head. "He knows what I know. Maybe he'll try to fool you. Even a lie can be important if it's the right kind of lie."

Now what the hell did he mean by that? Saunders watched as Farrel and Mr. Wall interrupted their meal to go to the bedroom, look over the place and put a chair inside the door. Then Farrel stood and thought it over.

He spoke to Mrs. Wall. "Would you object to having the bedroom door wide open, pushed all the way against the wall? I could sit a little distance away, then, out of sight. I'm afraid Parmenter would notice if it were open just a crack."

"I don't mind, no."

Farrel finally got it the way he wanted. He came back and finished the piece of chicken on his plate, unabashedly drank down a bottle of beer. There were a few minutes of silence, then sounds from outside. Steps crossed the porch.

Saunders choked on a crust of rye. Prickles ran across his skin. My God, he thought, I'm all atwitter. He downed the last of the beer to cover his choking.

Farrel had risen quickly and retreated into the dark bedroom. Wall went over to the door. The hinges of the screen door squeaked and there was a sudden light rapping on the panel. Wall turned the knob, pulled the door in, standing in such a way that Saunders could see the caller outside.

He was a tall man. The first impression that Saunders got was one of a consuming sickness. Brilliant eyes stared forth from beneath gray lids. A patch of scarlet blazed on each bony cheek. The hand he held toward Wall trembled with ague. The clothes were new. There was something funny about them, Saunders thought, as if the man had bought them outsize ·with the expectation of gaining weight. He took off his hat as he entered. His hair was thin, brushed close to his skull. It had once been red and now the amount of white in it gave it an orange cast.

Wall shook the man's hand, turning him meanwhile toward the room. He looked over at Mrs. Wall, nodded a voiceless greeting, and then his eyes settled on Saunders. Saunders thought that an instant suspicion flared in them.

"Glad you came early. Glad you're here," Wall was stammering. "Heh. Heh. Yessir, long time no see. You know the wife. This ... this is Mr. Saunders. Parmenter, Saunders. You two ought to have some friends in common." He sounded breathless and worried.

Parmenter ignored Saunders. "What does that mean?"

"He's with the railroad. Come, sit down."

Still wearing the suspicious look, Parmenter allowed himself to be seated. Mrs. Wall scurried around, bringing cold beer, more chicken, wanting to know if Mr. Parmenter wouldn't like a ham sandwich, too.

Parmenter looked the food over, promptly fell to. He ate like a wolf. Saunders watched, fascinated. Parmenter filled his mouth, and then worked his jaws, and the mass of food inside bulged and moved visibly behind the gray skin. Saunders almost felt sick.

"Beer, Mr. Parmenter?" Mrs. Wall had leaned close to him, an opened bottle, a glass, in her hands. He reached abruptly for the bottle and upended it. It gurgled down into the mass of food. Parmenter swallowed, then crammed in more ham sandwich and chicken. He sat crouched over the low table, his knees touching the tray, his skinny hands hovering over the food when they weren't busy lifting it to his maw. Saunders had never seen anything like it.

The Walls were obviously trying to conceal some surprise and discomfort. Mrs. Wall, rather pink in the face, retreated to a spot near the kitchen. Wall fumbled with his pipe.

Parmenter went on stuffing his cheeks, washing the mass down with beer. His glance occasionally skipped around the room, a swift shuttered look, and once when he happened to meet Wall's eyes he tried to smile. The effect in Saunders's opinion was ghastly.

What a way to eat, Saunders thought. He's like a beast. If Mrs. Wall had hesitated about handing over that beer, he'd have ripped it from her fingers. At this moment Parmenter picked up one of the pickled eggs and crammed it, entire, into his jaws.

Suddenly Saunders got a very uncomfortable impression of what life might have been like in Islas Marías. Enough frijoles to keep body and soul together, no doubt. Tortillas, chili. Nothing like this ham, though, or the cold fried chicken, the fresh rye, the spicy pickled eggs. He tried to imagine five years of Mexican prison fare and felt his stomach shrink.

Parmenter followed the egg with a chicken leg. He paused to wave it, half eaten, towards Saunders. "What about him?"

"Heh, he's with the railroad."

"Came down to see me?"

"Yeah. It's this way." Wall had his eye on Saunders as if he had expected him to speak up. "A lady called the Special Agent's Office. Said she's your wife's sister."

A bitter, pinched amusement seemed to flicker in Parmenter's face.

Saunders took up the tale. "A Miss Walker."

"Sure," Parmenter agreed, beginning to gnaw the chicken. "I know."

"She's worried about your daughter. She wanted us to find out if you were back in the country, if your daughter were with you. Someone in the office remembered you'd known Wall, that Wall lived down near the border. We called him right after he'd heard from you." He couldn't tell whether Parmenter believed it or not, or whether he suspected Wall of getting the railroad cop down here. The man's bony face hung over the food, his jaws distorted by chewing, his eyes skipping feverishly from item to item on the tray. He'd made remarkable inroads on Mrs. Wall's hospitality.

"She's very worried about the girl," Saunders added.

Parmenter looked up at him, squinting. "You tell Libby she can kiss my—" He seemed suddenly to notice poor, fluttery Mrs. Wall in the background. "—kiss my foot," he finished. He picked up a half sandwich. Then he gave Saunders a really hard stare. "What business is it of yours, anyway?"

"We're doing you a favor," Saunders said, feeling his way. "The girl is missing, a report on her disappearance filed with L.A.P.D. You were with the company a good many years, you've had a bad break. We're just trying to help."

All at once Parmenter seemed to lose interest in the food. He put down the half-eaten bread and ham and moved back into his chair. "Peg's eighteen. Grown-up. If she had a scrap with Libby—and who wouldn't?—and has left home, I can't help it."

"The situation is complicated by your wife's condition," Saunders said, watching closely.

Parmenter looked indifferent. "Is Marie sick again?"

"Peculiarly so," Saunders answered.

He waited. Parmenter didn't seem to know what to do with his hands. He folded them, unfolded them, pulled up the creases in the loose trousers, inspected his knuckles. He wanted to ask what Saunders meant; but caution and silence had become ingrained.

Finally he muttered, "What's that supposed to mean?"

Saunders ignored the query. Let him chew on it. "If your daughter joins you, do you plan to set up a home for her?"

Parmenter blinked, looked away. "What with? I'm broke."

"Later on, then? After you find a job?"

"Maybe."

There was an odd moment of silence then, broken only by Mrs. Wall's drawing a deep breath.

Parmenter was sitting perfectly still, his face controlled, as if balancing on some point of thought. He gave Saunders a quick glance. "You didn't come down here to rake over the Lobo Tunnel wreck, by any chance?"

Saunders shrugged. "I don't see how you could add to what we know."

"You look kind of young," Parmenter said, sizing him up. "I guess you came on after I left. Did they ever catch that—what's his name—that section hand they wanted?"

"We're investigating some leads," Saunders answered stiffly.

"Never got him," Parmenter summed up. He was silent again, studying over something in his mind. "You know

... funny thing ... I heard some rumors about Lobo Tunnel down there in Islas Marías. One of the screws told me they had an old Mex in there who claimed to have caused the wreck at Lobo, along with a couple of others. One in New Mexico. One in the Panhandle. Hated Yankee railroads for some imaginary reason."

"Did you get his name?"

Parmenter shook his head. "No. He's still down there, though. He killed a pal over a bottle of pulque." Parmenter brushed his trousers and stood up, implying that this was all he knew.

Mr. Wall also stood up, kind of flustered. "We didn't have much of a visit. Can't you come back before too long?"

"Can't do it," Parmenter said briefly. "I've got to get to L.A. and find a job."

"You going to stay in L.A.?" Wall asked.

Parmenter didn't answer the query, but evaded it by saying, "Wherever I go, I'll need a stake." His glance passed Saunders's quickly. He looked over at Mrs. Wall, hovering in the background, and said, "Thanks for the eats. You'll never know how good it all tasted."

"I'm glad you liked it." She smiled, but her examination of the empty platters seemed confused, as if she couldn't quite figure out where all the food had gone. "Well ... come back when you can."

"Maybe I'll see you folks in the city. I never want to come near the border again. Good-bye." Parmenter stepped over to the door, Wall following. They went out upon the porch and Saunders heard a brief mutter of parting. He glanced at the door, found Parmenter standing in the light, staring in at him while Wall made some remark. Memorizing his appearance, perhaps, so he'd recognize the railroad cop if they met in L.A. Saunders felt a prickle of irritation.

He tried to review the interlude just past. Had he handled Parmenter right? Should he have pressed him about his own part in the Lobo Tunnel affair, tried to worm from him the source of the money on which he'd gone to Mexico? No, he decided not. The amazing and unexpected nugget of information, the Mexican in Islas Marías who admitted causing the wreck, was worth far more than Parmenter's faded memories. Funny that Parmenter had volunteered it.

Maybe he wasn't quite the crook Ryerson and Farrel seemed to think he was. Maybe they had him all wrong.

There was a final good-bye. Parmenter left the porch, and Mr. Wall came in and closed the door. The next instant, cat-footed, Farrel appeared in the open bedroom doorway. He made brief business of thanking the Walls for their hospitality and co-operation. He turned to Saunders. "Let's see where he goes." He led the way to the outer door, stepped out swiftly.

Saunders made his good-byes, feeling awkward. It seemed pretty abrupt the way Farrel was handling it, though neither Mrs. Wall, clearing the table, nor Mr. Wall, busy filling his pipe, showed any annoyance. Mrs. Wall spoke as Saunders was leaving.

"I thought he'd make you tell him what was the matter with his wife."

"So did I," Saunders said from the doorway. "Maybe he wasn't surprised, though. Maybe he already knew."

"Maybe he didn't care," she said softly, picking up a plate.

It was completely dark outdoors. Saunders found his way to the car, started around it to the other side, when Farrel spoke in a whisper. "Get behind the wheel and drive off. I'll meet you down the road. That next corner."

"It's a pretty stiff walk," Saunders said.

"He's making it."

"He came out on the bus?"

"That's what I want to find out."

Saunders drove away. He looked for Parmenter but didn't pass him. There were paths through the fields, of course, and one of these may have provided a short cut. Saunders reached the next intersection, pulled the car up beside the road, killed the motor and the lights, and waited. It seemed a devil of a long time before Farrel climbed in beside him.

"He wasn't on the road," Saunders said, starting the car. "He's pretty cute," Farrel muttered, looking out at the dark. "What's he got to hide? I thought maybe he'd try to get a lift. This is a funny business."

"He's waiting at a bus stop away over there." Farrel jerked his head in the direction past Wall's place. "He didn't want to ride with you, even to speak to you again. He thinks he put something over. He wouldn't take a chance of spoiling it."

They drove towards town and Saunders tried to think what Parmenter had put over, and he couldn't figure it.

Subconsciously he wanted praise from Farrel; wanted the old hand to tell him he'd done well. Without realizing that he was digging for approval, he said, "Well, there's one thing. That Mexican prisoner in Islas Marías. He confessed he caused the wreck."

"Sure, that was it."

"That was what?"

"That's what Parmenter planted."

Saunders felt his face redden, was glad that the light from the dash wasn't strong enough to betray his embarrassment to Farrel. At the same time he was aware of a rush of resentment. How could Farrel decide so quickly that Parmenter had tried to pull a fast one?

He tried to keep the resentment out of his voice, however. "What was his motive?"

"A red herring," Farrel said indifferently. "Something to get our attention off him. Have us running down there trying to locate a lead." Farrel stretched his legs, lay back against the seat, his hat propped over his eyes. "Do you mind driving back?"

"Of course not. You drove down." He waited, wondering if Farrel wanted to nap. "What do you think Parmenter will try to do next?"

"Head for the loot," Farrel answered promptly.

"Maybe there isn't any, now."

"There's something," Farrel said, not explaining how or why he'd made up his mind about it. "Tomorrow we'll start on the other end, the people who collected the claims."

"Did you have any ideas about some of them?"

"Plenty," Farrel grunted.

"In particular?"

"It had to be something mighty fat. Parmenter got a big slice, and there must have been enough left to make the bite worthwhile. Now the two biggest payoffs weren't for deaths—you'd think death would be it, the worst, but these were only injuries." He jerked himself up a little in the seat. The wind sang at the open windows, night smells filled the car. They were passing a long irrigation canal and Saunders could hear the frogs and crickets. "A fellow named John Snowden got the jackpot, over two hundred thousand. He was young, a little over thirty, and he was a genius. He'd graduated from Cal Tech. Designed rockets, had ideas about satellites. Moon travel, God knows what. He got a bump on the noggin when the train piled up and then afterwards he was blind."

"Good God," Saunders said, thinking of the waste.

"Now I dug this up later on," Farrel went on. "See what you think of it. When Snowden was in high school, he used to have some sort of hysterical attacks. He'd collapse. He was high-strung and very nervous, and he'd have headaches and complain of rainbows blotting out his vision."

"Oh-oh."

"I located a couple of his teachers. They were crazy about him, he'd been the star pupil; but he was a perfectionist, a fanatic. He drove himself. When things didn't go right, he'd go off into a tizzy." Farrel was smiling faintly. "At the time of the wreck he was on his way out here to work on some project he'd had a hand in before. It was all top-secret stuff, I could never get a whiff of what it was all about, of course. But I did pin this down. Snowden had been in on the start of the project and something he'd originated had bugs in it."

The lights of town were coming closer through the night.

"Did the railroad pay off on a real injury," Farrel said softly, "or were we buying rainbows?"

6.

Saunders said, "If it was fake, how could Parmenter have known?"

"There's one thing that could have happened," Farrel answered. "Snowden could have had an attack on the train, called the porter for help. The porter would have reported it to Parmenter."

"Had an attack before the wreck?" Saunders thought about it. "And then the porter was killed."

"That's it."

"Was anyone traveling with Snowden?"

"He was alone in his compartment."

"You think Parmenter could have made a deal right there? In the middle of everything?"

"I don't know." Farrel straightened up, looked out at

the passing lights, the quiet streets of the town. "There was a second case sort of like Snowden's. A woman, Sonya Myles. A Russian dancer, married to an American. She'd been top of the heap in Europe but after her marriage and coming over here, hadn't done too much. She was coming to L.A. to sign a movie contract ... *maybe*. The wreck left her with an injured spine. She couldn't move her legs. Negotiations for the movie work were dropped, of course. She collected almost as much as Snowden."

"Was she in the same car?"

"One compartment between them."

"Same porter?"

"Of course."

"It wasn't just the money made you interested," Saunders decided. "If something happened before the wreck, the porter would have known about it. It was the fact that the porter was killed in the car where these two big claims originated."

"Uh-huh."

"This business with Snowden and his rainbows—anything corresponding to that with the dancer?"

"Not that I could find out."

"What about death claims? Weren't there some big ones?"

Farrel shook his head. "Not in the same class with Snowden and the Myles woman. You see, these were young people, they both had tremendous possibilities ahead of them—fortunes to be made, with any luck, and in Snowden's case a brain the government depended on was put out of commission."

Saunders turned a corner into the boulevard that led north. "Where are they now?"

"Snowden lives at the beach, on the coast above Santa Monica. The Myles woman and her husband have a ranch in the foothills of Riverside County. Bought it after the settlement. It's a whopper of a place."

"She didn't get that for peanuts. She's accounted for a chunk of her loot, at least. What about Snowden?"

"He got married. I went to see him after he bought his beach place. I don't think it cost him over fifteen thousand. There didn't seem anything fancy about the life he was living. He explained that he was saving the settlement for medical care, hoping to get some improvement in his sight."

"Somehow he sounds like our best bet."

Farrel was still looking at the lights. "Could be."

Saunders stepped from the elevator, looked automatically down the hall towards Betsy's door. There was a light under it.

He thought about ringing her bell, and then looked at his watch and decided that it was too late. Maybe he'd run into her again in the morning.

He went into his own place and glanced around half expectantly before remembering that his mother was gone. He went into the bedroom, shed his clothes, hung up his suit, put the gun away, dumped the shirt and underwear and socks into the hamper in the bathroom. Then he remembered that he was getting low on clothes, and checked up. Last pair of socks. Underwear remaining was old, mended. It would do, though. He went out into the kitchen in his pajamas. The coffeepot smelled stale. He recalled that his mother occasionally rinsed it out with a soda solution. He was looking for the soda when the door buzzer sounded.

It was Betsy. She had on a housecoat, her hair brushed back, make-up removed. She looked ready for bed. Saunders blinked at her.

"Come over for some Sanka and a cupcake," she offered.

"I'm … I'm …" He felt himself flushing. She stared boldly

in at his pajamas.

"We're rather grown-up now," she told him. "I think you could come over in a robe, and we could drink coffee and talk without anything happening. Anything we didn't want to happen, that is."

He felt the blood drain from his face; and she giggled.

"You've seemed pretty independent these last few days," she said. "Mama's gone. I like your mother very much, she's nice, but when you're around her you act like a baby."

He wanted to slam the door, but didn't. Betsy looked pretty cute with the make-up off, hair tied back, ready for bed.

He put on a robe and followed her back to her place, and she served Sanka and maple-nut-frosted cupcakes, and they talked. The funny thing was, when he went back to his own place to go to bed at a quarter of two, talking was all they had done. He'd been telling her about the wreck at Lobo Tunnel.

Farrel turned on the light and looked around. Mrs. Bellows had been in, picking up. The newspapers were gone. Magazines and books stacked. Pajamas on a hook in the closet. The bed made and the dresser dusted. In sudden suspicion he opened the bottom drawer of the dresser. There in the nest formed by papers and old clothes lay the empty bottle he'd planted behind Haines's bed, along with the one which still had whiskey in it.

He grinned a little. Dammit, he hadn't fooled her a bit. He mixed whiskey with some water from the bathroom, sat on the edge of the bed in his underwear, trying to figure out a new trick to play on the divinity student.

Shortly the whiskey took hold and he lay back and looked at the lights. His eyes twitched out of focus; the light blurred. Well, one more slug. He tried to raise himself and then fell on the pillow and was asleep. When he woke up the light was still on and dawn was in the window.

Peg Parmenter stirred on the bench in the bus depot, opening her eyes. She was cramped, chilled, and grimy. Silt had filled her clothes from the bottom of the irrigation canal. On the walk back to town—she'd been ashamed to catch the bus—her clothes had dried, but in drying had almost frozen her to death, and had remained stiff, wrinkled, with the silt ingrained. She knew that her coat was draggled, her shoes lumpish. It was awful what a soaking did to clothes.

She sat up, stretching her muscles, and looked at the clock above the counter across the room. It would soon be time for the bus to L.A. She thought with relief of her room at home, a hot bath, clean clothing.

She opened her damp purse, took out a mirror and lipstick. Over the mirror she saw a man looking at her from a stool at the lunch counter, and her instinct was to crouch low, to gather herself, to be ready to run.

Then anger followed. Anger at the unknown enemy—this man, perhaps?—who had searched for her, sure-footed and uncannily accurate in the dark. A faceless adversary who had seemed to see her when she couldn't see him, who had sent bullets seeking her flesh. She stared at the man for a long moment over the mirror, her heart throbbing with fright and rage, ready to scream if he moved towards her; but then after a little while she calmed down, deciding that this man at the counter was merely trying to flirt. The anger drained out of her and she felt scornful. He was young, she saw, too young to have the kind of background in which to have become involved with her father and to be her father's enemy. He was just a cocky kid trying to pick up a girl in a bus depot. She turned her back to him.

Her jaw shook, though, as she tried to apply the lipstick. The taste of fear was new in her mouth, as rank as the taste of the irrigation water, the weedy slime, the silt.

She thought over her errand here, her hopes for it, the way it had turned out. Of course, even in the beginning she had sensed a certain risk.

What should she do now? Pretend that nothing had happened? Go home and wait? Would her father contact her again, make excuses for not appearing, perhaps give more explicit directions?

No, the directions had been plain enough. Don't confuse yourself on that point, she admonished with an inner voice. Don't pretend you must have been mixed up in someone else's rendezvous. Only your father and you—supposedly—knew of that meeting place.

One other had found out somehow. Did this imply that something unfortunate must have happened to her father? She thought it over.

A slip, she decided. A slip, and now there was this sour taste of fear in her mouth and the urge, just below the surface, to crouch small and to run. There was no guarantee against future slips. Was it worth it? Was even the money worth it?

She put away the lipstick and mirror, forced herself to sit still and dispassionately consider. The money was worth it, she decided. The life she had lived these last few years wasn't worth repeating; an extension of it didn't bear looking at. Poverty had a taste of its own, like the ditch water. It had a voice, too, a voice like that of your penny-pinching aunt. A hoarse, bottomless voice like Libby Walker's. It had even a grain against your skin, like the mud on the bottom of the canal. You carried it around, gritty, prickling.

The knowledge that she was being unfair to her aunt, to the woman who had stepped in, who had tried to be both mother and father, only added to her irritable anger. To stifle her conscience, she forced herself to remember the scene in the school principal's office, where her aunt had taken her to explain that she needed dental work and there was no money for it and to ask help from the P.T.A.

Peg opened her eyes wider, fixing the scene in memory. *That fried my soul.*

Sweet charity—

The first thing I'm going to ask my father when I meet him is to teach me how to be a crook.

Pete looked up as Farrel came in. He noted the reddened eyes and the general air of untidiness, and was glad that Ryerson had come in and gone out quickly on another matter. Farrel came to his desk, peered through the inner wall of glass and, seeing Ryerson's desk vacant, said, "What's the word?"

"He's been and gone. What did you get from Parmenter?"

"What did you expect?"

"What you got." Pete nodded, ran a report form into his typewriter. "Give it to me and I'll write it up. It'll be on his desk when he gets back."

Farrel ignored the implication that he, himself, might better be gone. In a somewhat sarcastic tone he began to wind through the official phrasing. It all had a pattern. He described the ride to San Diego, the stake-out at Wall's place, Saunders's talk with the suspect.

Pete clucked through his teeth. "Well, wait a minute. Suspect. What's he suspected of doing?"

"Getting his hands on some dough is all I know. Isn't that enough?" Farrel said with dry irony.

"Maybe we'd just better call him a witness," Pete suggested.

"Okay."

While Farrel was signing the report, Saunders came in. To Pete's surprise, Saunders didn't look too hot, either. He looked tired and as if he'd missed some sleep, and as if something was puzzling him. He read over the report with an air of indifference, signed under Farrel's name.

Farrel said to Pete, "We're going out to Lobo Tunnel on our way up the coast."

"I'll tell him."

"We'll see Snowden today, the Myles woman tomorrow, some of the death-claims payees after that."

Pete nodded as if the routine reminded him of old familiar things. "Good luck."

Saunders was thinking to himself, It's six years old. What in hell can we do with it now?

The elevator dropped them to the basement garage, where Farrel checked out a company car. He drove, talking very little. Saunders thought he had an air of dragging tiredness, wondered if it was hangover. They went out through Glendale, then cut north and east, left most of the traffic behind. It was a funny detour if you were headed for the coast, Saunders decided. The miles fled under the tires, the air grew dry and the scenery withered. Now they were on the fringe of the desert, among Joshua trees and stubby hills.

Farrel left the paved road for a dirt track. They left the Joshua trees behind, the mountains turned sort of pink and got steeper. It was about noon when Farrel jerked the car to a stop and announced that they'd reached Lobo Tunnel. Saunders looked around at the hot, arid landscape. There wasn't a tunnel in sight.

"Over there." Farrel was pointing to some rails, to a cut in the side of a hill. "They've daylighted it since the wreck." It was rough walking. Saunders almost fell down when his feet slipped on a gravelly patch at a steep place. When they got to the cut, and stood there in the baking

heat, Saunders wondered why Farrel had wanted to come.
There was nothing to be seen here.

Farrel plodded around, seemed to be looking everything
over and checking something in his head. He glanced at
Saunders, who wasn't moving. "Let's have a gander at
that water tower."

They returned to the car and Farrel drove perhaps a
mile. The road petered out into a cow track and then into
nothing. They left the car and hiked. Farrel squinted from
under his hat brim. "There it is."

"There it was," Saunders corrected. There was a half-
collapsed framework, a few tank stays standing cockeyed
against the brilliant desert sky. "Where on earth did they
get water out here?"

"There's a spring," Farrel grunted. "Anyway, you're not
as far from everything as it seems. Little town named
Sagebloom just down the track."

"We didn't pass it."

"We'll go through it when we leave."

It was a little easier walking the ties; hard, though, to
adjust your step to the interval between ties. Saunders felt
as if he were mincing along on his toes. They were getting
close now. He noted that the rotting tank stood at the
bottom of a slight wash. There were odds and ends of old
pipe around, a platform where a pump may have stood.
A wooden duct, half buried in the sand, led off toward
the humped hills.

The end of the duct was hidden by a heap of dead brush.
Farrel walked over and kicked the heap apart. A little
rocky pool of greenish water lay revealed.

"Now, that's interesting," Farrel remarked. He seemed
to have got wind of something, Saunders was puzzled
what. He stood still, looking all around, and then became
engrossed in some scratchy marks on the hard earth. They
looked recent to Saunders—recent and meaningless.

Farrel nodded off down the track. "The culvert's new." Saunders could see the culvert's cement rim sticking out from the embankment. Farrel hitched his shoulders under his coat, as if the heat bothered him, and set off. Saunders went too, keeping to the ties.

The culvert was a big one, paved on the bottom, the ceiling shaped like an inverted U under which Farrel could almost stand upright. It must have been about twenty feet from end to end, channeling water from the small wash to a bigger drain on the other side of the track. Farrel went in out of sight and Saunders, on the embankment above, heard him grunt something.

Saunders, curious, went down to look.

Back in the shadows was some trash. Saunders decided that a hobo or two had made a temporary lodging here. There was even a small blackened patch against the wall, smoked by a fire.

Farrel had squatted above the heap of trash, was turning over the bits and pieces gingerly. He found a wine bottle with the neck missing, picked it away from the rest by hooking a finger inside it. There were some scraps of brown paper, some large and some small, torn up and half burned, and Farrel lifted these scraps one by one to his nose to sniff them. A weird performance, in Saunders's opinion.

A twisted rag lay under the papers. Farrel pulled it loose from the packed sand. It seemed to be a tattered sleeve from a shirt. It looked as if it had been here a lot longer than the papers, and apparently Farrel thought so, too, for he tossed it aside. When he had discarded the rag and had sniffed at most of the paper, Farrel spread one of the larger scraps on the paving and then raked up some small litter, sand intermingled with dry weedy leaves and little sticks, and made a small parcel. He stuck it in his pocket. Then he picked up the wine bottle with his hooked finger and came outside.

"They'll have a jungle here if you don't watch them," Saunders said, not quite sure Farrel knew what he was doing.

But Farrel was looking off down the track again. "The siding's gone. They've changed things around here. Daylighted the tunnel, fixed the culvert to handle the flash floods...." He sounded as if someone had been meddling with his business. "Well, let's go. Let's go have a look at Sagebloom."

7.

Whenever Saunders saw one of these out-of-the-way desert towns, he wondered why on earth people happened to be settled in them.

Sagebloom was typical. It was on no major highway and so had no traffic, no tourists. The government had not chosen to endow it with one of the monster air bases like those near Palmdale and Lancaster. It didn't possess glamour and atmosphere like Palm Springs. It looked dead. The bare rocky hills shut it in, the heat baked it, there was silence. Saunders couldn't see a tree, not even a decent-sized shrub, in the whole place. About twenty houses, most of them shacks, straggled here and there over the landscape, connected with the center of town by dimly defined ruts which passed for streets. A couple of the shacks had vines trained up their porches, and this was the extent of the greenery in Sagebloom. There wasn't even any sage.

The railroad depot and a couple of shanties made up one side of the business block. Facing these across the paved road which bisected Sagebloom were about a half dozen business establishments. Saunders noted a garage and service station on one corner. A general store, a bar, a barbershop, another bar, and a tool company made up the rest. The tool company advertised mining equipment. The best-looking of the lot was the second bar, a building almost new with a neon sign which read *air conditioned* over the doorway. Farrel spotted it. "Let's get cooled off."

There weren't many cars on the street. Farrel pulled in near the bar, got out, looked back at Saunders. "Coming?"

If he doesn't care, why should I? Saunders thought. Either Farrel trusted Saunders to say nothing about his drinking or he didn't give a damn. Saunders followed him into the dim, cool interior.

Farrel crawled upon a bar stool, pushed his hat back, rubbed his face. There was nobody else in the place but the bartender. When the bartender came to take the order, Farrel ordered a beer. Saunders stiffly asked for a lemonade.

When the drinks had been served, Farrel engaged the bartender in talk. They learned that none of the work-train crews had been in town for over a week.

Farrel glanced up casually from his beer. "Ever see a little guy hanging around—looks Slavic—" He continued, and Saunders realized that in an offhand way he was giving an excellent description of Versprelle.

The bartender couldn't remember anybody like that. The town was busy on Saturday nights, mostly, when the guys from the work-train crews, the scattered ranchers and miners, came in to have a time for themselves. The rest of the week it was pretty quiet. Like now. If Farrel's Slavic friend had been in on Saturday, he might have missed him. If he'd been around during the quiet days, he'd have remembered; and he didn't.

They went back to the car, and then Farrel remembered something more he wanted to ask the bartender. It was as bald a dodge as Saunders could think of. A double shot on top of the beer, he told himself. He stared stonily at the barren skyline.

Farrel drove all right, though. They left Sagebloom, the road took them down out of the sun-scarred land into a greener place, and then they were headed for the coast. Torn scraps of fog met them when they reached the coast at Malibu.

Saunders was recapitulating to himself the information he had on Snowden. A scientific genius, blind since the wreck. Farrel had dug up some interesting stuff about him. In high school he'd been subject to hysterical spells in which his sight had been blotted out by rainbows. A graduate physicist at the time of the wreck, seemingly on the verge of an important career, he had been on his way to L.A. to check some super-secret gizmo which had developed bugs.

The thing to find out, of course, was whether the bugs were Snowden's responsibility and whether their appearance was blamed on his work.

A fine chance to get that information, Saunders thought in irony, by two railroad dicks bucking the security police.

The coast highway wound above the crags, the scraps of beaches, and then dropped into a wide green valley. A row of houses faced the surf. Farrel pulled off the highway into the private road, rolled past the row of garages, and stopped. Saunders got out, feeling the nip of the sea wind, tasting a scraggle of fog. Beyond the edge of Snowden's garage he could see a big paved patio, furnished with lounges and chairs and a big umbrella. The furniture was of tubular aluminum with canvas cushions. The cushions looked faded and the big umbrella had a tear in it, and a section of fringe hung loose, whipping in the wind.

They walked through the patio. Their footsteps echoed ghostily in the enclosed space. The sky above was gray. It was hard to recall the heat, the dryness of Sagebloom. Saunders glanced at his watch. Almost three. A little over two hours from Sagebloom and he couldn't even summon a memory of the baking warmth.

The house was redwood and plaster, low and long, no windows on this side except little ones near the top of the wall. Farrel pressed a button and they waited. Farrel hadn't talked much on the way from the desert, and now he didn't look at Saunders as they waited; and for the first time Saunders wondered how Farrel liked having him along. The thought made him sort of uncomfortable.

All at once a soft masculine voice spoke on the other side of the door. "Who is it?"

"My name's Farrel, sir. I'd like to speak to Mr. Snowden."

A silent moment passed; evidently the man on the other side of the door was trying to place the name. "Farrel of the railroad police?"

"Yes, sir."

The door moved inward; a little reluctantly, Saunders thought. The man inside was tall, young, a little stooped. The thing Saunders noticed at once was how tanned he was. His light hair was sunbleached almost white. His eyes were hidden by dark lenses. He wore a short-sleeved sport shirt, dark blue, and gray trousers. Saunders was struck then by the strong, mobile-looking hand which held the doorknob. The tanned fingers were long and graceful, the wrist strongly boned. It was an artist's hand, a sculptor's hand, made to mold, to create.

"Hello, Mr. Snowden." Farrel walked in, offered his hand. Snowden took it at once, no fumbling whatever; and Saunders realized at once that Snowden could see.

Farrel hadn't missed it, either. "Well, you're doing a lot better."

Snowden smiled, his teeth white and strong in his brown

face. "Oh, yes, I've had good medical care and a lot of luck. Plus living out here, getting a lot of sun. You'd never know it by today, but usually it's fine." He moved back down the short hallway. "Come on in, sit down. Your friend, too."

Farrel introduced him to Saunders. Snowden nodded in greeting. He led them into an immense room whose windows faced the sea. The gray light from the beach filled the place, shone in the china knickknacks, the copper lamps, the vases on the mantel, the fire tongs on the hearth. It was a very well furnished room, Saunders thought, but not too well kept. Life with his meticulous mother had taught him to sense when a place went undusted, was casually used as this room was.

They sat down. Snowden offered cigarettes, tried to light them from a silver table lighter; it didn't work. He frowned above the dark lenses. "Damned thing's out of fuel." He fished matches from a shirt pocket. When the cigarettes were lit, he said, "What brings you all the way from L.A.?"

Farrel said, "It's still Lobo Tunnel."

"Never found out how it happened?"

Farrel said carefully, "Oh, yes, Mr. Snowden, we know how it happened. Some ties and rocks were piled in the opening of the tunnel. We just don't know who, or why."

Snowden's attitude seemed to stiffen subtly. "How can I help?"

"I don't know that you can. This is routine. You know that by now." He paused and Snowden nodded, seemed to relax again. "Now, a conductor named Parmenter, the conductor on that train—" Farrel paused again to cross his legs, to adjust the cuffs of his pants. He was looking at Snowden, too; but Snowden just went on smoking. "I suppose you remember him."

"Yes, I do," Snowden answered. "I couldn't tell you

what he looked like. After the wreck, after my eyes had gone out, he was awfully decent about helping and looking after everyone."

Farrel said casually, "He's been in Mexico for quite a while."

"Lucky stiff. I envy him. I used to love that country."

Farrel didn't explain why there was no reason to envy Parmenter. "He's back in the States now and we want to know if he contacts any of you, any of the passengers."

Snowden's sun-bleached brows rose above the lenses. "Why on earth should he do that?"

"He's a kind of peculiar fellow."

"He must be." There was a lot of astonishment in Snowden's tone; and Saunders wondered if it could all be real.

Snowden added, "Do you think he might come here to see me?"

Farrel refused to say what he thought. "If he does, will you call us?"

Snowden tapped out his cigarette and said uncertainly, "I guess it would depend on his errand. There's something here I don't understand. Does Parmenter represent some menace? Is he holding a grudge? Is he ... demented?"

Saunders thought these conjectures pretty farfetched.

"We're not sure what he means to do," Farrel said. "If Parmenter asked you for money, would you give him some?"

"Money?" Snowden seemed to be feeling the word over in his mind, as if it had form and he was afraid of it. "I haven't any money." He made an abrupt, nervous gesture. "I'd better explain," he added quickly. "My medical bills took a tremendous toll of the settlement I got from the railroad. And then I ... I formed a trust fund for my wife."

He's jumpy now, Saunders noted to himself. Farrel has a thumb under the edge of his shell and is getting ready to flip him over. Saunders was tense with expectation. Farrel was going to press Snowden, find out if he was vulnerable, whether he'd give Parmenter a bribe if Parmenter demanded it.

Farrel didn't do anything of the kind. He lapsed into a short silence, looking out through the great dusty panes at the gray sea and the beach. When he spoke it was quietly, offhandedly. "Do you ever get lonesome out here?"

Snowden seemed caught off base by the change of tone. "Lonesome?" He had to think this over. "Yes. Yes, I do. I'd play the radio all the time, but all the good programs are on TV now, it's just ... junk. It's hard to find good music. The doctors think I may be able to read again in a few months. That's going to be a great day in my life."

"What about records?"

"I can't read the labels. To hell with them." There was quick anger, loss of control which Snowden tried to conceal by changing position in the chair and by lighting a new cigarette. He coughed behind his hand.

To Saunders's surprise, Farrel stood up presently and moved as if to leave. "Don't bother letting us out. We'll shut the door." He went over to the hall entry and spoke to Snowden over his shoulder. "Give my regards to your wife, will you?"

Snowden looked as if Farrel had hit him then. Saunders was watching from across the room. Snowden sat in the light from the windows, and the sudden cringing motion was quite visible. "Well ... sure," Snowden stammered after a moment. To Saunders he said, "Glad to have met you."

"Same here, Mr. Snowden." Saunders felt awkward; he wasn't sure if Snowden were really half blind or faking behind the glasses, and whether he ought to feel sorry for him or be twisting his arm to make him talk. If Farrel felt any similar uncertainty, he didn't show it.

Outside in the car Farrel squinted against the gray light

and said, "I wonder where in hell his wife is."

Saunders almost didn't conceal his start. Well, Farrel wasn't as slow as he'd thought. Funny, though, that a man like Farrel would sense the air of faint neglect in the house. It hadn't been too obvious.

Farrel was nodding. "You caught that business with the lighter? Someone else used to keep it filled for him. And someone else used to read the record labels. His wife. Now she isn't there anymore."

Saunders smiled slightly, feeling disgusted with himself. Farrel hadn't needed any sixth sense about a dusty house. He'd just kept an eye out for the obvious.

Farrel hit a bar on the way back to L.A. He told Saunders he needed to phone. Saunders burned, but he waited silently in the car. If Ryerson caught on they could both be out on their ears. You didn't fool around with Rule G, working for a railroad.

Farrel was on the thin verge of being canned, but it didn't seem to worry him. He just kept plodding along in the routine related to the Lobo Tunnel investigation. The thought returned, He's like an old horse who sticks his neck in a familiar yoke. They'd seen Parmenter, they'd visited the scene of the wreck and interviewed the passenger whose claim had involved the biggest pay-off. Tomorrow they'd follow the rest of the pattern, visit the crippled dancer. Yes, it was a rut.

Saunders remembered something else. Farrel had said that to a cinder dick there's no closed file on a train wreck until it's solved.

Drunk or sober, Saunders surmised, Farrel kept Lobo Tunnel with him all the time.

Farrel came back faster than he had gone in. He slid behind the wheel. "I called Pete. Parmenter's sister-in-law has been trying to get hold of us. I think we'd better stop there on our way in to town."

Involuntarily Saunders glanced at the watch on his wrist.

Farrel added, "If you've got a date I can go alone."

Saunders controlled a flash of irritation. Farrel was taking a hell of a lot on himself in this six-year-old affair. "I'm going along; I want to meet the woman."

Farrel started the motor, put the car into gear. "She's a character. You'll see."

The bright hot light of the autumn afternoon was unkind to the shrubby desolation of the yard, the unpainted trim around the porch, the scabby brass doorknob. The faded blonde woman who materialized behind the screen matched the place, Saunders thought. Her voice was, as he expected, harsh and whining. "Oh. Mr. Farrel. I'm so glad you could come." She unhooked the screen and led them into the house.

Farrel introduced him to the woman.

"I'm pleased to meet you, Miss Walker."

She merely nodded, having eyes only for Farrel. She remained standing for a moment, while Farrel and Saunders seated themselves, then rushed away into another part of the house. When she came back she had some clothing over her arm, carried a pair of shoes. She practically dumped them into Farrel's lap. "There, look at them! Touch them!"

Farrel had reacted with surprise but was now examining the clothes. "Whose are they?"

"Hers. Peg's." She chewed a knuckle.

"She came back?" Farrel glanced up into her face.

She moved away slightly and averted her eyes. "I've been so distracted, worried about her—I stayed home. I called Mrs. Bonner and said I was sick. Need the money, Oh Lord how I need it ... Well, I was here when Peg came, so I'm glad. It was nearly noon. She crept in like a dying cat."

"Do you think she saw her father?"

"I'm coming to that." A shiver trembled through her. Saunders realized how terrifically keyed up she was, how possessed by an emotion that threatened to run away with her. Was it fear? "She'd been home for a half hour or so when the phone rang. I answered. I know it was *him*. He said, 'Is Peg there?' and when I said, 'Yes,' he just hung up." She stopped as if to give Farrel a chance to grasp the import of this.

"He didn't ask to speak to her?"

"He didn't think she'd be here!"

Farrel was obviously trying to follow her line of thought. "And then, the clothes—these were what she'd been wearing?"

She clapped her hands together, knotting the fingers. "Yes. Yes. Don't you see what's wrong with them?"

"There's ..." Farrel was rolling an edge of material between his fingers. "Dust? Sand?"

"Can't you feel the damp?" She rushed to him and pulled he stuff around, grabbed Farrel's hand and forced it along a seam. "Feel that?"

Saunders went over. He was puzzled by her air of outraged excitement. He picked up the end of something in the heap, pulled it free and then wanted to drop it swiftly. It had revealed itself as a silk brassiere. Wrinkled as it was, the shape of breasts molded by the damp silk was still distinct. They were young, round breasts. Libby Walker gave him a scalding glance and yanked the brassiere from his fingers.

Farrel put the clothing aside and picked up one of the shoes.

Her breath whistled through her teeth. "Look at the mud!"

Farrel hefted the shoe as if something in its weight interested him. "Still wet. Not just dampened, either—soaked. What did your niece say?"

"Nothing. She scarcely spoke to me. She bathed and changed her clothes, then waited around for a little while, then left. I think she expected *him* to call again. I think she was angry because I'd answered the phone. She's got some plan in her noggin. She thinks I might spoil it."

"Have you called Missing Persons to tell them she's back?"

Her face twisted. She seemed hung upon some terrible indecision. "I didn't call them at all, not even to report her missing. I ... I decided they might not pay much attention, a girl that old, not my child either."

Farrel set the shoes down. "When she comes in, see if you can't get her to agree to come downtown and talk to us."

She ignored the request. Her gaze was fixed on the clothes Farrel had put upon a table. "What do you think happened to her while she was gone?"

Saunders tried to lighten the situation. "Maybe she fell into somebody's swimming pool."

They both looked at him then. Libby reacted as if he'd struck her with the flat of his hand.

"Now that'd be something," Farrel grunted.

Saunders felt unaccountably ashamed of himself.

8.

The clatter of silver and dishes had diminished in the room below, the voices were dying out. Then Farrel heard Mrs. Bellows come up the stairs. She rapped at his door. "Aren't you going to have dinner?"

He was sitting on the edge of his bed in pants and undershirt. A bottle sat by his right foot. He picked this up, leaned across the bed and deposited it on the floor out of sight, along with the drink he had held in his hand. Then he went to the door and opened it and looked out politely at Mrs. Bellows. "I guess not."

"You ought to eat something." She started to say more, and then she must have caught the odor of whiskey because a pinched look came over her face.

"I'm not very hungry."

She half turned from him as if to go, indecision in her manner, something warning him that she meant to talk further and that he wouldn't like it. He wanted to shut the door; but she'd been too decent to him and he couldn't cut her off. She turned to face him again. "You're very foolish to punish yourself like this. Take my remarks as those of an old friend. She wasn't worth it. Someday you might ..." She put out a hand, not quite far enough to touch him. The fear of offending him struggled with the demands of her conscience. "You might meet your child again. You'd want to be in good shape then, wouldn't you? Who knows when that day might come?"

He didn't have any answer for her. He looked at her calmly, the way he could look at almost anything when he'd had enough to drink.

"I'm not the only one who worries," she went on slowly. "Would you be ... awfully angry ... if Mr. Haines came in to talk to you in a little while?"

It took a moment or so for him to realize what she meant, and then the ludicrousness of what she proposed brought an eruption of laughter, an inward frenzy of mirth, a towering alcoholic boffo. He stood looking at her, in appearance more somber than ever, while the crackling merriment echoed in his brain. Finally he muttered, "Well, why not?"

Afterwards he was not very clear about the visit of the young divinity student. He recalled sitting on the edge of the bed, the bottle between his feet, the glass in his hand, while Haines talked about something or other. He nodded in agreement, to encourage Haines, when he thought of it. He had begun to get the hazy idea that Haines had been admitted to this formerly happy-go-lucky establishment in order to work some miracle upon himself, and he fought off this impression because it was going to make him mad.

Part of the time Haines seemed to be sitting in a chair, part of the time on the edge of the table. His whereabouts seemed vague and fugitive. Mostly he was a resounding voice and a long brown face. Finally Farrel discovered himself on his knees, Haines close beside him and muttering over him in a prayerful attitude.

In the next instant, it seemed, like the snap of a shutter, the scene had changed utterly. He was wearing his shirt, tie, coat and hat and was hopping off a bus and headed for a bar.

He stumbled to the curb and glanced around him. This wasn't too far from the office. It was the middle of skid row. Neon glittered, there was the honk and rustle of traffic, and he was assaulted by the yammerings of barkers outside the shooting galleries and the all-night shows.

He went into the bar, got onto a stool, ordered a drink, fumbled for his wallet. It was then he noticed the stiffness in his hand. He brought his right hand close to his eyes and examined the bruises and scrapes across his knuckles.

Had he punched that sanctimonious young punk?

God forbid!

He tried to worry over it but the sense of oppression drifted away. He paid for the drink, tipped the bartender, sat looking into the bar mirror. All at once his thoughts seemed to clear and turn over, and he was thinking about Parmenter. A bright new conclusion glittered in his mind, as real as the display of bottles back of the bar. Parmenter was broke; flat-broke, strapped. How did he know this?

He found his own mind answering its question: Parmenter must be broke because he was so hungry. Only someone down to his last few cents would have stoked up as Parmenter had at Wall's house. Parmenter had tried to eat enough to do him for an extra day or two.

Something else was meant to follow this conclusion. He waited, watching the faint shiver of the liquor in the shot glass, his hands spread on the bar.

Parmenter would have to make his move right away. He had nothing to fall back on. His wife was in a state hospital, his daughter unemployed, the sister-in-law who kept his house an implacable enemy. If the source of the money on which he had gone to Mexico still existed, he'd head for it at once. For some reason then Farrel thought of Snowden's lonely house at the beach, Snowden alone in it, a half-blind man angry and afraid because his wife was gone.

"I should have asked him where she was," Farrel said. The patron on the next stool turned and glanced at him oddly.

If Snowden had been Parmenter's victim, Farrel felt sorry for him. He was a sitting duck under present circumstances.

"The dirty little blackmailer!"

"What did you call me?" demanded the man on the next stool.

Farrel looked at him in surprise. The guy had a thick neck and heavy shoulders, red skin, a tufty crew cut growing out, meanness back of his little eyes. "Go to hell," Farrel said.

Again there was the click of the shutter, a change of scene; and now they were in the alley behind the bar, getting ready to fight.

Across town Saunders paced his living room. It was getting late. He was nervous and frustrated. Betsy was home; he'd heard dance music from her radio, seen the light beneath her door. She had made no move to contact him, however; and for some reason he found himself unable to go over and casually barge in on her. On the table across the room lay his mother's letter, freshly torn open, in which she expressed a wish that he was getting along all right and in which she warned that she had decided to stay away two weeks longer because someone had invited her to their lodge at Tahoe.

Smoking and pacing, Saunders tried to analyze this silly inability to be offhand about Betsy. They'd known each other for months as casual friends and now there was this feeling that to go over there would be to reveal something about himself, some wolfish underhanded trait which might annoy her. Where had such a goofy idea come from? Why shouldn't tonight be like last night?

It wouldn't be, something warned.

On top of the other thing, Saunders thought, the evenings now seemed so damnably brief. It was a peculiarity of the day he had not noted before. Up until his mother's leaving, the time between his coming home at night and going to bed had rolled along in a leisurely routine. There was no silly sense of being rushed or cheated. Before dinner he had read the paper or looked at something on TV. When the meal was done, he'd helped his mother clean up. Afterwards he had occasionally gone out for a date, or to a movie with some old school friends; most of the time he had read or he and his mother had played cards.

Now there was this frantic sense of time rushing past, and the preposterous embarrassment about going to see Betsy.

Probably she expected him to come. After all, a girl couldn't always make the first move.

He went over to the window and looked out at the

night, the traffic in the street below, and listened to the grumble and mutter of the city. In an effort to get his mind off Betsy, he tried to think of other things. The job. Lobo Tunnel.

There wasn't even a tunnel there anymore; it had been day-lighted and now there was just a cut. No evidence of the wreck remained, not even to a rusty bolt. The water tower where the character named Versprelle had grown his patch of marijuana was falling down. What Farrel thought he'd found in that culvert was an optimist's dream.

Tomorrow they'd go see the crippled dancer, this Sonya Myles, and after that there would be other claimants; and then Ryerson would expect something to emerge. God only knew what.

After six years, he wanted miracles!

They were together in Ryerson's office at eight forty-five the next morning, and Pete, looking in through the glass partition, could see Farrel's puffed purple eye and make note of Saunders's air of twitchy nervousness. Pete smiled to himself. What a pair!

Ryerson was far too shrewd an operator to do things haphazardly, so there must be reason behind the selection; but Pete was damned if he could see it.

The page in his machine had an error in it anyway; with a sudden wry puckering of his lips Pete gave way to an impulse to type out his impressions of the pair.

Calvin Saunders: A matchless example of an upstanding, clean-cut, wholesome, American mama's boy.
J. Farrel: Let's be merciful.

Then Pete, with a final glance at the trio in the inner sanctum, ripped the sheet from the machine, wadded it completely and dropped it into the wastebasket. He couldn't imagine why he had felt the urge to write it down.

There was much more hint of autumn in these tawny foothills than in the city, on the desert, or at the beach. Here the land prepared for winter, for sleep, for renewal. The cottonwoods and sycamores had dropped half their leaves and patches of sumac flamed crimson and orange along the bottoms of the canyons. The oaks were dusty. The summer's grass was gone, shredded and blown away by the dry fall winds. Both sky and earth looked bright, but bleak.

Farrel had turned off the Corona Freeway to the Temescal Canyon road. This was the old Butterfield Stage route, pretty wild country before the road dropped down to Elsinore. Farrel drove through Elsinore, swung north off the highway just before reaching Murrieta. This secondary road was well paved but the turns were neck-twisting. Pretty soon Saunders was looking down into a wide dry gorge where cattle were grazing. Farrel nodded in the direction ahead. "We'll come to the gate pretty soon. I'll let you out to open up."

Barbed-wire fence now closed in the road; beyond it cows lifted their heads to watch. They were short-legged black cows, looked husky and cared for. The gate, when they reached it, proved to be a businesslike affair of white-painted timbers topped by barbed wire, smoothly operated by pulleys and weights. Saunders got back into the car. "How much farther?"

"A mile or so."

"They built this place after the claims were settled?"

Farrel shook his head. "Bought it. You'll see. The house is adobe, Spanish, built in the old style. It's a regular hacienda."

A gust of wind whipped leaves from the sycamores across the windshield. Then they emerged from the grove;

the road made a wide loop before a walled courtyard. It was just what Farrel had said, and made Saunders think of a movie set, something out of *Ramona*. Through the wrought-iron gate he saw a paved patio and a fountain. A woman in a wheelchair sat beside the fountain, her head back as if asleep.

They got out, closed the car. The woman had lifted her head and was looking at them. They walked into the courtyard. Oleanders and potted camellias made walls of greenery; vines climbed the house. There was a smell of smoke, a wood fire, and in the distance someone sang in a high-pitched voice.

The woman in the wheelchair made a sudden impulsive movement, gripping the wheel rims in her hands, turning the chair a little; Saunders saw that she meant to leave. Then she seemed to force composure into her manner. She waited for them, her head high, shoulders straight. "Yes ... gentlemen?"

Farrel said, "Mrs. Myles, I guess you don't remember me." He started to take out his identification; she snapped her fingers.

"Of course. Mr. Farrel." She put out a hand. Her manner was not exactly friendly or welcoming; it was as if she'd expected worse and meant to make the best of these intruders. "Well, what brings you 'way out here?"

"The same thing, Mrs. Myles. The wreck."

She showed none of Snowden's curiosity or interest. "You must be tired of that old thing by now." She glanced around briefly. "Shall we talk out here, or would you rather go indoors? I can offer you some refreshment. Coffee? Cold lemonade? Or something stronger, like a cocktail?"

"Thank you," Farrel said gratefully, not indicating which he preferred. "We don't want to put you to any trouble. If you wish, we can stay out here. This is my fellow investigator, Mr. Saunders."

"How do you do, Mr. Saunders?"

Saunders had been sizing her up. Goggling like a fool, most likely, he realized with a start. She was beautiful, a fragile doll-like girl all pink and white, slim-limbed, her hair pale gold under the sun, and with the most enormous hazel eyes he'd ever seen. Greenish, he thought, taking the hand she extended and bending towards her as if hypnotized. Her eyes are green as water and there's something unreal about them. They're too big, too perfect. He felt as if the hand he touched belonged to something not of this world, like a mermaid.

There was no blanket about her. She wore a white woolen robe, short-skirted like a dress. Nylon hose on long, lovely legs. Small feet in gold sandals. She withdrew her hand from Saunders's grip and looked over at the vine-covered veranda. "Lotti! Lotti, I want you!"

The singing stopped and a woman in a brilliant red skirt and a blue blouse came at once and Mrs. Myles instructed her to make a shaker of martinis. Saunders started to speak up, indicating he wanted his name kept out of the pot, and then decided against it. He was very curious about this woman; he wanted to make a good impression; he didn't want to make her think he was some sort of a prig. Farrel sat on the tiled rim of the big basin surrounding the fountain. He asked Mrs. Myles's permission to smoke, offered her a cigarette, lit up for all three of them.

She looked up at him over the cigarette. "Still the Lobo Tunnel, hmm?" The green eyes flickered; obviously the purple mouse that extended to Farrel's temple fascinated her and she was too polite to ask about it. To Saunders she seemed terrifically young to have done all that Farrel had said of her. She had already been a famous dancer at the time of the wreck six years ago; in fact, Farrel had implied somehow that she was a little past her first fame, unable to create the reputation in this country which she had held in Europe.

The only accent in her voice which Saunders caught was, if anything, British.

She went on, "I still remember the debate I had with my husband. To fly or to take the train. You know ... he'd flown so much over there during the war. He was tired of it. Tired and nervous." Her tone was light but a shadow crossed her expression, as at some old memory.

"You mentioned it before," Farrel agreed.

"We were different people then." She was quiet, remembering that other pair. "Children, I suppose you might say." She smiled at Farrel, at Saunders. "Now ... if I can help in any way—"

Farrel plunged into it. "The man who was the conductor on your train, a man named Parmenter—have you seen him since the wreck?"

"No. Never." She continued to smile.

"He's been in Mexico for about five years," Farrel said. "In trouble down there. Now he's coming home. We're anxious to know if he attempts to contact any of the former passengers for purposes of begging money."

She shook her head gracefully. "He should beg money of us? But this would be ridiculous!"

"You have money," Farrel pointed out with what seemed to Saunders deliberate crudity.

"We had some," she corrected lightly. "Not in the way I would have preferred to gain it. Now we are just ... farmers. Cattle farmers." A small motion of her hand indicated the house, the tall trees, and was meant perhaps to include the rolling brown hills beyond. "My husband handles the livestock, the range. I carry on the paper work. Do you have any idea of how complicated it is now to be in the cattle business?"

She seemed amused, almost on the verge of laughter,

and to Saunders she seemed so alive and so full of good
spirits, it was impossible to think she wouldn't rise and
walk from the chrome-wheeled chair when she chose.

There was a clatter of glassware from the shadowy veranda, and then a man came towards them carrying a
tray, a silver cocktail shaker glinting in the sunlight. He
was tall and broad-shouldered. His brown hair had turned
gray above the temples. He was extremely sun-tanned.
As a man, he had about the same grade of good looks as
his wife. They made a wonderful pair. Saunders felt a stab
of jealousy.

The man wore riding pants, boots, a suede jacket
trimmed in leather fringe. He put the tray containing the
shaker and glasses on the rim of the fountain, shook his
head at his wife. "Isn't it early for strong drink?"

"These gentlemen must have had a long warm ride,
Chuck."

Chuck Myles offered his hand. "Hello, Farrel." Farrel
introduced Saunders, and Saunders found Chuck's hand
to be hard, calloused, strong. A workingman's hand. He
turned back to his wife as she explained the errand which
had brought Farrel and Saunders out here.

"Did you see Parmenter since the wreck?" Farrel asked.

Myles was pouring drinks. "I don't believe so. Did we,
dear?"

"I'm sure I've never seen him. I recall him vaguely. I was
in so much pain, almost out of my mind, in that horrible
hour following the wreck..." She glanced from Farrel to
her husband. "I think that the conductor did something
for me, some kindness, some special favor. But now I
don't recall what it was." She rubbed the side of her head.

"I don't want to think about it," Myles said. He handed
Farrel and Saunders a drink apiece.

They sipped the martinis, and the dry wind rattled the
sycamores and sent spray drifting from the fountain. Saun-

ders began to feel foolish. These people, this pleasant and substantial couple, weren't the sort to be cowed by a character like Parmenter. Nothing so dirty as blackmail could touch them.

9.

Farrel said, "You might be interested to know that there's no Lobo Tunnel anymore."

"They've changed the route?"

"They daylighted the tunnel. Opened it into a cut," Farrel explained.

"To prevent wrecks like the one we were in?" Sonya asked.

Farrel shook his head. "It's just company policy. They daylight 'em right along where it's practical. A lot less upkeep."

A thoughtful look settled over her. "I have some confused memories. Wasn't Lobo Tunnel in the hills at the edge of the desert?"

"It's all desert in there," Farrel agreed.

Myles moved restively, changing his position on the fountain's rim.

"I remember thinking that a short while more and we would have been safe," she went on. "The rest is mostly noise and lights. It didn't seem to take long to reach the hospital in Victorville, once the ambulance came."

"I suppose you had been collecting your luggage, packing up the last of your things," Farrel suggested.

She gave him a glance in which blankness mingled with apprehension. "I guess we must have. I can't remember much that happened just before the wreck. We'd been in the lounge car and we'd had a silly argument there. I've tried to make Chuck tell me what it was about, and he says it wasn't important."

"Compared to what came after, it was nothing," Chuck Myles put in. He lifted the silver shaker. "Does anyone want a refill, or should we start thinking about lunch?"

"Did you lose anything in the wreck?" Farrel asked. "Jewelry, money, anything not covered in your claim?"

A funny stab in the dark, Saunders thought, and a point which must have been cleared up long ago when the claims were settled.

"I don't believe so. Didn't you ask me that before? It was months, of course, before I began to be interested in anything like that. There were the operations and then I had to get used to the idea that I ... I wouldn't walk again." No word of the hopes about the movie contract. Her air of mild distress, of confusion, seemed slowly to abate. "What would any missing thing of mine have to do with the wreck, with what really caused the wreck, anyway?"

"Nothing," said Farrel frankly. He didn't explain why he'd asked this.

"Well, what about the wreck?" Myles demanded. He still held the shaker, his attitude still implied that this palaver had better be ended in favor of lunch.

"I thought you knew," Farrel said. "I thought I'd told you about the stuff piled in the tunnel."

"Yes. That. It seemed to me I read later that you fellows had some theory about a section hand."

"You must have heard it. It wasn't in the papers."

Myles shrugged. "I picked it up somewhere."

The conversation veered off upon lunch again—Farrel politely declined to eat—and then to the management of the ranch. Myles insisted that they come with him to see some new breeding stock. They went into the veranda, rounded the house, walked down a broad roadway lined with trees, to the barns and corrals. The house was old,

Spanish, sleepy; but this was all new, all up-to-date. Myles displayed the new cattle in a big corral, more of the stocky black kind which Saunders had noticed on the hills. The cattle looked at them peacefully. Saunders thought about Mrs. Myles; he had decided that Myles had taken them away from her to spare her further questioning by Farrel. Farrel had seemed somewhat of a boor.

Why should he try to pin her down, whether she'd lost anything in the wreck never accounted for?

The questions had upset her. And she couldn't answer. Myles was right in bringing them away. Saunders tried to show some interest in the cattle, to please Myles, but he'd never lived in the country and knew very little about stock. Myles reeled off some facts about breeding lines. It seemed that certain desirable qualities were highly inheritable.

When they returned to the courtyard, Myles insisted on a final drink for them. He offered lunch. Mrs. Myles was not in sight.

Farrel said thank you, they'd have to be leaving. He and Saunders went back to the car.

Driving through the windy sycamores, Saunders couldn't keep it in. "Why did you prod her like that about what she might have lost?"

Farrel rubbed his neck under his collar. "Just testing."

There was more than that to it, of course, and Saunders retreated into anger.

As soon as they got into Elsinore, Saunders said, "I can feel those martinis. I want to eat."

Farrel glanced at him curiously. "Sure. Where?"

"Drive around."

It wasn't a very big town and the selection of cafés was limited. Finally they settled for hamburgers; Farrel had beer, too, obviously wanting to keep the glow from dying.

In the semi-light of the booth at the rear of the café, he looked calm, almost drowsy.

Saunders felt an irritable urge to stir him up. "You asked Snowden and the Myles couple about Parmenter. Before, you said that Parmenter's chance must have occurred because the porter was killed. Yet you didn't ask any of them about the porter."

Farrel just shrugged. "It wouldn't do any good ... now. If we'd got on it right after the wreck, while there still must have been some uncertainty, we might have had a chance." The waitress brought the beer and poured it for him, and when she was gone he went on. "For a short time Parmenter and the people he was dealing with must have been on edge, waiting to see if the porter had given anything away. But what we had, finally, was too indefinite."

"What you had?" Saunders echoed blankly.

"It's in the files. A passenger in the rear car said that just before the wreck a porter stuck his head in from the vestibule—this man was in the corridor outside his compartment—and asked if he thought there was a doctor in there. Meaning in the last car. And the guy said he didn't know but he'd try to find out. He went to look for *his* porter ... and *smash*, that was it."

A cruel edge came upon Saunders's temper. "I didn't see that in the official reports."

"It's in there somewhere."

The hamburger was greasy, and Saunders got mayonnaise on his hands from it. "That's all there was?"

"It could have been enough," Farrel said, "if we'd worked on it right away."

"How can you work on somebody who's blind ... or who is screaming from the pain of a broken back?"

"It didn't stop Parmenter. He worked on 'em." Farrel was handling the greasy sandwich with distaste. He put it down finally and went back to the beer. Watching it gurgle down, Saunders thought, How can he pour it in on top of those martinis?

"What about other claimants?"

"We'll talk to them."

"But you think it's either the Myles couple or Snowden? Don't you?"

"Or Snowden's wife."

"I'll admit, Snowden's history ... that stuff of being blind with rainbows ... makes you think of tricks. But Mrs. Myles's injuries must have been real enough. Something like that would show up in an X ray."

"It showed up," Farrel said mildly. The glass was empty; he looked around for the waitress. "She'd suffered a terrific fall. Or a blow."

"That's much more in line with what would happen in a wreck than Snowden's blindness."

"Yes, it is."

Saunders wrapped the oozy sandwich in a couple of paper napkins and tried again. "If Snowden had been suffering an attack of hysterical blindness *before* the wreck ... called the porter ... asked for a doctor—he might have let something slip, such as that it had happened before, he only needed a sedative, or something like that."

Farrel nodded.

"Then, when the crash came, and he suffered added shock, and the condition didn't clear up—well, as you say, he'd have no way of knowing the porter wouldn't be at the investigation, telling the truth about everything." He frowned at Farrel, wished Farrel had been paying closer attention. "Then—the idea of putting in for a big claim must have come from Parmenter. Parmenter must have told him the porter was dead."

"Not necessarily. The girl Snowden married was traveling on that train. She was his secretary. She wasn't injured in the wreck and she might easily have seen what happened to the porter."

Saunders felt that Farrel had in some niggling way blocked him in an important theory. There was always this background, the innumerable details he didn't know; and Farrel was too indifferent to brief him thoroughly. Well, Ryerson should find out soon enough. When nothing developed. When he had to realize at last that no new look at old facts would work with Farrel there, Farrel in his rut.

Saunders tried to think of some way to disclose Farrel's slovenly methods to the Chief, but outside of simply telling Ryerson he could think of nothing; and somehow a bald betrayal wasn't in him.

In his own corner of the booth, Farrel sat looking peacefully at the refilled glass. He sensed Saunders's anger but seemed insulated against it. The end was coming, of course, as inevitable as sundown. Saunders would finally get a bellyful and report him, probably on Rule G, and then Ryerson could can him. Farrel had no doubt whatever that Ryerson had saddled him with the young punk for just that purpose.

Of course if he could pull Lobo Tunnel off the fire, the execution might be stayed. For a little while.

The side of Farrel's head ached, the temple where the flesh was swollen and purple; and occasionally the blacked eye was shot through with a sparkling hot light. He couldn't remember much of what had happened in the alley. He was still miserably ashamed of the way he had treated Haines. Haines had a skinned place on his chin, matching the spots on Farrel's knuckles. Farrel had sneaked out without breakfast in order to avoid Mrs. Bellows.

Winding up Lobo Tunnel might save his neck on the job. Nothing could change what was happening to the rest of his life.

At eleven o'clock that morning Peg Parmenter heard
her aunt leave the house. She got out of bed quickly, went
into the bathroom and washed, then put on make-up,
combed her hair, and dressed. She went into the kitchen
and poked around, looking for something to eat. She
warmed some coffee. There were eggs in the refrigerator,
bacon too; but she didn't feel like cooking. She found a
stale doughnut in the breadbox, dipped this into the coffee
when she had poured it. Then she hurried into the living
room and stood beside the phone. She stood tense, her
nails digging her palms, willing her father to call now;
but nothing happened. By and by she went to the mailbox
in the wall and investigated—she found a notice from her
aunt's church, a gas bill, a couple of ads. She stuck them
back in the slot.

When her father had first contacted her she had been
filled with courage and excitement, but these were draining
away. Her father was abandoning her. He had other fish
to fry.

There was a chance, of course, that she had somehow
bungled the meeting near San Diego, though she couldn't
see how. She was, in fact, now trying to convince herself
that what had happened down there was an accident, an
encounter with some local farmer afraid of trespassers,
some ill-tempered fanatic with a gun. Someone with a
corn patch to protect. Someone waiting for a chicken
thief. The shooting had had nothing to do with her father.

An inner voice warned, too, that such lulling of herself
was dangerous; but this she ignored.

She stood in the middle of the room, edgy, burning with
impatience. She knew that Libby Walker must have gone
only as far as the grocery store. When she worked, she

was gone before eight. She was taking another day off to watch the girl.

To spoil things, Peg thought fiercely.

Sure enough, presently her aunt's steps sounded on the porch. Peg fled for the rear of the house, snatching up coat and purse, letting herself out noiselessly into the rear yard. She walked for about six blocks, until she came to a main thoroughfare. Here on one corner stood a large fountain-lunch and candy store, a hangout for the school gang. Peg had formerly been one of its faithful customers, but since her graduation she felt a little out of place there. The high school crowd seemed suddenly juvenile. Her classmates were settled in jobs or going on to college.

Now, however, she needed a place to pass some time and to think, so she went inside, ordered a Coke from the boy behind the counter and then strolled over to the large magazine display with the glass in her hand.

It was a big, cheerful store. The youth of its trade seemed to have rubbed off somehow upon its interior. The jukebox music was lilting, the fountain glittered. At the rear of the store, behind the candy counters and the hobby displays, were three telephone booths. These occasionally drew in adults off the street. Most of the fountain and candy trade was teen-age.

She took a magazine back to the counter, sat on a stool, paid for the magazine and opened it to read. While she was thus engrossed, her mind more than half occupied by her personal tangles, a man entered and walked directly back to enter a phone booth. He was in it only a minute, not long enough to have made a call. He left the store at once. The boy at the fountain didn't even notice him, nor did two couples in a booth, nor did Peg Parmenter.

Four minutes later one of the phones rang in the rear of the store. The soda jerk put down a glass he was drying and went to answer. The public call boxes were often used to relay messages for teen-agers, from family or friends, a favor the store extended in the name of good will. The boy came out after a moment and called to Peg.

"For you, Peg-o."

Her mouth grew pinched. "My aunt?"

"Didn't sound like no doll, Doll." He winked at her.

She slipped off the stool and went back, warily. The moment she put the instrument to her ear, she had a sudden hunch that it would be her father. "Peggy?" said the phone.

He was the only one who called her Peggy. To her mother she was Marge. To her aunt—mostly, these days—she was Now, listen!

"Here, Dad. Speaking." Her wrist started to shake.

"Can you meet me?"

"Sure. Where?"

"Know where the Union Depot is?"

"Yes."

"Hop a bus and meet me there in a half hour."

"How will I—" She swallowed in embarrassment. "How'll I know you?"

"I'll know you, kid. Just wait for me."

Forty-five minutes later she was still waiting, in one of the big leather lounge chairs, in the main room at the depot. It was a terribly big place; Peg felt lost in it. She had watched the hurrying people for a while, but now she just sat, blank-eyed.

He sat down all at once in the chair next to hers. He turned his face to her, and though the years had been long, her memories washed in the vagueness of childhood, she knew him at once. Knew him and was shocked. He looked ... sick, starved. A wave of revulsion shot through her as he put a hand in her direction.

He said, "How're you fixed for money?"

She wasn't surprised, somehow, at the lack of preamble

nor the nature of his first question. She was his child; her mind worked as his did. "About fifteen dollars."

"Can you spare five?"

"More if you need it." I can raid Aunt Libby's purse again, she thought.

"No. Five's okay. You'll need ten. You're going to run an errand for me. Take a little trip." He was leaning closer now. She could see the small inflamed veins in his eyes, his stained and broken teeth, a jagged scar that cut across one eyebrow. "Will you do it?"

"Sure I'll do it." She fumbled with the purse, getting out the shabby wallet. There was still sticky dampness in its seams, from the soaking in the ditch. She lifted her glance to his face. "I'm sorry we missed each other ... down there."

"So am I." He wasn't looking at her but at the bills between her hands.

A thought fluttered at the back of her mind. A warning. He must have been watching the house, following her, to have known he could reach her by means of the phone in the candy store. She hadn't been in the place for ages.

Since he'd been so close, on her heels you might say, why hadn't he approached her near the house? Or in the store while she idled near the magazines?

Perhaps he's scared of Aunt Libby, she told herself. Her hands had mechanically divided the money; he had accepted one of the bills.

The truth was—she knew it certainly, coldly—he wanted a crowd around them. He didn't want anyone to see them together who might know her.

In case something happened. Something bad, like—

He twisted the bill in his fingers. "You'll get this back a thousand-fold, Peggy. Trust your old dad."

She thrust the warning from her mind.

10.

They were approaching Corona when Farrel said, "Keep an eye out for a place to phone. Something I want to find out from Pete."

"Don't you need gas?" Saunders asked, planning to fox him out of going into a bar. "Pull into a service station, why don't you?"

"This'll do."

It was a bar. Farrel went in and Saunders waited grimly. When Farrel came back and climbed behind the wheel, he spoke as if continuing some delayed conversation. "Nothing on the wine bottle. The stuff was marijuana, though."

Saunders was momentarily at a loss. "You mean that dusty stuff you found in the culvert?"

"That's right." Farrel sat as if thinking. "We ought to go up there, I guess. Somebody's in the reefer business and it could be Versprelle. He could be back." He rubbed a hand along the wheel, chewed at his lower lip. "Easier, though, to go in without being spotted after dark."

"You mean, tonight?" Saunders was thinking of the desolate hills, the broken water tower, the general air of loneliness and isolation.

"Why not?" Farrel started the motor. "I'll tell you what I want to do this afternoon. I want to go over to the Sheriff's Office, the Narcotics Detail, and see if I can't get a line on that bugger. I want to see if Versprelle might have been cooped up until recently. Somewhere."

"Isn't it stretching things to figure that Parmenter and Versprelle got out of jail at the same time? They didn't have anything to do with each other. Or it didn't show up."

"Don't reject something just because it looks like a coincidence," Farrel muttered.

In the L.A. Union Depot, Libby Walker waited until Peg was a good distance from the ticket window. Then she went up to the wicket. The man behind the counter looked at her incuriously and waited. She had seen Peg slip from the house. Several times she had almost lost the girl. Now she was nervous, bitter with a sense of guilt.

"My ... my niece was just here. She was going to buy my ticket, too, but I guess she forgot." The lie was so bald, her voice weak and squeaky; he was bound to be suspicious. She waited for his accusation. "I'll need a ... a round trip," she got out, when he said nothing.

"Where to?"

Her heart thumped painfully. She controlled a quiver that started around her mouth. "The same place. The place my niece, that pretty girl—"

"Sagebloom?"

"Sagebloom?" she echoed blankly. She'd never heard of it. The word meant nothing to her.

He was taking a ticket from the rack, shortening it, stamping it with a rubber marker. His motions were bored, mechanical. She took money from her purse, scarcely daring to breathe. He told her the price and she passed in a bill and received back some change. She put the ticket and the change into her purse. Then she circled the last group of chairs warily, and stood half hidden behind some racks of magazines and paperback books. She could see Peg across the big room, standing in an aisle, talking to her father. They had no suspicion of her presence. She watched carefully to make sure that the ticket didn't pass from Peg to Parmenter. It didn't. Peg kept it in her purse.

What a desperate time she'd had following, keeping out of sight! But now she knew Peg's destination—wherever

Sagebloom was—she could follow and thwart her. It was what Marie would have wanted her to do if Marie had been able to comprehend what was going on.

Peg must not be involved in his schemes as Marie had.

She mustn't end as Marie had, either.

Across the big room, Parmenter and the girl had turned towards an exit. Libby was muddled with indecision. Should she follow, risk being seen, risk a tirade from Peg and perhaps worse from her criminal father? It occurred to Libby then that she and Peg had a rendezvous on a train and that she had no notion of when it left.

She waited until they had crossed an open patio to the lunchroom, then walked over to the information center. She learned that since Sagebloom was on the main route north, all the trains went through it; but only two made the local stop. One of these trains left at three o'clock and the second at ten minutes of seven. The trip to Sagebloom took less than an hour.

She decided that Peg must mean to take the three o'clock train, since she had already bought her ticket; and it wasn't yet quite one.

She left the depot by another exit and walked around. This part of L.A. had all been transformed within the past few years, Old Chinatown torn out to make room for the Union Depot and other structures recently demolished to provide access to the freeways funneling in and out of the downtown area. But Libby Walker strolled unseeing and unhearing amid the chatter of hydraulic hammers and the grunt and roar of earth-moving equipment. Her mind was filled with bitter thoughts of Peg, of Peg's treachery and sullenness. She climbed the slight rise towards the Civic Center, paused suddenly to look back.

"I ought to leave her to her fate," she said half aloud. "I've done all that Marie could have asked." She thought of the years just past, Marie's succession of sicknesses, the final commitment to the State Hospital, her own hard labor to keep Marie's home waiting for her. There had been days when she had dragged home hardly alive, beaten with weariness, to find Peg ready to pounce with some demand—clothes, cosmetics, money for the candy store, some phonograph record which had become a fad.

The memory of ugly scenes crowded Libby's mind. She was incapable of grasping the utter selfishness of the young. She had forgotten the longings of her own girlhood. In Libby's youth she had been docile and patient; the older sister, expected to watch over the flightier Marie.

Her parents had trained her to be sober and responsible. She had been taught the value of money, money earned by hard work, spent frugally. A demand for fripperies and foolishness would have been a negation of that teaching. It had never occurred to Libby that she had been denied something which was her right, a part of youth itself. She clung to her pinch-penny philosophy and attempted to impose it on the girl.

Now she stood undecided, looking downward into the maw of a freeway ramp where raw earth was being scraped aside to create a highway.

"I ought to let her go."

Then she thought of Parmenter. His appearance, even at a distance, had shocked her; the gray-lidded eyes, the scarlet patches on his cheeks spoke of a cancerous illness. The clothes, too big—he got them cheap, Libby thought. He wanted new ones, and they had been what he could afford. Stolen, perhaps, peddled on the back street of some Mexican town. He seemed to give off an evil effluvium. How could Peg endure him?

Something bad would happen to Peg if she were allowed to continue in his company.

Unwillingly Libby began to retrace her steps in the direction of the Union Depot. She must find some way to get on the train without being seen by her niece. There were many passageways in the bowels of the big station. She would find one where she could wait, out of sight, until the train left for Sagebloom.

Later, getting on the train, she was nervous, expecting Peg and her father to confront her at any moment. Once inside the coach she sank into a seat by the window, turned her face from the other passengers. She felt empty, not having had any lunch. Thirsty, too. There was a tap at the end of the car but she didn't dare use it. On the heels of this discomfort, anger flared in her. Here she was, doing a decent, a helpful thing; and acting like a criminal about it. Scared. Afraid of a shrew-tongued girl and an evil man.

"I ought to get off the train and leave her to her own devices," she muttered. The bright light of afternoon lay on the coach ramp, hurrying and happy-looking people rushed around. Embraces were exchanged. Libby felt quite alone, almost sick, and miserable.

Saunders had read the reports of the investigation until his eyes felt hot. This was a mountain of stuff.

It seemed that every last scrap of the barrier piled in the tunnel had been traced to its source, down to the last bolt. The timbers had been ties, partly, and partly some of the underpinnings of the old water tower. A rusted pump had also come from the water tower. Two section hands had testified that Versprelle owned a pair of bolt-cutters, new ones; and the bolts holding the pump had been sheared off clean with such a tool. There was rather indecisive evidence that Versprelle had not left the vicinity after being discharged three days before, but had been seen in Sagebloom as late as the afternoon of the wreck.

Saunders thought, Well, that sounds like a hophead. He'd probably been high on his own reefers. Crazy for vengeance. It's a wonder, though, Saunders added to himself, that Versprelle had taken on the railroad instead of committing some petty revenge against the foreman. He must have known the real reason for his discharge, perhaps even the part the railroad dicks had played in it.

There was photographic evidence that Versprelle had been at the scene of the wreck, enjoying himself. Soaking up the tumult, the agony of people who were innocent of any injury to him. At this moment Saunders remembered that Farrel seemed to expect to run into Versprelle tonight at the water tower. A funny jolt of fear ran through his nerves and he wondered if Farrel knew exactly what he was tackling. This wasn't in Farrel's pattern, his dogged routine.

Tonight could be the switch, the break. A niggling uneasiness settled in Saunders; whatever came along that was new he had expected to discover for himself. Hadn't Ryerson expected it of him?

He looked across the office. Ryerson was out. Pete had leaned back in his chair, relaxing, taking a cigarette break. It seemed to Saunders all at once that the place had a dismal, oppressive atmosphere. It was like the outer office of a jail. The light was gloomy, the room bare and big, impersonal.

Pete glanced his way, smiled a little, winked. "Where's your pal?"

It was ridiculous to think of Farrel as anything resembling a pal. "My associate in this affair," Saunders said, deliberately formal, "has gone to the Sheriff's Office to try to get a line on Versprelle."

Pete said nothing. His face grew blank. Saunders caught a whiff of suspicion. Was Farrel out tanking up on dutch courage?

But when Farrel came in a little later, he seemed no more liquored up than usual. It was hard to tell about him. Probably late in the evening he'd be in pretty gay shape; he appeared to have developed the knack of sipping his way through the day without going too far.

They discussed plans for the night. Saunders wanted time to meet Betsy at home. He needed to take some clothes to the laundry. He ought to write a letter to his mother. Farrel seemed agreeable to starting out fairly late. Probably he had a few errands of his own. Liquid ones.

Betsy came up the front steps of the apartment house, getting keys from her purse. She looked trim and neat, but a little tired, too. Saunders was waiting in the vestibule. He'd been there almost fifteen minutes.

She nodded at him rather distantly, but in spite of an impression of rebuff he followed her into the elevator. The door shut them in together.

She looked at him, and he took a couple of stumbling steps and put his arms around her. He was awkward without meaning to be; they fell against the wall. Betsy wriggled free. "Wait, please." She punched the button for Stop and the little cage hummed to a halt. They were between floors, hung in a void. Betsy put her hands on either side of his head and pulled his face down to hers and kissed him. It was a terrifically intimate and lingering kiss. Saunders felt his complexion growing red; he felt like a fool.

She let him go then. Without thinking, he yanked out his handkerchief and scrubbed harshly at his mouth, at what he felt must be lipstick marks a yard wide. Betsy watched him curiously.

Finally she said, "Are you going to be home all evening?"

"No. I've got to work."

"Too bad." She turned briskly, punched the button for their floor, and the little cage rose again.

"What's that supposed to mean?"

"Just an experiment I meant to conduct."

"Yeah? What kind?" His male ego rose with its neck feathers in fighting-cock arrangement.

"Quite scientific," she murmured in the same smug tone.

"Such as how to make a sap out of a sap?"

She didn't answer. The automatic mechanism opened the door and she stepped out into their hallway. She looked back at him over her shoulder. "You'd better take your white shirts to the laundry. Those colored ones aren't your usual working clothes."

"I'll do what I damned please."

"Your mother knew you'd forget."

"What are you? A nursemaid?"

The look she now gave him reminded him, somehow, infuriatingly of Farrel. He tromped down the hall on her heels and when she opened her door he went into her apartment. He grabbed her elbows, yanked her around to face him. "What was supposed to happen tonight?"

All at once and more infuriatingly still, she seemed embarrassed. Her gaze dropped and all the boldness seeped from her manner. "If we're going to have a row, close the door, won't you?" Her lips trembled a little; she turned her head quickly as if to keep him from seeing. In that instant a warning bell clanged in the depths of Saunders's mind. Here was an expert playing a game at which he had proved himself a boob. He took his hands from her quickly, stepped back.

She went over to the couch, slipped off her jacket, dropped it with her purse and gloves. She fluffed her hair away from her neck. She took a cigarette from the purse and lit it. She waited.

"I'll see you later," Saunders muttered. He went back into the hall, to his own apartment. He shut himself in. He tried to figure out what had happened.

At first she had seemed on the verge of brushing him

off. That had made him nervous, so that in the elevator his approach had been clumsy and immature. Then she'd stopped the elevator and shown him how it should be done. He turned red, again, at the memory.

He hurried into the bathroom, to the mirror above the basin, to inspect himself for lipstick stains. There were a few faint ones. Probably she used some kind of practically indelible goo.

He went on with his analysis. He wanted to find out where and how she'd made such a fool of him. That remark about the experiment ... Facing himself in the mirror, Saunders growled, "What in hell *was* going to happen tonight?"

Was Betsy the kind of girl who might ... uh ... be promiscuous just to find out something about a fellow? Saunders squirmed at the thought and the squirming revealed to him his idealization of this minx.

The dig about the shirts ...

Automatically he was spreading a shirt on the floor and piling the rest of them on it out of the hamper. He tied the bottom shirt into a bundle with the arms and the corners of the tail, took it back to the living room. He lit a cigarette, smoked furiously, walked to the windows and back around the room. He was remembering the way Betsy had looked just before he'd released her and jumped away. There had been something soft and yielding, a little frightened ... What had she expected him to do at that point?

He tried to imagine a continuation of the scene and came upon the horns of a dilemma. The most exciting course of action wasn't what his ideas about Betsy allowed him to suppose.

He went downstairs, locking the place, and left the shirts at the cleaner's shop on the corner. He ate in a kosher café next door, then took the car from the garage and went back downtown.

Farrel was in the office, all the dusty files on Lobo Tunnel on a desk before him. Saunders had a sudden hunch he hadn't eaten anything. Probably had a bottle on his hip.

The night sergeant, Burns, was in the inner office at Ryerson's desk. Everyone else, The Chief, Pete, the other investigators, had gone. The place echoed to Saunders's steps as he crossed the office.

The flesh around Farrel's injured eye looked tight and greenish. There was a lot of silver in his hair under the lights. Despite an outer appearance of weariness, Saunders sensed excitement. He leaned, put a fist on the desk. "What's new?"

"Don't know yet. Something's up." Farrel stacked the Lobo files, stood up, carried them to the cabinets. When he had deposited the folders and shut the drawer, he shrugged to settle his coat, reached back and patted something on his hip. The gun—maybe. Saunders listened cynically for any hint of a liquid gurgle, heard nothing.

Farrel came back. "Collins was in Union Depot today looking for a baggage thief. He saw Parmenter there with a young girl."

"He knows Parmenter?"

"Remembered him from Lobo Tunnel in spite of the changes made in Mexico. Parmenter and the girl had a long confab. The girl bought a single to Sagebloom."

Saunders straightened in surprise. "His daughter?" He caught the ominous flash of anger in Farrel's face, didn't pause to analyze it. "Look. This is a twist. There's never been the least connection between Parmenter and the scene of the wreck—nothing outside the train—" Farrel nodded at him. A lot of wild surmises rushed through Saunders's mind. Could Parmenter be planning some crazy repetition of the Lobo disaster?

"We don't know what connection there is now, if any," Farrel said. "Maybe we'll find out, though. Tonight."

11.

Libby Walker waited until the last possible minute before leaving the train. She examined the paved area between the small depot and the tracks from the shelter of the car vestibule. The sun was quite bright. There wasn't anyone out there except the station agent, looking over some crates on a baggage truck, and the porter with his step, just below. Some mechanism under the train hissed softly. The porter stood looking up at her as if she were crazy.

"Is this Sagebloom?" she stammered, still hanging back to give Peg time to show herself.

"Yes, ma'am." Plainly the neat, small man with the chocolate face found the peering woman an odd customer. "Am I the only passenger to get off here?"

"I guess you are, ma'am." He flicked a finger towards the wooden step as if politely urging her to come down.

She crept down to the next-to-last step and stopped again. "I ... I may have left something at my seat."

"I'll get it for you, ma'am." He started up the steps but she suddenly found her courage, or a sort of desperate fright sent her running. She hopped down out of the car and sprinted into the station. There she stood in the small waiting room, hearing only her heart pound; and when she thought to look outdoors again, the train had gone.

The train had gone, and Peg hadn't been on it.

Instantly the conviction smote her that she had been tricked. They'd seen her following, spying. Peg had bought the ticket to throw her off the pursuit. Parmenter was clever, as clever as the Devil from Hell. He'd planned it. He'd sent her out here on a wild-goose chase.

Libby Walker gnawed her knuckles in frustration. Her eyes filled with tears. But after a few moments of seething anger, another idea occurred to her. Was it possible that Peg would come on the later train, the seven o'clock train?

The thought that she might have to wait here for all those hours sent her hurrying to the other windows to look at the town. When she summed up the array of establishments facing the depot across the street, she gasped. Why, it was nothing but a ... a wide place in the road! And she was again convinced that her coming here had been the result of trickery.

Parmenter would have no use for such a tiny village! There was no cover here for him, no crowds, no maze of streets nor towering buildings.

She hurried to the ticket window in the far wall. The station agent had come inside. When he saw her he came to the window.

"When does the next train come through for L.A.?"

"Six o'clock." Under the green visor, his glance was curious.

"I ... I seem to have made a mistake in getting off here," she said to cover her confusion.

He put out his hand. "What's your ticket say?"

"Oh, I mean ... it's for Sagebloom, all right. But I didn't know the sort of town it was. So small, and all." Her voice sounded husky and harried. She licked her lips.

"Well, yes, it's not a big place."

Under the conviction of trickery, the other idea persisted. There must be some reason Peg was coming here! "What sort of—" She tried to find words. "What's this place known for, if anything?"

"Known for? It's a kind of jumping-off spot, I guess. Mines up in the hills. We haul a lot of freight for them. Some alfalfa farmers down the other end of the valley. Once in a while we see a few of them."

She felt her throat clog mutely. She was unable to come out baldly with what she wanted: what would bring a crook to Sagebloom? Then, as she turned from the wicket, she recalled the significant fact that Parmenter himself was presumably not coming here. He was sending Peg. She looked out at the wan, dusty little town and realized why it must be Peg and not her father. He was far too clever a character to expose himself in such a place while working some shady scheme.

Anger, and hatred for Parmenter, rushed through her. She stumbled to a bench, sat down, tried to collect her thoughts.

She remembered a time, almost six years ago, when Marie had begun to write her hazy but ecstatic letters about Parmenter's cleverness and his immediate prospects for wealth. She had sensed that Marie was involved in his affairs; by the time she had come to California, Marie was not interested in explaining. Parmenter had deserted her, run off to live like a king in Mexico, and Marie had faded. There had been the burden of keeping up the home and looking after the child.

Now the child was grown and the situation was repeating itself.

Peg's secretiveness of the last two days, a certain glitter in her eyes when she felt she was not observed, warned Libby Walker. The girl was as big a fool as her mother. Without guidance, she would end as Marie had.

And again, through angry tears, Libby muttered, "I ought to disown her."

Though Libby wasn't the type to patronize a bar, eventually hunger and thirst drove her across the street to eat a bite and to wet her whistle with something cold. There were two bars; she chose the less shabby. The bartender took one look at her and produced a menu from behind some bottles. She had a pastrami sandwich, chokingly dry, and some buttermilk.

The afternoon dragged endlessly. At last, in the rear of

the general store, she found a cubbyhole lined with books, a branch of the County Library. She tried to concentrate on a book of Bible quotations, standing in the dusky corner, but the words made a jumble in her mind. Under the righteousness she felt over her errand here, a sense of danger was making itself felt.

Parmenter was a reckless and ruthless man. He would be playing for high stakes. He was using Peg as a cat's paw.

When the six o'clock train came through, headed south for L.A., she almost got on it.

Dusk settled over the desert, a shadow on the land. Long after the humped hills and the little canyons lay in darkness, the sky remained clear and greenish, an open vista into space. A dry wind whipped through Sagebloom. Some cactus owls hooted faintly in the distance. The neon signs came on over the bars and the windows of the general store lit up.

The station agent noted that a passenger got off the seven fifty-three from L.A. Two in one day was unusual. More unusual, both were women. He looked around for the other one, the one who had thought she'd made a mistake, and couldn't see her.

This one was young, pert and pretty. She gave him a glance as she walked through on her way to the street. Something in her eyes was bold and haughty. Owns the earth, the station agent thought. Got a good figure. Bet they're real, too. He looked out from a window on his side of the building, saw her silhouetted against the lights across the street. She was pulling her coat closed over her breasts, ruffling her hair off the collar. The desert wind had touched her with its evening chill.

She hesitated there for several minutes, looking the town over. She seemed to be seeking landmarks, something pre-

viously described which she must find. Finally she went
across the street to the sidewalk, strolled up and down,
her purse swinging.

All at once he caught sight of the other one, the older
one; and she was doing the damnedest thing—crouching
in the narrow alleyway between the general store and
Louie's bar, peering out in the direction of the girl. Her attitude expressed a furtive fright. He thought of going over,
trying to talk to her, remembering her distraction at the
wicket; but at this moment a car stopped outside the
depot, edging over the broken curb, and a man came in
to ask about train arrivals from L.A. He was a big good-
looking man, husky and wind-burned, the kind they hired
up at the mines. The station agent explained schedules
and offered a timetable. When he looked out again at the
street, both the girl and the older woman were gone.

At eight-twenty Farrel and Saunders parked behind the
station and went in for a talk with the agent. The agent
was eating a sandwich out of a waxed paper sack and
drinking coffee from a thermos. He told the two investigators about the women who had arrived, one early and
one late, and about the peculiar behavior of the older
one.

Farrel and Saunders separated for a quick scouting trip.
Saunders went first into the general store. No one was
there except an elderly clerk who was getting ready to
close. He was pretty deaf and his memory was poor. He
thought someone had been in during the afternoon, a
strange woman, and that she'd looked at the books in the
back; but he couldn't describe her. Young? Old? Fat?
Thin? Nervous? Excited? Might be. Might not. He
squinted at Saunders and chewed a coffee bean between
his beautifully artificial teeth, and jangled keys on a ring,
and tapped a foot. A total loss from Saunders's view-

point.

The tool shop which specialized in mining equipment was locked. Saunders could hear metallic hammering from somewhere; he went through a narrow passage to the rear. Here was a brightly lit open shed, a small forge, an anvil, two men and a dapple-gray horse. The horse seemed asleep. The two men were bent anxiously and amateurishly over a horseshoe on the anvil. The forge flared.

"Have you seen anyone go by here during the last half hour?"

They looked up. "A woman. Ran by fifteen, twenty minutes ago."

"What did she look like?"

The man holding the horseshoe in a pair of steel nippers wiped his face with his free arm. "Oh. Older."

"Did she say anything?"

"Didn't hear it if she did."

"Where was she headed?"

The man with the hammer nodded off towards the dark. "Out there. I guess she didn't know where she was going, come to think of it."

"What do you mean?"

"Big gully back there. Folks who live around here steer clear of it. There's a footbridge off yonder—not the way she was going, though."

Saunders hurried along, found the gully, explored its dark and cavernous lip. He couldn't see or hear anything down there, went back to the car for a flashlight, and returned. The drop was straight down, water-cut, perhaps twenty feet. Deep enough to break a neck if you went in unaware. He walked and shone the light in, and peered. And found nothing. He went back to the forge. The horseshoe was back in the fire and the men were resting, propped against a wooden shelf, smoking. The horse had his eyes open.

"You didn't happen to hear a scream?"

They shook their heads. The one who had had the hammer said with a trace of hesitation, "No scream. Thought I heard shot, though."

"When was this?"

"Wasn't no shot," said the other, the older man, positively. "A truck pulled out about then. Backfired. That's all."

"A truck that big doesn't make a noise like a .22," said the other.

"You thought it was a .22," Saunders said.

"I got me a .22 target pistol, use it on jackrabbits, and that's what it sounded like to me," he answered firmly.

"Backfire," the other muttered, tapping out his pipe.

Saunders went back to the street, headed for the bar. Sure enough, Farrel was inside talking to the bartender. Something slid across the bar and went out of sight fast as Saunders came in. Now who does he think he's fooling, Saunders thought. He went up to Farrel. "I can't find the girl. The older woman either—I guess it didn't have to be the aunt. It could be someone who lived here."

Farrel got off the stool. "It's the aunt. She ate in here this afternoon. She knew somehow that the girl was coming here and got here ahead of her." He walked out, Saunders following. He looked at the street, the few cars parked, an occasional car or truck going through on the highway, the signals blinking against the dark, down the track, and shook his head. "They aren't here now. How in the hell did they disappear like that?"

"A couple of men out back, shoeing a horse, saw the older woman go by. She was running. Then one of the men thought he heard a shot."

Farrel was looking at him, frowning. Saunders was nervously aware that Farrel was displeased.

"They didn't bother to go look?"

"Well, the other man swore it was a backfire from a truck."

"We've always got one of them," Farrel muttered. He went behind the row of buildings and found the forge, but he didn't get any more out of the men than Saunders had, and it seemed to disgust him deeply.

Then afterwards Farrel had to explore the gully. Trying to figure the time, later, Saunders guessed that it must have been close to nine-thirty before they left Sagebloom for the Lobo cut. There had been no sign of either woman, no place for them to wait out of sight except the open desert or one of the dim shuttered houses up along the hillside.

At the car, unwilling to give up, Farrel said, "Well. Any ideas?"

"They're gone, all right."

Farrel gave a dissatisfied look around, crawled in behind the wheel. It took no time at all to leave Sagebloom. For a short distance the road climbed a slow rise beside the tracks. The moon was up, the rails shone silver in the dim light. A green block signal made a pinpoint of color in the far distance.

The road swung slightly north, leaving the tracks. Joshua trees stood silhouetted in the moonlight like misshapen giants. Saunders looked out at the desert night, the dead world of empty hills and little canyons, and thought suddenly of Versprelle, the weedhead who might or might not be waiting for them at the water tank. Their whole errand seemed a crazy one, and Farrel with a crazy faith in its possibilities; and that afternoon, Saunders recalled with surprise, he'd been influenced enough to feel nervous over it.

Why the hell should anyone be there now, he thought, sliding a glance over at Farrel.

Farrel was rubbing his neck at the back, under his collar,

the habitual gesture—Saunders decided that he must be trying to ease some tension. Maybe the drinks had keyed him up. Maybe he'd begun to sense the ridiculous aspects of this trip.

Saunders felt the urge to needle. "You expect Versprelle to be in the culvert making his reefers?"

"I don't know."

"Isn't marijuana a pretty common weed? Couldn't some have simply grown wild nearby, bits and pieces settled there when the plant had dried?"

Farrel gave him an odd glance. "It needs water."

"There must be some seepage from that old duct."

Farrel didn't reply, just quit rubbing his neck and put both hands on the wheel, looking straight ahead at the road in the headlights. Saunders felt the smallness of his victory, taking the wind out of Farrel like that. An old horse, trotting faithfully in his rut—you didn't cut him with a whip.

They came to the unpaved turnoff, swung from the highway, headed back in the direction of Sagebloom. The hills were sharper, steeper now, and some of their odd pink color showed in the moonglow. Farrel drove as if he had memorized every bump since the previous trip. He didn't go as far as before, braked to a stop and doused the lights. When he got out, he closed the door silently. Saunders did the same. He heard Farrel slap his hip, and knew that the motion was mechanical, a part of the pattern in which Farrel moved.

"It's going to be a long hike from here."

"We've got all night," Farrel said. "Did you bring the flashlight?"

"Right here."

Farrel hadn't moved away from the car. "There's something on the tracks up there."

Saunders looked, hair rising on his neck. He couldn't

see anything at first. "Is it moving?"

"I think it's lying across the rails."

They walked cat-footed through the dark and came to the tracks, and climbed the slight rise to the rails, and Saunders could see something just ahead, something like a raggedy sprawled bundle. He half lifted the flash and Farrel said, "Hold it."

Farrel grabbed the flashlight from his hand, cupped his fingers over the glass before snapping the button. Saunders saw the shape of Farrel's fingers, red, almost transparent over the bulb; and then they were bending over the thing on the tracks.

A little light seeped through Farrel's carefully spread fingers and shone on a battered face. Farrel bent, touched her; and then straightened. "No pulse. She's getting cool already."

"Who is it?"

"Libby Walker. Parmenter's sister-in-law."

"How the hell—"

"Wait here." Without explaining, Farrel went off into the dark, walking the ties. He was gone a long time, and Saunders finally decided he'd gone on to the cut, the water tower beyond, to the culvert where he'd found the scraps of marijuana. Saunders felt very uncomfortable there by the dead woman. He moved off a short distance and listened to the owls in the distance, and the dark seemed big, hollow, and lonely. Farrel came back by way of the road. "Saunders?"

Saunders skidded down off the ballast. "See anyone?"

"Not a soul."

There was the far-off hoot of a hunting owl, and then the gradual growing of a new sound, a faint vibration in the air.

"You're not supposed to move them," Farrel said, "but we're going to have to this time. There's a train coming."

Saunders saw then that the train had been supposed to cover what had really happened to Libby Walker.

12.

The train came up the rise from Sagebloom, the noise of its diesels shaking the night. The long eye of its light swerved and leveled, then spread around them like a great cold flash of sunlight, illuminating the dry earth, pebbles, a few scrubby bushes, the body of Libby Walker, Farrel and Saunders standing motionless, the dark bulk of the car. With a grating roar and a rush of wind the train swept past them.

When the clacking of wheels was dimmed by distance, Farrel said, "Go back to Sagebloom and call the Sheriff's Office. This isn't L.A. County, you'll have to find out just where we are. These desert counties have radio cruisers and one of them might be near us. See what you can do." He put out his hand, offering something; and Saunders reached and found the keys to the car. "Don't come back after me. I'll ride in with the Sheriff's men. You go through that town until you find out what happened to the girl."

It was about twenty minutes back to Sagebloom. The trip calmed Saunders a little. The bartender offered his phone and advised that there was usually a cruiser in the district, not too far.

After Saunders had contacted the local Sheriff's Office, he called Burns, the night sergeant, in L.A. Burns would get hold of Ryerson and tell him what had happened here.

Then he went over the town as Farrel had told him to. He found the men in the smithy shed, the horse still unshod and sleeping, the men playing blackjack on a bench with a tattered deck of cards. They didn't know any more about the woman they'd seen running than they

did before. If she'd made it to the gully, she'd probably
fallen in and broken her neck. They were curious now
about Saunders. He took out his official identification
and introduced himself, and explained the necessity of
finding the missing girl.

The older of the two men, leathery and wind-burned,
informally friendly, who said his name was Joe Shelly, offered to go with Saunders to the various houses up along
the hills, to keep Saunders from possibly breaking *his*
neck in the dark, and Saunders accepted gratefully. The
paths and the rutted tracks which passed for streets were
hard to navigate by moonlight. They knocked on nineteen
front doors—a few of which threatened to collapse under
the knocking—were peered out at, occasionally invited
in, once were offered coffee. Everyone they talked to was
interested in the thought of a young girl having disappeared in the town. Nobody had the least idea how she
might have done it.

Then by means of a lantern from the smithy they explored the gully. They found a dead cat and a snake,
which, alive or dead, they left strictly alone. There were
no human bodies in the deep wash.

When they got back to the shed again, the younger man
and the horse were gone. "Fred got tired of waiting," Joe
said, snuffing the lantern. "Tell you what I think. Maybe
the gal hopped a bus. Greyhound goes through here for
Mojave a little after eight. Any reason she couldn't be on
it?"

Saunders cursed his own lack of perspicacity and rushed
off to do more telephoning. There was still time for the
Sheriff's men to intercept the bus on the long stretches between here and Mojave. One thing about the desert, it
took time to get across it. He turned from the phone to
find Joe Shelly at his elbow.

"'Nother idea. Maybe she hitched a ride."

Saunders felt his hopes sag. If she'd gotten a ride a little
after eight, going south, she'd be in L.A. by now.

"Thanks," he said to Joe.

Joe nodded in the direction of the long empty bar, the
bartender shining glasses, looking at them. "Set you up a
beer," he offered.

"Thanks. Can't." Saunders was unconsciously abrupt,
plagued by the sense of failure.

"I see. On duty, huh?"

Saunders nodded, thinking wryly of Rule G; and then
he remembered Farrel, an acknowledged drunk, out there
in the night with a dead woman, no drink on him. There
were times, maybe ... No. He cut off sharp any feeling of
sympathy for Farrel.

Farrel squatted on his heels in the dark, lit a cigarette,
waited. His head hurt, the side where he'd either cracked
someone's knuckles or the brick wall of the alley, he could-
n't remember which. He felt horribly let down for lack of
a drink. He felt mad and tired about Libby Walker, and
he thought of her, not as she lay now, stiffening on the
desert earth, but at home, a small worn woman with a
terrific sense of righteousness in her. She had loved her
disobedient niece. The girl's defiance had grieved her. And
her hatred of Parmenter had breathed through every word
she had spoken about him.

Farrel had already gone over the ground with the flash.
Near where her head had lain on the track there were
gouts of drying blood; and he had decided that it had
been here that she had received her fatal injuries. He
couldn't imagine the small, wiry woman lying still under
such an attack, however—she must have been uncon-
scious, knocked out previously.

There was just one way she might have got here from
Sagebloom, and that was by car; and Farrel was of the

opinion she wouldn't have come willingly any more than
she would have lain still to have her head beaten in. So it
meant, probably, that she had been the running woman
glimpsed by the two in the shed. She'd been running for
her life and she had lost.

I should have tried to gain her trust, he reproached himself, enough so that she would have called me before coming up here.

He shifted his heels, feeling the strain in the tendons of
his ankles. The cigarette tasted flat, sour. He threw it
away. He heard the faint sound of a motor far away, not
a car; and for a moment thought of a section car before
he realized it must be a plane. The idea of the section car
brought Versprelle to mind. I wish he'd come along right
now, Farrel said to himself. He's the boy we need. This is
his special little patch of country. He could have seen
something if he was out there scouting a location for his
next crop of marijuana.

Still unsure about the sound of the motor, he climbed to
the track and tried to sense any vibration from the rails.
But the sound, whatever it had been, was gone now. A
plane, undoubtedly, on its way to one of the big fields
around Palmdale. Planes were thick in that neck of the
desert.

He was still standing there when the Sheriff's car swung
off the highway and swept the scene with its lights.

Farrel introduced himself and sketched his business up
here. The two deputies looked around. Pretty soon others
would be here, men from the coroner's office, and then
Farrel would tell the whole story as he knew it. He knew
that Libby Walker's death was his business only indirectly.
He worked for the railroad, and in only so much as her
death involved the interests of his employer was he supposed to meddle in it. His real business concerned Parmenter and Versprelle and the Lobo Tunnel.

For a moment as the deputy's light illuminated Libby's battered head, Farrel wished that a file existed where you stowed old wrecks and got on directly with the business of catching a murderer. The wish was brief. What Saunders thought of as Farrel's rut, a long-ingrained sense of where his job began and ended, corrected the urge to branch out into homicide.

Saunders, slumped against the car door, had been dozing; but he woke suddenly and looked out at the deserted unfamiliar streets. "Hey!"

"Let's have a look at Parmenter's place," Farrel growled.

Saunders pointed out that by now L.A.P.D. would have answered a request from the other county to check up on material witnesses like Peg and her father. Farrel agreed with a grunt but didn't change direction.

The neighborhood was abed, the houses darkened. Saunders looked at his watch in the light from the dash; it was just past midnight. He felt stiff and exhausted, a black taste in his mouth, grains in his eyes. He nodded forward as Farrel braked to a stop at the curb. He looked out. They were beside a corner house, the Parmenter place. The yard, dimly lit by a lamp on a pole across the street, seemed even more grown up with ill-kept shrubbery. The front door must be around the corner, facing the other street. On this side there was nothing but windows, all of them dark. Saunders stifled a yawn.

"Right there," said Farrel, pointing, "is the gate to the rear yard. Keep an eye on it, huh? I'm going to rattledy-bang on the front door."

If L.A.P.D. had found Peg or her father here, Saunders thought, they'd have them downtown by now, holding them for the men from the other county. Or the city cops could be staked out here, waiting, and could tell Farrel to take himself off. But all Saunders did was shrug. "Okay."

Farrel got out and shut the door noiselessly and walked away around the corner, not on the pavement but on the straggly lawn.

Saunders could hear him when he knocked. He sounded as if he was trying to beat the door in. It should rouse anyone inside; scare them to death if they had anything to be nervous about. No lights came on in the windows visible to Saunders. Farrel pounded again, and then again. Finally he came back and got behind the wheel. Saunders expected him to start the motor, but Farrel didn't. He slumped down against the cushions.

"Who're you waiting for?" Saunders demanded.

"I want to get my hooks on that girl or on Parmenter before L.A.P.D. gets them," Farrel said.

"You'd have to turn them in."

All private police agencies, no matter how big or how powerful, had this one inflexible rule: you co-operated with the local law.

"Sure I'd turn them in."

"Maybe Parmenter is more than just a material witness. You said Libby Walker hated him. Maybe he hated her— a lot."

Farrel grunted. It was hard to tell what he meant by it. It could have been agreement, or even admiration for Saunders's insight, or just surprise at the low level of his intelligence.

"The train isn't the only means of getting into Sage-bloom," Saunders said. "The Greyhound bus goes through at about eight o'clock."

"The person who killed Libby Walker had a car," Farrel said. He sounded as if he might be deliberately suppressing an interest in the matter, forcing his mind off the murder and back to Lobo Tunnel.

"Well, if Parmenter's broke, that lets him—"

"Cars are stolen every day in L.A."

"How did the girl get out of there?"

"Remember that brassiere her aunt showed us?" Farrel's tone wasn't in the least lascivious; he might have been talking about the size of Peg Parmenter's shoes. "If she has anything to go with what's inside it, she wouldn't have any trouble hitching a ride."

Saunders remembered Miss Walker's angry snatching of the garment from his fingers, felt himself flush there in the dark.

Farrel said, "Hell, we'll give it ten minutes and then beat it." He propped his hat over his forehead and muffled a sound that was half yawn and half groan.

Saunders saw what Farrel wanted to do. He wanted to get hold of the girl or Parmenter, or both of them, and try to use the threat of involvement in murder to pry out some item relating to the Lobo Tunnel wreck. Saunders stared through the windshield at the dim dreary street and felt his own taste for the job deteriorating. This business of sitting here in the dark was the worst kind of grind.

He knew this urge for excitement, this restlessness and desire for experiment, dated from the time his mother had gone off on her vacation. Somehow up until then he'd been satisfied with everything. Even placidly content. Now it all, somehow, ought to be different. His passes at Betsy were part of it. As far as the job went, he wanted to use his mind, outwit other minds who were pitted against his, make it all a puzzle and a chess game and a subtle kind of war. The way Farrel did it turned it into a treadmill. Like sitting here, waiting like a bump on a log.

An itch prickled to life between Saunders's shoulder blades and worked its way nerve by nerve to the ends of his fingers. I wish to God I was home in bed, he told himself. It was then that he heard the light, hurrying footsteps in the empty distance.

"Don't straighten up," Farrel grunted.

The steps whispered closer. High heels, a young lithe step, not quite running. Now and then a louder tap as if a heel struck an irregularity in the paving.

From the corner of his eye Saunders saw the figure which darted up to the rear gate. He turned his face then. The wooden gate, painted white, swung out and then shut with a harsh click. He didn't hear the house door, but a moment later a light came on in the rear room.

Farrel said, "Let's wait a few minutes. Maybe she'll get into her nightie. It'll be harder to dash out, then."

They waited. Minutes ticked by. Saunders wondered how long Farrel thought it took girls to get undressed; and then he remembered that Farrel had had a family of his own, once, according to the remark made by Mrs. Wall. He'd have to quit thinking of Farrel as an old bachelor.

Now that the girl was there, almost within sight and reach, Saunders was aware that L.A.P.D. was apt to show up at any time. By now they must have checked the house, gone away with plans to return. He wondered if Farrel felt any suspense over it, and decided that he didn't.

The light went out suddenly behind the window. Farrel stirred in his seat, then froze as the white gate banged open again. A running figure started up the block. Saunders caught sight of a small bundle or case, an overnight bag perhaps, dangling from one arm.

They were out then, rushing to catch her. Farrel could move with unexpected swiftness, silent as an eel, when he wanted to, belying his usual sloth. They must have been on either side of her before she realized what was happening. She turned her face from one to another without slackening speed. Then she stumbled, caught herself, put a gloved hand to her mouth. From between her teeth came a sharp terrified screech.

Farrel's tone was soothing. "Miss Parmenter? We'd like to talk to you. We're police officers."

She gave a heavy, throaty gasp and stopped in her tracks. She looked back at the gate, then measured the two men. "Leave me alone."

"We can't do that, Miss. Let's go back to the light where you can examine our credentials."

"I won't have anything to do with you! Go away!"

Farrel took out his leather case and offered it, though the light was too poor to read by. "We want some information about your father."

She hesitated on the verge of panic. "I don't know where he is. Please let me go."

Farrel didn't say anything. He put the case back into his pocket. His figure looked solid and unmoving there in the dim light. The girl's eyes flickered past him. Then with a gasp, a kind of ducking motion, she was away and running for the gate. They went after her, not as quickly as she, and Farrel rapped on the wooden panel. They could hear her hissing breath in the dark, inside the gate, and by and by she said, "Go away. I don't know anything about my father."

"We'd like to know what you talked about with him in Union Depot today," Farrel said reasonably.

"N-no!"

"Give us a few minutes."

Silence. Then soft steps, the click of a door latch. She'd gone inside the house.

Farrel jerked a thumb at the gate, indicating that Saunders should stay there. He went around to the front and Saunders could hear him pounding as before. The rear of the house seemed to contain a terrified, listening stillness. Saunders acted on a sudden hunch. He went into the back yard, closing the gate softly, and approached the dim outlines of a window. "Miss Parmenter. Can you hear me?"

There was a faint stir, a rustle. He sensed that the window was open, if only a little, and that she stood there inside.

Farrel pounded again. Saunders said, "He's pretty stubborn. He'll beat on the door until you let him in. Some of the neighbors are going to get tired of the noise and call L.A.P.D. and then we'll have lots of company. Why not talk to us?"

She must have remembered Farrel's introducing himself as an officer, for she asked instantly, "Who are you?"

"We're railroad police."

No answer to this. She might have been debating. Or perhaps had run into another part of the house to get away from the sound of his voice. Saunders waited, feeling his nerves twitch. It had been a hell of a day. He was bone-tired from all that running around in Sagebloom. Bullying this frightened girl wasn't quite his line.

But after all, as Farrel would have said, they were working for the railroad. "We just want information," he said hopefully to the window. "You don't have to be afraid of us."

After a moment the light snapped on and he could see her in there, in the middle of the room by a small table with a lamp on it, a tall shapely girl in a white blouse and gray skirt. A coat lay on the back of a chair. She stood looking towards the window, brushing at her cheeks with the back of one hand, and Saunders guessed she'd been crying.

She spoke clearly. "Go around to the front door and I'll open it."

It could be a trick. She'd have them both at the front while she could be skipping out at the back. Suddenly Saunders thought, Hell, I hope she gets away with it. I'll go home to bed.

When he reached the front of the house the porch light

was on and Farrel had his hand on the knob, a look of expectation on his face. The door opened slowly, she seeming to hold it against Farrel's pressure.

She was an exceptionally pretty girl in Saunders's opinion. She had ivory skin, full red lips, somewhat heavy straight brows above thick-lashed gray eyes. Her hair was dark and curling and she wore it shoulder-length. The figure was stunning. "I'll look at your identification," she said nervously.

They offered the credentials through the doorway and she studied them without touching them. Then she stepped back, wordlessly inviting them in. She didn't say anything about sitting down. She stood in the center of the room, tense, high-breasted, shoulders back, and waited.

Farrel didn't waste words on preamble. "Tell us about your meeting with your father."

She seemed to expect the question, to be prepared for it. "He telephoned and asked me to meet him at Union De pot."

"Was your aunt in on this?"

"No."

"She was out when the call came?"

"I ... I suppose she was."

"What did your father want?"

"He asked me to run an errand for him."

"In Sagebloom?"

This caught her by surprise. She tried to cover the moment of confusion by looking around at the room. "Where's that?" she stammered.

"You were there."

There might have been more—an admission, some honest facts—but at this moment the bell rang. Saunders answered. A couple of L.A.P.D. detectives were outside. Saunders knew them. He shrugged and opened the door.

13.

The two L.A.P.D. detectives came in, greeted Farrel, and one of them said to the girl, "Are you Peg Parmenter?"

She nodded, her eyes like saucers. The two city detectives offered their identifications and she looked at them dazedly. To Saunders the room seemed suddenly crowded, the girl hemmed in by men. She must have felt something of this, too; she retreated to a corner and sat down as if trying to make herself small.

One of the L.A.P.D. detectives, a tall gray-haired man named Scoville, said to Farrel, "You in on this?"

"In a way," Farrel said. "We just got back from Sagebloom."

"Something to do with the railroad?"

"We're trying to find out. The job we went up there on is the Lobo Tunnel wreck—if you remember that."

"I remember it. My wife's aunt was on that train." He nodded over at the girl. "Go ahead."

The L.A.P.D. men were willing to wait for Farrel because co-operation between city police and private agencies worked both ways. There would be times when the railroad cops would be called on in L.A.P.D. matters. It was the network of all law-enforcement agencies working together which made them so much more effective than if they had worked alone.

Farrel lit a cigarette. Saunders knew that he was disappointed because he didn't have the girl to himself. She was much more frightened now, and more on guard. He couldn't promise or cajole—what happened next depended on the L.A.P.D. men.

But Farrel was going to give it a try. He went over to Peg Parmenter's corner and sat down near her, and said,

"We know you and your father were together in Union Depot today, and that at this time you bought a ticket to Sagebloom."

She clenched her hands. "I didn't use it! I didn't go!"

"You got off the train at Sagebloom a little before eight o'clock tonight," Farrel went on calmly. "The station agent saw you go across the street and walk up and down there, swinging your purse, as if you were waiting for someone. Who were you waiting for?"

She ducked her chin, her gaze dropping. "It was ... a wild-goose chase. I didn't meet anyone." The tone had a touch of panic. Defiance, too.

"Whose idea was it for you to go to Sagebloom? Your father's?"

Her glance flashed up at him. "He hasn't done anything wrong!"

"Why did he send you to Sagebloom?"

"A friend of his was going to be there and I was to give this friend a message."

"Like what?"

"I didn't read the message," she said quickly.

"You have it here?"

"No. I ... I lost it on the way home."

Farrel inspected the cigarette, decided to crush it out, took a minute over it. "How did you get back to Los Angeles?"

"In a truck. I asked the driver if he minded my riding and he said he didn't. He was just pulling out when I got the idea of leaving. I just decided ... all at once ... that Dad's friend wasn't coming and that I'd better go."

"What was the driver's name?" He found her gaze blank and puzzled and repeated, "The truck driver. Do you know his name?"

"Of course not. I didn't find out anything about him. I just caught a ride."

"What did you talk about all the way to L.A.?"

"Just ... impersonal things."

"Do you know of any way we could get hold of him?"

"No. And why should you?"

"We'd like to check your story," Farrel said patiently.

"You have my word for it," she said nastily. She was getting her nerve back.

"Have you seen your aunt since noon today?"

The girl snapped, "She's asleep in her rear bedroom. I hope you're quiet enough not to wake her."

"Did you see your aunt in Sagebloom this evening, Miss Parmenter?"

She'd been ready with another snappy retort, a denial of whatever he meant to ask; but this caught her unprepared. She didn't say anything at all for a few moments, just looked blankly at Farrel. "What was that?" Farrel repeated the question. All at once Peg Parmenter looked at the other men in the room, at Saunders, the L.A.P.D. detectives. "Is that what you're all here about? Did she follow me and make up some story about me?"

"We're investigating your aunt's murder," Farrel said, letting her have it between the eyes. "We need to know if you saw her in Sagebloom."

The next few minutes were pretty hectic. Peg Parmenter was at first stunned—briefly. Then she had a touch of hysterics, real ones as far as Saunders could tell. Then she sprinted off to have a look in her aunt's room and prove to herself that Farrel was lying. The neat, plain bed in the scantily furnished room seemed to unnerve her. She began to cry.

The L.A.P.D. men asked permission to look through her aunt's belongings. She gave it with a nod. She stood in the hall to weep. She looked taller than ever and quite alone. At one time she peered at Saunders over her cupped hands and cried, "That's why I let you in! To keep her

from being waked up by that awful banging on the door!"
She seemed to blame him for some duplicity in this connection.

One of the L.A.P.D. men came out to talk to her. "Your
aunt was a great Bible student, is that right, Miss Parmenter?"

She sobbed that it was.

"Did she keep a diary of any sort?"

"I don't think she did."

They got her back into the front room. Saunders brought
her a glass of water from the kitchen. When she was a
little calmer, Scoville took up the questioning.

She was beginning to accept the idea that her aunt was
dead. Saunders sensed how she was examining the shocking fact, turning it over in her mind, testing it for implica-
tions. She told Scoville, "She had no right to follow and
spy on me. I wasn't doing anything wrong. If she hadn't
been so angry and jealous of Dad—"

"How did she know you were going to Sagebloom?"

"I can't imagine." She thought this over, too, and added,
"She wasn't on the train. I'd have seen her get off. That
little burg isn't any bigger than a minute." Peg's voice had
turned cold, now, and she was obviously thinking of her
aunt's distrust of herself.

Farrel said, "Your aunt must have met someone in Sagebloom who had a reason for killing her."

"Not Dad!"

"Who were *you* intending to meet?" Farrel said point-
edly.

She straightened in the chair, pushing her breasts out inside the thin cotton blouse. "An old friend of Dad's, who
was going to help him."

"Help him *how?*"

Her glance fluttered around the room, and Saunders
thought, She's trying to decide how much to tell and what

to hold back. The girl was attempting a battle of wits for her father's sake. Remembering Parmenter's sickly, almost repulsive appearance and his unpolished behavior, Saunders was puzzled. The man had been gone for years, had deserted this girl and her mother, had obviously sent them nothing of his windfall. Then, remembering the money angle, Saunders found himself studying her more closely.

She began cautiously, "Dad said that a friend of his was willing to stake him with a sum of money. He said he'd done a favor for this person, and the friend had never forgotten. I was to go to Sagebloom and meet this friend and collect what he had for Dad. I don't know anything about the person, not even whether it was a man or a woman. It was someone who would recognize me...." Her voice turned husky and stopped. She sat quiet in the chair, her eyes big and startled between the thick fringe of lashes. She seemed to have been struck by some irrelevant idea.

"Yes?" Scoville urged.

"Someone who would know me," she stammered. "That's all."

"But you left before this friend of your father's showed up?"

She nodded slowly. "Yes. I ... just all at once I got nervous."

"You thought there might be some danger?" Scoville suggested gently.

"It was the ... dark, and the deserted street, and not knowing anyone," she answered in almost a whisper.

Scoville said, "Won't your father be disappointed and angry because you failed him?"

She looked down at her hands. "I don't care."

"When do you expect to see him again?"

From the expression on her face, Saunders thought that this was a point Peg hadn't decided for herself. She shrugged. "I don't have any date with him if that's what you want to know. I don't know where he's living, either. I don't have any idea how you could catch him."

Farrel said, "What frightened you tonight in that town? What scared you so much you ran out before anyone could hand you the money?"

"J-just the dark, and a kind of ... lonesomeness," she stammered.

"You saw something. Someone," he accused.

"Nothing. Nothing." She shook her head as if she never intended to stop.

And there the matter rested. She wouldn't admit meeting her aunt or having talked to anyone except the truck driver who had given her a lift to L.A. Under their prodding she recalled the kind of truck, the company name painted on the door, and quite a lot about the appearance of the driver. Saunders decided that she actually had come home in this way. L.A.P.D. would locate the driver and his story would check with hers. In this connection he recalled that one of the men at the horseshoeing shed had claimed to have heard a truck start at the same time the other thought he'd heard a shot. Saunders wondered if the two sounds could have been mingled, if Libby Walker's life might have been snuffed out at the moment her niece was running away from Sagebloom.

Farrel took up a new tack. "You were making a quick getaway tonight, from this house, when we met you. Where were you going?"

"To a friend's." Her tone was firmer now. She seemed to feel that she had put the worst of the fight behind her.

"Any particular friend?"

"A girl I know. She's always asking me to come over to spend the night."

"As late as after midnight?"

Peg stared him down. "She works late. She wouldn't mind."

"Why did you want to get out of the house?"

"I thought my aunt might have missed me, and that in the morning I'd catch hell for being out late."

Saunders told himself, She's had time to think that up. Maybe she thought it up while she was crying about her aunt in the hall. He wondered why she had been running from the house. Had she been running from the place where her father might find her? One thing Farrel seemed sure of, she'd been scared to death by something up there in Sagebloom. Could it have been something she might have feared could have followed her here?

The questions went without answers. To Peg's obvious relief, the L.A.P.D. men made no move to take her in. They warned her not to try to leave town, suggesting that she stay with friends and let them know where she was. Peg promised dutifully. She agreed, too, that she would be available if they needed her to come down and sign a statement.

She wasn't crying when she let them out and closed the door after them. If she felt grief over her aunt's death, if she was appalled by the grim ordeal of the approaching funeral, she was bearing up quite well.

In the car, leaning over to put the key in the switch, Farrel shook his head. "That's a cool one."

"She was more rattled in the beginning than she was at the end," Saunders pointed out.

"We didn't ask the right questions," Farrel said. He ticked his tongue behind his teeth. "I wonder if she got the jack, after all, and has made up her mind to keep it for herself."

"The same idea occurred to me. It would account for her haste in leaving Sagebloom, and for running away like she was when we met her."

"I don't know, though. I can't see a payoff and murder

in the same picture. Parmenter was using the girl as a
cat's paw, using her to collect from someone he's afraid to
meet himself. That person could have mistaken Libby
Walker for Parmenter's messenger. In fact, I like that theory."

Saunders had to admit it was as good as any.

"If Libby was murdered, in error, that way, it means
Parmenter's victim isn't in a paying mood." He started
the car. They pulled away down the dark street. "But
what could have scared the girl in time to save *her* life?"

Saunders thought, We'll never get that out of her. He
said, "Her father might have warned her." He saw Farrel
smiling at the idea, and resented the unspoken argument.

The car turned into a main boulevard and headed for
downtown.

"Tomorrow, early," Farrel said, "we'll go see John Snowden and Sonya Myles."

Saunders, in the midst of the dull tiredness, the grainy
itch for sleep, was surprisingly aware of the vividness of
his memory of Mrs. Myles. He remembered all of her, the
pale gold hair, the green eyes, on down to the lovely legs
in their nylon hose, the crossed ankles, the slender dancer's
feet. Then he checked himself. Why, he thought, her legs
by now ought to be withered by the paralysis. He glanced
at Farrel, half minded to discuss this.

But Farrel said, "We've got to trick Snowden somehow.
We're going to find out how well he can see."

Peg Parmenter turned out the lights in the living room
and went back toward her bedroom at the rear of the
house. She looked in at her aunt's neat bed, puckered her
lips in thought, then stepped in and looked at the array of
books on her aunt's bureau. These were Bibles, Bible com-
mentaries, and collections of religious quotations and po-
etry.

Peg looked these over without touching them. She opened a couple of bureau drawers idly, shut them again. She walked out into the hall and stood quiet in indecision.

Peg had no intention of following the suggestion of the L.A.P.D. men; she meant to stay here in the house. Actually, her first flight had been headlong, without a well-considered target, and the idea of remaining where she was, now that the interview with the police was over, was rather welcome. Too, she gained a sense of safety from the visit of the officers.

Not those two railroad dicks. They were nobodies. She knew though that the police, the *real* police, must have an eye on her. And so much the better. She'd had two bad scares and she was beginning to feel that the job of errand girl for her father wasn't the profitable picnic she had hoped. There was still the money, though ... somewhere. She'd be cagey and careful—much more careful—from here on in.

She should be hearing from her father soon. In her mind she began to compose the story she would tell him. If he hadn't heard as yet about Aunt Libby, she could use that as her trump card, the climax, the punch line to emphasize her danger and her expectation of a larger share of the reward—when it appeared.

The phone rang in the living room. She lifted her head at the sound, unconsciously smoothing the blouse at her waist, straightening her belt. Then she walked quickly back into the front room. She picked up the receiver and said, "Hello."

No answer. The wire was open. No sound came through it.

"Hello. Who is this?" she said into the phone.

Nothing.

An odd prickling started at the nape of her neck. "Is

this a joke?"

No one answered that it was.

"If you don't want to talk, get off the line," she said, much more flippantly than she felt. With the phone at her ear she was looking at the room, the big shabbily furnished living room, and it looked strange and menacing, the furniture all dark humps and odd shapes in the thin light cast from the open door to the hall.

There was a click and the line went dead. She tapped the buttons in the base, and the phone came alive again with a dial tone. She hung up the receiver.

"Now wasn't that corny?"

She asked it of the silent room, but her own thoughts answered instead. It hadn't been corny. It had been scarey ... scarey as hell. She was cold all over. Someone had wanted to know if she was home. And now they knew.

She tested the front door lock and the latches on the windows before going back to the rear of the house.

She wouldn't be alone here. Not all night. She knew with dreadful certainty that some plan was afoot to bring her company.

She sat on the edge of her bed, rubbed the goose bumps on her arms, and tried to think. She remembered vividly the experience down there below San Diego, surrounded by open deserted fields, chased by someone who seemed to see in the dark, hugging first the ground and then the ooze at the edge of the canal, and emerging finally dripping and half frozen. She recalled tonight in Sagebloom, walking the funny little one-sided street, looking across into the dark beyond the railroad station and seeing the glitter of blued steel. What had warned her that it was a gun, pointed at her?

The silly fat middle-aged truck driver, who had needed someone to talk to to keep awake, had saved her life. Intuitively she knew it.

And now, she knew, it needed saving again.

14.

But the police wouldn't have left her alone. Not entirely alone. They must be around somewhere. She was an important witness in a murder case. She had sensed that they had been of more than half a mind to take her down and lock her up, that her youth and her straightforward story had saved her. Probably they were outside, on what they called a stakeout, right now. She doused the light and went over to the window and peered from behind the blind at the street. Beyond the straggly bushes were the sidewalk, the curb, the empty asphalt paving ill lit by the street light at the far corner. No car. No watchful cops. Nothing.

She put on the bedroom light again and hurried off into the front of the house and peered at the street there, the cross street, and it was the same.

They'd gone. Even the railroad dicks were gone.

Peg, like most citizens, had no idea of the workload carried by the municipal police; but it occurred to her now that they might have other business which would prevent them keeping a watch over her, even had they wished to do so.

She thought, I could call them back. But then, of course, there would be a great many more questions. She'd have to tell them about the thing that happened down there below San Diego, and she might even have to admit that the yarn about waiting for Dad's friend had been a lie. Dad hadn't called the person a friend. He'd said that a party owed him money and was too embarrassed over the long delay in payment to face him. That was a lie, too, of course, as big as any she'd told; but it made the whole affair sound a lot more like blackmail than the way she had put it. Funny thing, blackmail was exactly what she thought the old man was up to. For some reason, his looks, when she had met him in the depot, had convinced her that Aunt Libby's muttered vilifications had been the truth. Aunt Libby had known a lot more than she'd even hinted at. It was a good thing she hadn't kept a diary. The diary might be dangerous.

Peg stayed in the lighted hall, standing, to think. It made her nervous now to be within sight of windows, even with the blinds drawn. An urge to hurry raced through her, but she was without direction, not knowing which way to turn. If she ran away now, she might meet in the dark street the very one she intended to flee. What to do?

Hide.

Could she hide here in the house cleverly enough to outwit a searcher, and comfortably enough, warm enough, to endure hours of waiting?

She tried to think of a spot fulfilling these requirements. Under the beds ... silly. Closets? A searcher would look first in all of them. There was an attic of sorts. In the hall, almost over her head, was a square opening shut with a wooden panel. A bird had gotten in up there somehow last year and Aunt Libby had crawled up to try to catch it and put it out. There was about a three-foot leeway between the hall ceiling and the timbers of the hipped roof. It might be a good place to hide except for the fact that if you were cornered up there there was no place to go.

She leaned against the wall, wrung her hands, tried to force the fright out of her mind so that she could think clearly.

Call the police! screamed something inside her brain.

The money isn't worth it.

She half started towards the front room, the phone, when a new thought clicked into place. She thought of the closet floor in her mother's room. It had been her father's room too, of course, in the years when he had lived at home. She recalled very little of those days. She'd been so young, and the years between had fogged the memories. It was funny that now she recalled the hidey-hole under the floor. She hadn't thought of it in years.

The house, like almost all Southern California medium-sized bungalows, had no cellar. There was a crawl hole in the cement foundation, a square opening shut with a little door, left to give access for underfloor inspections and repairs. In the closet in the bedroom, moreover, some former tenant had taken up a portion of the flooring and replaced it with an unhinged trap. The panel was easily removable. She even remembered, now, her father's guess as to why it had been made. The bathroom adjoined the closet; big drains branched there below. Her father had said that someone had had to clean out the pipes and had opened the closet floor to get directly at them. What she was thinking now was how hard it was to see the panel unless you knew it was there. The edges fitted snugly and the flooring matched all the way across—the trap must have been made of the boards which had been taken up. Best of all, now that it was night—the closet had no light in it.

She had a vague half-memory of someone telling them about the closet opening before they moved in, either the former owner or the real-estate agent who had shown them around.

Her father had opened it up once. She didn't know why. She could remember him, though, squatted at the edge of the open hole.

If I crawled down there, she told herself fearfully, her hands gripped across her stomach under her breasts—I could get away if I had to. I'd go out through the little door in the foundation, to the yard.

She wavered in indecision, one part of her mind convinced that this was the solution, the other part yammering for her to call the police.

She thought desperately, Why, they might not even believe me! They might not see anything to be frightened over. After all, the shots in the dark down there by those open fields might have been fired by some farmer angry at trespassers. (I thought of that before. It's still a good explanation!) And this call tonight—a wrong number.

If they did believe me, they'd take me in. I'd be mugged, booked, all that humiliating routine.... She remembered, cringing, her aunt's dragging her into the principal's office to ask for help on the dental bill.

If the cops shut me up for safekeeping, I'd be of no use to Dad.

She swung around abruptly and walked into the room which had been her mother's. It was not often entered and had a faintly unused musty smell. She didn't snap on the light. She adjusted the hall door so that a thin beam bisected the floor, leaving the rest in gloom. She went to the windows and examined the drawn blinds. They were old and cracked, and she thought about trying to cover them with bedding ... a spread, an old blanket ... but no. If anyone came, got into the house, the presence of such stuff at the windows would fix their attention on this room.

She'd have to take a chance.

She went to the closet, peered inside. It was dark in there, pitch-dark. She knelt and crawled forward on her knees, feeling with her finger tips for the edge of the trap.

She shivered, thinking, It's so damned dark in here. And then she realized how black it would be under the floor. There could be spiders down there, spiders and mice—She quivered with nervous dread and sat quiet, trying to make up her mind.

She heard something come up on the back porch. Very quiet, slow, and cautious. There was a brushing sound, as of hands running along the wall, searching for the doorknob. Terror shot through Peg like an icy galvanic shock. She fumbled up the panel in the floor, leaned over the blacker space below, her brain thrumming with shock.

She couldn't remember whether the rear door was locked or not. Up until this moment she had taken for granted that it was, that she'd locked it automatically on running in after her encounter with the railroad cops, but now a terrible doubt seized her. The thing ... shape ... fiend ... *murderer* ... on the back porch could be coming in!

She heard the latch rattle. She inched her knees over the edge of the hole, dropped her legs, meanwhile precariously balancing the trap so as to drop it into place over her head. She slid forward a little at a time. She felt solid earth under her shoes. Then she was kneeling, a little off balance, ready to crouch lower and slip beneath the floor. She put down her free hand to brace herself.

The hand encountered something. Fabric. Clothing. Rough wool like a man's coat. In the instant before new shock bolted through her on the heels of the old, her fingers found a flapping empty sleeve.

Under the wool was a humped solid shape.

Someone was already down here!

Her lips jerked back off her teeth and her throat opened, and as she clawed her way up she let out a screech that must have been heard for blocks. She pounded from the bedroom into the lighted hall and stood there with her face to the ceiling, still screeching. Away off on the edge of consciousness she was aware of a swift withdrawal from the porch, the gate latch snapping.

In panic, she rushed off in the opposite direction. In the front yard she met the next-door neighbors, the middle-aged couple named Crown. Mrs. Crown was in a flannel nightgown and Mr. Crown had his suspenders hanging. They must have rushed out at the first scream.

The Crowns had been pretty good friends of Libby's and hadn't been too approving of the stubborn, difficult girl; but now Mrs. Crown sheltered Peg in her flannel arms while Peg poured out a tale of Libby's death and her own fears—even in terror nicely censored. Mr. Crown offered to go in and find what had scared her so.

"When I screamed, they ran away," Peg remembered, shivering.

The Crowns exchanged a look; they were obviously puzzled and almost as scared as Peg. "We ought to call the police," Mrs. Crown suggested.

Peg wept that the police had been at her for hours over Aunt Libby's death and that she couldn't stand seeing them again.

Mr. Crown said, "Ma, you take Peg inside and hand me out my pistol. I'll check up and lock the place and she can stay with us."

Mrs. Crown put Peg to bed in one of her flannel gowns, after giving her hot milk and a patent sedative. Mr. Crown came in later and held a whispered conference in the hall with his wife.

"Nothing over there. Maybe she imagined it."

Mrs. Crown nodded. "She's in a state, poor child." She drew a deep sorrowful breath. "Libby dead ... I can't quite believe it. I won't really believe it until I see it in the morning papers." She glanced expectantly towards the front door. Under the shock and sorrow, her manner held a touch of excitement. "A sweet religious person like that—who'd kill her?"

He hefted the old-fashioned gun. "I'd like to know!"

"Maybe they've caught him already, and it'll be in the paper, too." Again she glanced towards the front of the house. "You're usually awake early—bring in the paper as soon as you hear it thump the porch."

He nodded grimly.

In the bedroom, wide-eyed, Peg listened to the strident whisperings from the hall. She felt grateful, almost humble, toward the Crowns though she didn't intend to let them know all of her business. She was wondering now if out in the dark somewhere eyes watched the house next door for her return.

She was wondering, too, if in the scramble to get out of the trap in the closet floor she'd had the sense to drop the covering in place.

And who was down there …?

Saunders stepped from the elevator. The hall was sleepy-quiet, closed-smelling, brightly lit. He went over to his door and took out his keys, threw a glance toward Betsy's apartment. The white door was shut and to him there seemed something prim about it.

He thought about Betsy as he undressed. He wished that he could decide about this aggravating girl. He yearned to be on sure ground with her, immune to awkward indecision, masterful. His mother would be coming home before too long, and then—well, things would be different.

He tried to picture himself settling back into that comfortable existence as his mother's pet, and felt a sort of shock.

He examined his appearance in the mirror as he brushed his teeth before getting into bed. Red-eyed. Whiskers showing. A kind of cynical look around the mouth. He looked like a man, he told himself. What in hell had he been thinking of to let his mother care for him like a kid? He couldn't even keep track of his laundry without her.

He washed socks, a final chore, standing almost asleep above the basin.

I wonder what Betsy really thinks of me, he asked himself as he wrung out the last sock.

"I'll bet she thinks I'm a regular fairy," he said half aloud, relishing the naughty word.

He crawled into bed, buried his head in the pillows, and began to snore.

Across town, Farrel was investigating the stock in his bottom bureau drawer. He had about three inches left in the bottom of a fifth. He poured it all into a water glass and sat down on the edge of the bed to drink it. Around him the house was very quiet. In the distance, over in the freight yards, a diesel switcher hooted. A slight breeze flapped the window blinds. The air was cold.

He thought about Lobo Tunnel, and an irritable frustration rose in him at the thought that after all this time the wreck had somehow claimed another victim. He had no inner doubt but that Libby Walker had been involved, innocently or otherwise, in Parmenter's blackmailing activities. Parmenter's scheme was based in some manner on the wreck, on one of the occupants of that car where the porter had died. Farrel sipped whiskey and rubbed the back of his neck. He noticed that the turned-back cuff of his shirt was quite soiled, and tried to remember when he'd sent anything out to the laundry.

Back to Lobo. The point which Saunders had brought up, that the marijuana scraps in the culvert might have been the blown debris of wild weeds, disturbed him. He'd have to remember to ask someone who knew whether the weed would be apt to spring up without attention in such a place. As Saunders had pointed out, it grew easily. There must indeed be seepage from the abandoned duct which had once brought down water to the tank. Suppose the crop which Versprelle had tended so long ago had shed seeds which had somehow survived? Possible? It seemed so.

Farrel put the glass of whiskey on the window sill on the other side of the bed and stretched out on the counterpane. He folded his hands under his head and looked indifferently at the ceiling. He'd felt chilled on first coming in, but now the whiskey was warming him. Across the room his coat hung on a chair, and he thought about getting a cigarette from his pocket, and then let it go. He was beginning to feel drowsy. Farrel had one recurring anxiety regarding himself. He was afraid that sometime he'd be drinking and smoking, and pass out and set himself afire.

He had a reason for living, for not wanting to die; but it was getting dimmer. He thought now briefly of his wife, of her young face and slender body, the long-ago fragrance of her hair, her soft hands cupping his chin, her lips moving against his own. She was somewhere, right now. Happier, he'd be willing to bet, than she had been with him. It wasn't his wife he had wanted to see all these years. If she hated him as she must, to hell with her. He would liked to have seen his little boy.

He jerked his mind away from these tormenting memories.

We've got to get Versprelle out of the way, he decided.

We've got to catch that bastard and clear up his end of the Lobo Tunnel wreck so we'll know just where we stand with Parmenter. Parmenter's sending the girl to Sagebloom tonight has created confusion. He had a reason for sending the girl, and creating confusion might be it; or it might be something else that would actually tie Parmenter to the cause of the wreck.

Up until now Farrel had thought of Parmenter as an opportunist, seizing a chance which had presented itself without warning. This night's work had muddled the image. Parmenter could have actual contact with Versprelle, improbable as it had seemed.

Catch Versprelle, then.

Catch the weedhead and take his fun away. By now,
Farrel thought, he'd be on horse. They always went from
marijuana to heroin. He'd never known it to fail. Take
away Versprelle's drug, and shut him up where he couldn't
get any more, and within a few hours he'd be telling anything you wanted to know.

Farrel's eyes dropped shut and he slept. The breeze under
the blind grew colder, filling the room. When the light
was gray, Farrel awoke, a choking cough filling his throat.
He staggered into the bathroom to spit phlegm, to run a
glass of water and drink it. He rubbed his hand over his
face. Under the stubble of beard, his skin was icy.

He crawled under the covers and shut his eyes and was
instantly asleep again. He slept until Mrs. Bellows rapped
on the kitchen wall below, signaling that breakfast was
ready.

15.

They sat facing Ryerson across the big desk. It was eight
o'clock. In the big outer room the other investigators were
just beginning to come in. They were hanging up hats
and coats and looking over the stuff Pete had filed in the
rack of pigeonholes by the door. Across the air well a girl
in an office opposite lifted her skirt to straighten the line
of her hose. Pete and several investigators stopped what
they were doing to watch bug-eyed.

Ryerson was ticking a sheet of paper between his big
fingernails. "A report from Sugrue in Mojave. He's been
trying to run down some complaints about marijuana
peddling in the work crews. Some of the foremen have
been having a rough time. Thefts and knife fights. Grudges.
Reefers come high when you're out on the gang at the

mercy of a single peddler."

"It could be Versprelle again." Farrel's voice was rough, husky, the result of his sleeping so long uncovered in the chilly room. He hadn't shaved too skillfully. His shirt was definitely in need of laundering. The flesh at his temple was less swollen, yellow in color. His hands trembled.

Saunders didn't seem to be in too sharp a shape, either. The Chief's cool eye noted a certain distraction, as if Saunders were unhappy on the job or had other more important things in mind. Saunders said, "Hell, it could be anybody. Peddlers are a dime a dozen. Why should it be Versprelle again?" He ignored Farrel's narrowed look at him.

Ryerson seemed to think about it. Or perhaps he was thinking that these two whom he had sent out to work as a team were no longer pulling together. He said slowly, "Well, it's possible—not probable—that Versprelle has come back to work under another name. The gangs have quite a turnover. Sugrue is pretty sure that the source must be one of the section hands. Anyone coming out from town to make contact would be pretty obvious."

"Is Feretti still up there?" Farrel asked.

It took Saunders a moment to remember that Feretti had been the foreman who had discharged Versprelle several days before the wreck at Lobo.

"He's out in New Mexico," Ryerson answered.

"Can't he be transferred back here? He'd spot Versprelle quick enough."

"Feretti's about ready for retirement," Ryerson said. "I'd hate to bring him back, go through the red tape of a transfer, and then have it not be Versprelle after all."

Saunders thought, Farrel's 'way off the beam and Ryerson knows it. He wondered at the Chief's patience. Then he realized that Ryerson must also have been thinking of Feretti or he wouldn't have known about the retirement.

Ryerson was working his way around to something. "I

have another idea I want to talk over with you. See what you think of this. We could plant a couple of investigators in the section gangs." He glanced from Farrel to Saunders, a measuring look. He seemed to expect them to say something in reply.

Farrel said, "It might work." He rubbed his hands together. "Who'd be in on it? I mean—the foremen—"

"Nobody," Ryerson answered, shaking his head. "You'd be on your own."

At this moment Saunders caught up with the conversation and realized what Ryerson was proposing, and that it applied to himself. He straightened in his chair. "You mean, go out on the road and—" He caught a flash of himself naked to the waist and wielding an enormous hammer on a spike in a railroad tie. He found Ryerson's eyes examining him oddly. "I see." Both Farrel and Ryerson were now looking at him in the way they once had before, at the beginning of this damned case—as if he were awfully young and green to be here passing as a man. Saunders felt himself flush; he wanted to curse, to walk out. Instead he found himself asking, "Won't we seem sort of ... inexperienced? Compared with the regulars?"

Ryerson shrugged his heavy shoulders. "As I said, the gangs have a big turnover. There's nothing much to breaking in, if you can handle the work." He had laid the sheet of paper, Sugrue's report, on a stack of others. "Think it over and let me know."

Saunders thought ... *let me know if you're man enough to handle it* ... Then his glance flicked over to Farrel and he wondered if Ryerson's doubts concerned his partner.

Farrel was staring out of the window into the air well. The offices across the way had a lot of girls in them, file clerks moving around, some of them satiny brunettes and some twinkling blondes. Farrel didn't seem to be looking at the girls, though. He seemed to be thinking seriously, perhaps about his capabilities as a section hand.

On his part, Saunders was wondering with a peculiarly personal interest just what life was like in a work gang. He had seen the gangs out along the tracks many times. A couple of his investigations had taken him to the outfit cars where the men lived. His general impression of things, looking back, had been one of hard work with little chance for relaxation or amusement, isolation, a rough give-and-take among the men, no privacy to speak of, plus sketchy accommodations for personal grooming. He gave Farrel a second glance, but Farrel was still looking out of the window.

"Now," Ryerson said, as if putting aside the other matter, "what about this morning?"

Farrel turned his head. "I'd like to check on Snowden and Mrs. Myles."

Ryerson tapped his big nails on the shiny wood. "And see what they think of the murder last night?"

"Yes, sir."

"If one of them had anything to do with it, he'll be on guard."

Farrel nodded. "If he is, that'll be interesting, too."

Ryerson hesitated a moment. "The Sheriff's Office will be handling the murder."

"Parmenter figures in it somewhere," Farrel answered. "We want to know how Lobo Tunnel made him wealthy, don't we?"

Ryerson smiled slightly, as if he had tested Farrel in some way and now was satisfied.

There was fog in the canyons facing the beach. The sunlight was thin, the sea looked cold. Farrel was driving. He said, "When we were here before, Snowden made a great point of not being able to read. What I want to know

now is how *far* he can see."

"Why don't you hit a few service stations in his neighborhood?" Saunders asked. "If he sees well enough to drive, he'll be buying gas."

Farrel nodded. "Good idea."

When they were close to Snowden's house, Farrel turned into a service station, parked away from the gas pumps, went into the little office. Saunders got out to stretch his legs. They'd been on the road almost an hour and a half, and traffic had been heavy. Inside the little glass-walled building he saw Farrel take out his ID and show it to the attendant. A couple of minutes later Farrel came back to the car.

"This is it," he said shortly. "The Snowdens have a credit card on this company. But the boy says it's always Mrs. Snowden who drives."

"She wasn't there a couple of days ago. I somehow got the idea she'd walked out on him."

"The boy mentioned that he hadn't seen her lately." Farrel got in behind the wheel. "He hasn't seen Snowden driving alone, either."

"Well, if Snowden had plans to head for Sagebloom, he might have been careful about being seen alone in a car."

"You're so right."

Farrel drove a short distance down the highway, then turned into the private road behind the houses facing the beach. They passed the numbered garages until they came to the Snowden place. The scene was as before, the paved patio, the furniture of tubular aluminum and faded canvas, the big umbrella with its whipping tag end of fringe. On one of the chairs a cat sat, licking itself. It was a big gray cat. It looked at Farrel and Saunders carefully for a moment, then jumped from the seat and rushed out of sight around the house. Farrel went to the button on the redwood wall and pressed it. They waited.

The door opened, and instead of Snowden, whom they had expected, a woman looked out at them. She was thin, with mousy brown hair and an uncertain mouth, no figure to speak of; and bright red toenails peeped from her rattan sandals. The clothes, in Saunders's opinion, were a mistake. She wore a black cotton blouse and a full pink skirt. The black blouse had been washed with something which had left lint all over it, and the pink skirt should have been filled out better than she filled it. Her blue eyes peered at them worriedly from glitter-rimmed spectacles.

"Yes?"

"Mrs. Snowden? I guess you don't remember me." Farrel was taking out his ID when she made a harried, impulsive gesture.

"Yes! You're from the railroad. A detective. Mr. ... Mr. ..."

"Farrel, ma'am."

"I remember." She nodded quickly. She made no move to widen the door and ask them in. "I wasn't expecting visitors. You caught me by surprise, or I'd have known you right away."

"Is your husband here, Mrs. Snowden?"

"John?" She blinked past them at the patio, a searching glance. "I just got here, I haven't looked around for him. Usually he suns himself out here, or walks on the beach, in the morning."

"He isn't indoors?"

She looked at Farrel's shoes. "I don't believe so. I haven't heard a sound. Why don't you try the beach first?"

She's certainly brushing us off, Saunders thought; and took a steadier look at her. She was young, younger than you thought at first because of the lank mousy hair and the curveless body. The collarbone made a ridge above the neck of the blouse and the elbows jutted. The line at the bottom of her face was in every sense a jawbone. She was not graceful, not soft, not friendly. Saunders thought, She must have a damned brilliant mind for Snowden to have wanted her. Certainly she hasn't got anything else.

She shut the door after a silent bobbing of her head, and they went out to the beach. There were a couple of women walking a couple of dogs, a lot of curlews and a few sea gulls, nothing else; and you could see for miles. "What the hell's she giving us?" Farrel growled in his new hoarse voice.

"She wants us away from there," Saunders said, jerking his head back towards the house.

A grimly pleasant look settled in Farrel's eyes. "Damned if she doesn't." He turned back, with Saunders following.

This time Farrel didn't ring the bell, he pounded; and the door snapped open like a lid, with Mrs. Snowden a jack-in-the-box to spring at them. She rushed out and closed the door and leaned on it. There was sweat around her mouth. The flesh above her collarbone twitched in a nervous quiver. "Please go away. John's ... John is ill."

"May we see him, Mrs. Snowden?" Farrel persisted.

She caught her breath. "No. Please go away."

"We won't be here long enough to cause him any discomfort."

Her eyes blazed behind the twinkling mask of the glasses. "You've hounded him, broken him, accused him—" A little spittle came out upon her lips; she wiped it away with a shaking hand.

"We've accused him of nothing, ma'am. We keep track of the people in the wreck at Lobo because the case has never been closed—"

"You think *he* did it?" She leaned wildly towards Farrel, her voice almost a scream, the glasses slipping down her bony nose.

"Of course we don't." Farrel seemed oblivious to her near hysteria. He looked at her thoughtfully for a moment.

"If he's sick from some emotional upset, couldn't it be because you had deserted him, Mrs. Snowden?"

She stared at Farrel for a short, terrible space of silence. Then she ran for the patio lounge and flung herself on it, face down. She sobbed and ground her teeth and beat knuckly fists on the faded canvas cushions. "Go on in, then. Damn you. Damn you."

"It's an invitation," Farrel muttered. He went in.

Saunders didn't know what to do. The woman was going to pieces and he felt that one of them ought to keep an eye on her. She seemed on the verge of some violent act. Running out into the sea, for instance, trying to drown herself. Saunders walked over to the lounge where she lay writhing and weeping, stooped and touched her shoulder gently. "Did you just find him? Just since we were here the first time?"

There were muffled wailings. "Yes ... yes," she cried at last.

"How long had you been away?"

He thought she'd never get it out. Her glasses had come off; she threw them at the house wall. By some miracle they bounced and didn't break. She choked and slavered. "Only a week. God help me. Only a week!"

"Have you called a doctor for him?"

Sobs and cries. Her face was reddening, what he could see of it, from scrubbing it on the canvas. "... won't do any good. Too late now."

To hell with her. Saunders caught the infection of her terrible despair. Snowden must be dead. Saunders turned and hurried after Farrel. He found Farrel in the living room, using the phone. Farrel looked at him in the gray light let in by the big windows which faced the sea.

"Go take a look."

Saunders went into a carpeted hallway, pine-paneled, with fluorescent lights set flush with the walls, with planters here and there full of thick-growing greenery. He passed the open door of a big kitchen, then a room lined with books, containing a desk, a workroom.

Three bedrooms opened off the far end of the hall. One was empty even of furniture. The circus wallpaper implied that the place was ultimately intended for kids. The second bedroom was full of rag rugs and colonial maple. It looked so tidy and unused that Saunders subconsciously named it the guest room. In the third bedroom, which was kind of plain but usable, there was a big bed in the middle of the opposite wall. Snowden was sitting in the bed, propped up with pillows.

For a moment Saunders had the vivid impression that Snowden was watching him through the dark glasses, which were incongruous worn with pajamas and robe. Then he saw that though Snowden was fairly erect, he was held so by the pillows. There was something broken, caved-in, about the way he lay. The bedclothes were tossed and twisted about his legs. Saunders hurried over and touched Snowden's spread hand with his fingers, almost jumped back at the unexpected warmth of Snowden's flesh. He bent close and couldn't hear any sound of breathing. Had Snowden just died?

On the mahogany bedside stand stood a half-filled glass of water and two prescription bottles, both uncapped and lying on their sides, empty. To Saunders it suddenly had the pat unreality of a stage setting, and he felt an instant's suspicion.

Something was really wrong, though, with the man in the bed.

He could hear loud splashings, a faucet running, Farrel yelling for him in the distance. He hurried back into the hall.

Farrel was in the kitchen filling a coffee maker at the sink. "Get that damned woman in here!" He jabbed an electric cord at a wall outlet.

"He's dead, isn't he?"

"There's a pulse. Not much. We've got to get coffee into him. God knows when the ambulance will get here. They'll have to find this place." He fussed with the electric pot, cursing people who lived on faraway beaches. Saunders went back to the patio.

Mrs. Snowden was sitting up, blind eyes turned to the sun as if she might be praying.

"You'd better come help, ma'am."

She tried to find him through unfocused eyes. Saunders got her glasses off the pavement, put them into her hand. She jerked them into place behind her ears. "What can we do? We don't even know what he took, or when—"

"Farrel seems to think hot coffee is indicated."

She stumbled after him into the house.

Farrel said, "Come get this gizmo working." He rushed out, found the bathroom, wet some towels there while Saunders bumbled on his heels, trying to help. Farrel went into the bedroom, stripped the covers off Snowden, ripped his pajamas to the waist, began to slap him with the dripping towels. He threw a look over his shoulder. "Get his feet on the floor. We're going to walk him."

Snowden didn't walk, he hung between them like a broken-legged man. They dragged him back to the bed, and Farrel made Saunders rub his feet and legs while he slapped him with the towels. There was no response from Snowden; he was like a dummy.

"Maybe we're doing the wrong thing." Saunders recalled some mistakes in first aid he'd heard about. Hell, Snowden might have had a heart attack, tried to relieve it with medicine, and now they could be killing him. He looked down at Snowden's long tanned legs, hesitating.

"He's a dead duck anyway," Farrel growled. "What we're doing isn't going to make any difference." He bellowed at the door, "Where the hell is that coffee?"

She came in after a minute or so, her skinny arms shaking, rattling the cup in its saucer. Saunders held Snowden's head up and Farrel tried to pour the liquid into his mouth. It went all over the sheets and down Snowden's bare chest; Saunders didn't think that any of it went down his throat. What might have happened next was problematical, in view of Farrel's ideas of resuscitation. Outside, at this moment, a siren whined briefly, tires crunched on the sandy drive, a car door slammed.

Saunders muttered, "Thank God," under his breath. If they'd killed Snowden with their efforts, he had no doubt that the widow would have sued the railroad.

16.

The intern was tall, slim, with an antiseptic smile and cold gray eyes. He and the stocky, white-jacketed driver went into Snowden's room and worked over him for a few minutes. Then the driver came out and asked Saunders to help him bring in the stretcher. They went out together to the ambulance. The driver opened the rear door. The stretcher was a big chrome-wheeled affair. Saunders looked closely at Snowden when they had the stretcher in place beside the bed. He couldn't see any change.

"Is he going to die?"

"He's in pretty bad shape." The intern looked at Saunders with a touch of suspicion. "Let's see, I caught something about your being with the railroad."

Saunders flipped out his identification. "Railroad police. We came here on a routine inquiry, a wreck that happened some time ago. Snowden was in it."

The doctor nodded dryly. He was tucking a thick white covering up around Snowden's ears. "I see. Anything to do with what happened here?"

"I don't think so."

Before they got Snowden out of the house, a couple of Sheriff's deputies arrived in a county cruiser. The intern cut them off sharp. Mrs. Snowden was running around in a coat, now, carrying a handbag, and Saunders knew it would take all of them to keep out of that ambulance with her husband. For himself, he had no intention of trying.

Farrel said, "We'll go along. She might talk to us there."

The hospital sat on a knoll, back from the beach. It was a low white stucco building, looked like a ranch house. A neat sign, stuck in a big bank of ice plant, said *Las Ondas Hospital.*

The ambulance had made better time. It was parked at the emergency entrance, empty. Farrel parked the company car on the graveled lot, got out, studied the place. "Hasn't been built long," he decided.

Saunders had never seen grounds as raked, plucked and pruned as these were. There didn't seem to be as much as a leaf out of place. They went around the building to the front entry. The door was a single enormous pane of glass with a golden bulb for a knob. Inside were white plaster and gray tiled floor, the receptionist and the PBX girl behind a grill on the other side of the room. The receptionist directed them to the waiting room.

They sat on a foam-rubber couch and waited. There were a couple of pictures on the wall; they were modernistic, scratchy lines and angles with here and there the suggestion of a form which might or might not be intended to seem human. Saunders gave up looking at them. He glanced at his watch. They waited. When he looked at his watch again, almost fifteen minutes had passed. He began to feel impatient.

Mrs. Snowden came in and glanced around with an

uncertain air. She didn't seem to recognize Saunders and Farrel for a moment. Her gaze was blank, exhausted. When she finally took in who they were—they were standing politely by then—she half frowned and turned her head towards the door.

"How is he?" Farrel asked.

"Not ... not doing too well."

"Do they know what he took?"

"They think—sleeping pills."

"Are you going to wait here?" Farrel asked, and added, "If you want to go home, we'll take you."

The offer seemed to confuse her. "I ... I don't—I hadn't thought about going home."

"If they expect any sudden change, of course, you'll want to be here."

She shook her head. "They don't expect that." She came farther into the room. She looked at a chair for a minute or so as if wondering why it was there. Then she decided to sit down. She looked and acted, Saunders thought, exactly like a woman who had suffered a horrible and unexpected shock. After a moment she said hesitantly to Farrel, "I guess John owes you whatever chance he has. I just—went to pieces." Her chin dropped. The mousy hair crept forward along her cheeks.

Farrel shrugged. "In our business we're used to emergencies." He sat down on the couch again, Saunders following suit. "Do you mind my asking, had you heard from your husband? Had he given you any warning he might be thinking of something like this?"

Her shoulders quivered. "I shouldn't have gone away. He's been difficult, angry and irritable so much of the time—but I shouldn't have given up. When his eyes improve ... and they will ... he'll be his old self again." She lifted her gaze to Farrel as if suddenly taking in his question. "A warning? No, I had no inkling he was as desperate as this. I was just anxious over him."

"Can he drive?"

She studied the query as if it puzzled her. "How could he?"

"How would he get groceries, other necessities, then?"

"Our neighbors would have brought him anything he needed."

Saunders and Farrel exchanged a glance. Saunders wondered if Farrel had the idea he did, that Snowden was a proud, sensitive man to whom any dependence on neighbors would be galling.

"Did he have a car at his disposal?"

"The jeep," she said. "I took the station wagon."

"Has he ever attempted suicide before? Or threatened it?"

The idea seemed to appall her. "Oh, no! Never!"

"Then he must have been under a recent severe strain."

"More than the trouble with his eyes? I suppose he was." A certain stiffness came into her manner. "Didn't you come to see him to try to prove his injuries were faked?" When Farrel didn't answer at once, she added, "That's what he told one of the neighbors yesterday."

Saunders thought, Snowden must have known better. They'd explained their errand better than that.

Farrel asked, "And this neighbor called you about it?"

She nodded. "I was staying with a cousin in San Pedro."

"Your husband's claim was settled over five years ago," Farrel pointed out. "The amount of damages was decided by a jury in a California court. Any degree of recovery since that time couldn't set aside the judgment."

Inside the glitter-rims her eyes widened. "Couldn't it?"

"No, ma'am."

I'll bet she already knew it, Saunders thought. He wondered if she had led them into this byway to distract their attention from something else. And again he remembered the staginess of Snowden's appearance in the bed, the half-filled glass, the empty prescription bottles. Well, maybe Snowden had wanted her to catch on quick and be sorry for having left him.

The Sheriff's deputies came into the outer office. Farrel and Saunders excused themselves to Mrs. Snowden and went out to meet them. The four held a brief conference. The Sheriff's men had talked to some of the neighbors before coming on to check Mrs. Snowden's story. Farrel and Saunders identified themselves and Farrel explained their presence at Snowden's place. He mentioned the Lobo Tunnel wreck, the railroad's continuing interest in the people involved, Parmenter's absence in Mexico and Libby's murder last night. It was an involved tale but the Sheriff's men followed it with obvious interest. Farrel mentioned in closing that there was no direct evidence to connect Snowden with the crime in Sagebloom, nor any confirmation that he was Parmenter's victim.

In their turn the Sheriff's men offered what they had learned from the neighbors. One couple had come home late, past one in the morning, and had noticed Snowden's lights on in passing the house. A woman several doors from Snowden thought that she had heard a nearby garage open, a car come in, sometime quite early in the morning; perhaps around four. No one they had been able to contact had seen Snowden around the place during the late afternoon and evening. If this was a case of attempted suicide, of course, he could have been indoors working himself into a suicidal mood.

If it was a case of attempted murder ... one of the deputies' eyes settled briefly on Mrs. Snowden in the other room ... then the possibilities were almost limitless. Snowden might have been out with someone who had brought him home later to give him whatever he had taken.

It shouldn't have been hard to poison a near-blind man. And again Saunders thought of the stagy layout on the bedside stand.

Farrel and Saunders promised to check with the deputies later in the day, and left. There was a long drive ahead to the Myles place.

In the car, turning into the highway below the knoll, Farrel speculated, "He could have gone to Sagebloom last night and knocked off Libby Walker, thinking she was Parmenter's messenger. Then at home in the cold gray dawn it may have occurred to him that killing the go-between hadn't taken Parmenter off his back." Farrel tromped the brake to keep from running up on a slow-moving truck. "He could have seen that all he'd done was to give Parmenter a bigger bite on him!"

Saunders frowned at the crowding traffic. "Or ... he might be completely innocent. It could be that he's never heard from Parmenter since the wreck—and that he just got tired of living alone and half blind and decided to check out."

Farrel grinned disbelievingly. "Now, that'd be something!"

Mr. and Mrs. Crown were homebodies and they seemed to expect Peg to stay right at their heels. By ten o'clock she realized uneasily that they considered her their charge and that they intended to keep an eye on her. Peg began to feel jumpy and nervous. Aunt Libby's surveillance at its strictest had been a spotty affair. Aunt Libby had had to work.

Mr. Crown was partially retired, had only a seasonal job as a watchman at a race track. Right now he was free. He spent the morning in the yard, transplanting some shrubs, trimming others. He offered to go next door and trim the greenery if Peg would go with him and supervise.

Mrs. Crown said nonsense, Peg was going to help her bake a cake. She explained to Peg that she loved to bake. Bake and sew. She'd show Peg a thing or two in the next few days.

Peg had no way of knowing that the Crowns had been unwillingly childless during their long marriage, and that they considered that she had been allowed to run wild like a young colt. Without knowing this, she still sensed their urge, to take over her life and dictate to her.

"Your father would want you here," said Mrs. Crown firmly. She took cake flour from the cupboard, shortening from the refrigerator. "Now, we'll just make us a nice marble cake with maple frosting. You'll love it."

Peg said, "If Dad calls, I ought to be next door to answer the phone."

"Mr. Crown's in the yard. He'll hear the phone if it rings."

Peg was silent for a moment, until a new idea occurred to her. "I should look through Aunt Libby's things. There might be a clue as to why she was killed."

"You just leave clues and suchlike to the police." Mrs. Crown sifted the flour and baking powder. She got flour on her hands and down the neck of her house dress. "You're safe here with us. Don't you remember how scared you were last night?"

"I wonder what the police are doing." This remark, at least, was sincere.

"According to the morning paper, they're on the verge of catching the murderer," Mrs. Crown assured Peg. Mrs. Crown didn't believe all she read in the papers, but she enjoyed relaying the news. "They've got roadblocks out on those desert highways, and they're asking everybody to report any hitchhikers."

"I was a hitchhiker."

"They don't mean you, child. You wouldn't have killed

your Aunt Libby."

Peg sat on the kitchen stool, silenced for the moment. She thought back over the previous night. For some reason the events that followed the visit by the cops didn't seem so terrifying by daylight. Someone had fumbled at the back door, sure. Why hadn't she just yelled out at them, threatening them with the police? That business of trying to crawl under the house ... it was goofy. As for what was under the floor, well, it didn't seem now as if it was what she had thought. She wanted to go and have a look, in privacy.

Her chance didn't come until almost noon. At about a quarter of twelve, Mr. Crown, in the front yard, was busy gossiping with a neighbor. Mrs. Crown was hunting for their cat. The cat was pregnant, on the verge of having kittens; and Mrs. Crown was determined to keep her from having them in some remarkably undesirable place like the top shelf of the linen closet. Peg chose this time, when both the Crowns were occupied, to slip off to the house next door. She was baffled, then, to find the rear door locked.

She got a screen off and window open, and crawled into the room at the back of the house which had once been her mother's. She went to the closet. The trap had dropped into place.

Aunt Libby had been a great one to prepare for emergencies, like the failure of the electric lights; and in the kitchen were candles and matches. Peg brought a candle, knelt on the closet floor, lit the candle and stuck it by its own drippings into a corner. Then she pried up the trap. The candlelight was pretty dim but even so she could see that what lay below the trap was nothing at all like a body. There was a hump of stuff there under the protection of an old coat.

She threw the coat aside. What was beneath was old

yellowed newspapers and other trash. Peg sniffed at the moldy odor.

Some of the stuff was tied into a bundle; she pulled this out. It seemed to be a bundle of typescript and some pictures. She slipped the string aside and pulled the pictures free; and sucked in her breath at what she saw. This was a wreck, a train wreck, a bad one.

The typed pages seemed to be the record of a trial, or a hearing of some kind. Page after page dropped through her fingers, nothing on them except brief questions and answers. Peg shuffled it all together again, and at this moment she heard Mrs. Crown calling.

She dropped the papers and photographs back into the hole and threw the coat over them, fitted the trap into place and blew out the candle. When Mrs. Crown rattled the knob of the back door and yelled for her, Peg opened at once. Mrs. Crown peered anxiously past her into the house and Peg waited, all innocence, a robe and gown over one arm, cosmetics and a toothbrush in her hands.

Mrs. Crown wanted to know why she'd come over, and how she had gotten in.

"I climbed in. I ought to have a key," Peg hinted. "All my things are here."

Mrs. Crown promised to get the key from her husband. She insisted that Peg put the night latch on before closing the door.

When they reached the house next door, Mr. Crown was in the living room with a couple of strange men. He explained to Peg that they were reporters. They wanted to talk to her and to take her picture.

Peg looked dutifully grieved for the picture and parried their questions skillfully. She appreciated the attention, in a way; but she sensed too that these men had an angle somewhere, possibly were trying to get a line on her father, involve him in her aunt's death. She made plain—providing they believed her—that he could have had no part in the murder.

One of the reporters, the younger and more hopeful-looking, asked for her theory of the crime.

Peg thought it over. She was aware of her effect on the young man. He was, she saw, studying her thick lashes and creamy skin, and her figure. "Aunt Libby was a very religious person," she said slowly. "She wasn't afraid to speak up when she saw something going on she thought was wrong. I have an idea that while she was in Sagebloom she saw someone doing something they shouldn't. And she spoke up about it. She approached them and tried to correct them."

In her mind's eye Peg could see Aunt Libby's nodding forefinger, the peering gaze that seemed to probe for sin, the lips that moved and spilled scalding reproaches. A sudden conviction seized her. Why, what she had just told the young reporter, the yarn she had concocted on the spur of the moment, was exactly what must have happened!

"Your aunt was a righteous sort of woman," the young man muttered sympathetically, scribbling on a paper pad.

Peg nodded. "She must have noticed someone doing something evil." And a voice within answered: she must have seen whoever it was, across the street in the dark beside the Sagebloom depot. She must have glimpsed the hidden figure and the pointed gun, and grasped the murderous intent.

A pride glowed in Peg, pride at her own cleverness which she was careful to conceal.

She had not only her father's secretive nature; her aunt's pecking and quarreling through the years had taught her to keep her ideas to herself. Usually they had invited disapproval.

But now she glowed within because she realized that

she had seen all the way to the middle of the crime. She had guessed its riddle.

The answer lay in Aunt Libby's nature and in what she could have seen to excite her last night in the little desert town.

I know. I know. I'm the only one who does, Peg thought, looking at the two reporters and the Crowns with a feeling almost of pity.

17.

They left the little town of Elsinore behind. The rolling foothills lay ahead, frosty with the look of autumn, the sky hazed. Dead leaves blew across the road from clumps of sycamores. Saunders stretched; he was tired of riding. It was a hell of a distance from the beach to here. He thought about the plans discussed in Ryerson's office that morning. "Why doesn't the Chief ask them to bring Feretti back? It would be a hell of a lot simpler than putting us on a work gang."

Farrel said, "I heard that one of the Feretti kids had a bronchial disease. Feretti moved to New Mexico over three years ago, bought a place there, hoping the kid might get better. Now he's settled and is going to retire before too long. I guess that's why Ryerson won't ask for his transfer back here."

"Big family?"

"Whole string of kids. Some must be married and gone by now."

Saunders smoked in silence, thinking over Ryerson's plans. Ryerson would manage it through Personnel some-how, no one would know who they were. They'd be on their own in the work crews. It occurred to Saunders that he and Farrel would be expected to put out a decent day's work. No gold-bricking or loitering allowed. No coffee breaks, he'd bet. He knew that he himself was soft but when he thought of Farrel's physical condition he wanted to shudder.

Farrel turned the car into the side road that led to the Myles place. The stocky cattle still roamed peaceably behind their fence and watched the passing car with mild interest. The big gate to the patio stood open when they arrived, but Mrs. Myles in her wheelchair was not there to greet them.

They got out of the car. Saunders tensed the muscles of his back to get the stiffness out of his shoulders. Farrel looked tired, the eye he'd blackened previously was red with strain. "There's somebody," he said.

The woman named Lotti was sweeping the patio with a scuffy broom. She waited while they walked in through the arched gateway. She brushed a lock of hair off her face. "Yes, sir."

"We'd like to see Mrs. Myles."

She hesitated. "I think she's resting."

"We've come quite a way. We won't keep her long."

"Very well." She stood the broom handle against the fountain's rim and walked away. She stood very straight inside the brilliant cotton dress. Saunders thought that there was something Indian about her, a wild grace and strength.

She came back in a few minutes. "Mrs. Myles will see you indoors."

The house inside wasn't exactly what Saunders had expected. The room to which they were admitted, facing directly on the paved porch, was big enough; it was also dark and kind of shabby. The furniture had been there a long time; it was all heavy stained oak with red velvet cushions and something about it spoke of age and use. Mrs. Myles rolled into the room through a curtained doorway. "Mr. Farrel, Mr. Saunders." She nodded at them and Saunders found her strange eyes hypnotic. "You're back so soon? Have you learned something?"

"There's been a murder in the case," Farrel said abruptly.

She looked at him as if she must have heard him incorrectly, or as if she doubted what he had said. "In … in relation to the Lobo Tunnel wreck?"

"There must be some connection."

"And you're now investigating this murder?"

"No, ma'am."

She propelled the chair forward, stopped near the fireplace, where a small fire glimmered. She motioned towards a settee. "Sit down, won't you?" She folded her hands in her lap, waiting until they were seated. She had on a short robe, blue, some kind of brushed wool that looked soft as snow. Her fine legs gleamed in their sheer hose. "You're not investigating the murder?" she repeated.

"It's still Lobo Tunnel," Farrel said, looking straight into her face.

She spread her hands, wordlessly implying an inability to help.

"At least we're getting some action," he added.

"Not of a nice type. Who was killed?"

"Parmenter's sister-in-law."

With her head turned slightly aside, her greenish eyes strayed over to Saunders as if she expected some clarifying comment from him. "How would this concern the wreck?"

Farrel now seemed to be gazing into the fire. The fireplace was like an immense blackened stone throat in which the flame leaped like a tongue. "Parmenter was blackmailing someone. Or trying to. He knew something about the wreck he'd never told."

She waited as if thinking this over. "That's why you asked me, when you came here yesterday, if Parmenter had been to see me to ask for money."

"Yes, ma'am."

"Why should he blackmail us?"

"I don't know that he has." Farrel seemed to rouse himself from the contemplation of the fire. "We need information. We need to know what went on in your car just before the wreck. We need every scrap, every detail, that you can recall."

If her husband were here now, Saunders thought, he'd wheel her out of the room.

But she seemed less perturbed, less bewildered, than before. "I wish I could help you. I've explained so many times—I just can't recall clearly what happened just before the wreck. There's a ... a period of blankness. We had been in the lounge car and Chuck and I had had an argument. He didn't really want me to try this Hollywood thing, you see. I think the argument must have been about that, though he won't admit it."

The woman named Lotti appeared at an inner door as though inaudibly summoned. Mrs. Myles glanced her way, then looked at Farrel and Saunders.

"What would you like, gentlemen?"

"A double bourbon if you've got it," Farrel said frankly.

Saunders felt like blushing for him. I ought to turn him in, he thought. To Mrs. Myles he said, "I'd appreciate a cup of coffee."

They'd had lunch on the way through L.A. Farrel had pulled his usual stunt of fiddling with a sandwich, filling up on beer.

Mrs. Myles nodded to Lotti. The woman vanished.

Farrel said, "You don't find them often like that anymore."

She smiled slightly. "No, you don't."

"When you were having the argument in the lounge car," Farrel said, "did you notice where the train was?

Still out on the flat desert? Or had it reached the hills?"

He was trying to time her, Saunders saw.

"We were in the hills, I'm sure," she said at once.

"It's not much over five minutes from the first of the hills to Lobo Tunnel," Farrel pointed out.

She shifted her ankles. The gold sandals glittered in the firelight. "I suppose I could be mistaken. Though ... since it's all so jumbled, the argument and our return to our compartment and the wreck must have followed each other by moments."

"You don't recall seeing Parmenter in the train corridor, near some other compartment perhaps?"

For the first time a look of weakness and distress appeared in her face. The firelight had lent her a ruddy bloom; but now Saunders saw that this was false. Actually, she was almost ill. He thought, This is hell for her. She doesn't want to remember the horror of the wreck, the agony, the frightful chaos.

"I don't remember," she answered finally in a murmur. Her tone added, Please don't force me to remember.

"I wish you did," Farrel said harshly. "I wish we could pin that cookie down and find out where he was when the wreck happened."

"He was with us ... me ... at some time—" Her throat was shaking; she kept her hands clenched, obviously to keep them from shaking too. "I have an impression of kindness, of such help as he was able to give."

Saunders said, "Do you remember how you got out of the train? Were you carried by Parmenter?"

She shook her head. "I don't know."

Farrel asked, "How long was it before you checked your belongings, what you'd had with you on the train?"

Saunders thought, that again.

She seemed to summon an air of patience. "Chuck took care of all that. It was a long while before I was interested in that luggage, Mr. Farrel."

"How much of the luggage was open at the time of the wreck?"

"Why, none—" She stopped short. "Funny." She seemed poised upon the brink of some inner discovery. Her lips hung slightly apart and Saunders could see the gleam of her teeth. Her eyes were thoughtful. "It was as if a shutter opened, for an instant. I could see the inside of the compartment, the shade drawn halfway at the window, the brown earth rushing by outside, as plainly as—as if it were yesterday. And all the luggage locked and stacked together by the door. And something else...." She narrowed her eyes and stroked her temples with her fingers; Saunders had the feeling that she looked right through him at the scene her mind painted. "Something there in the corner of the compartment. But I can't quite see what it was."

The silence hummed. They waited. Suddenly she tossed her hands.

"Your husband—"

"No." A look of disappointment, letdown, came over her and she turned her face swiftly. Saunders thought that she suppressed a desire to cry, from weakness or frustration. "It's gone now, all faded away. It was just a flash ... a look at nothing...."

Farrel said with conviction, "You'll remember all of it one of these days." Lotti had come in with a tray, glasses tinkling, coffee steaming in a cup for Saunders. She paused to hand Mrs. Myles a glass of what appeared to be orange juice.

After a few minutes of refreshing themselves, Mrs. Myles said, "And the murder concerns the wreck? You haven't said how."

"The sister-in-law must have become involved in Parmenter's business."

"In the blackmail?"

"If my idea's the right one, and there was blackmail."

"Now you say it's just your idea." Her gaze skipped to Saunders, to see if he agreed. Saunders kept his face blank.

"Parmenter has a hold over someone, and he's broke," Farrel answered. "I don't think he's a man to quibble about where his money comes from. Doesn't that add up to blackmail?"

"It could. First you must find who's hiding a secret and what the secret is. That's right, isn't it?"

"That's right."

"And you've come here searching for *our* secret?"

"If you have one."

They seemed to Saunders to be sparring at each other with thin and deadly and invisible weapons.

"You want us to account for all of the money we obtained from the settlement with the railroad?"

He shook his head. "That's putting it optimistically."

She was leaning towards him now. The greenish eyes were quiet and intent in her lovely face. "We bought this place. You can see what a large place it is, and you know what property sells for, anywhere in southern California. Even here in the foothills, far from Los Angeles. It's not at all cheap."

"I guess it isn't." Farrel had lit a cigarette without offering her one or even asking permission to smoke. He was forgetting his manners, Saunders thought.

"There were large sums spent for doctors. I had to *try*, you see, even though I sensed from the beginning that my case was hopeless. It's not easy to look at legs you used to dance with ... to see them lie like two sticks, flesh kept on their bones only through unremitting massage, your foot put into a shoe every morning and the shoe taken off at night as you would shoe a dummy in a store window—"

Under the steady pressure of her words, Farrel had the grace to look discomfited.

"It's not easy to meet your husband each morning and look into his eyes and try to see if he is growing tired, if the distance between you has increased, if in his soul he has begun to sense the long, long desolation ahead. A crippled wife." She moved her tongue across her beautifully shaped mouth. "It's no fun being a crippled wife to Chuck, Mr. Farrel."

Saunders was so swept by embarrassment, his ears rang with it. His face was hot, he couldn't look at her. He was glad, immensely relieved, that her husband wasn't present to hear her confession. He wished himself back in the car, headed for town. But Farrel appeared no more discomfited than before.

Her voice thickened. "Chuck had a very bad time in the war. He was a flyer, as I've mentioned. He wasn't wounded physically but he saw things and endured things no man should have to see and endure." She seemed to be thrusting into their unwilling hands all the sorrowful tag ends of her life. "He needed happiness and love, a lot of gaiety, reckless excitement. We would have had those things if it hadn't been for your railroad, Mr. Farrel."

Farrel didn't answer. He finished the double whiskey, crushed out the cigarette into an ash tray, and rose. Mrs. Myles still stared at him across the big stone hearth.

She said, "There are no secrets here. No skeletons in the closets—just clothes I'll never wear again."

He nodded gravely. Perhaps—give him credit, Saunders thought, whether he deserved it or not—perhaps he was more embarrassed and touched than he seemed.

She swung the chair around on its wheels, looked at Saunders. "Do you believe me?"

His throat was dry as dust. "Yes, ma'am. Certainly."

"Leave us alone, then."

Farrel nodded again. Did he mean they wouldn't come back? She apparently took it for a promise; a smile broke out and she offered her hand to Saunders.

They said their good-byes and went outside, and Saunders got the shock of his life. Chuck Myles sat close to the open door on a bench, his elbows on his knees, idly turning a piece of harness in his hands. He looked up at Farrel and Saunders as they passed. They turned and he stood up. His tanned face was dark with congested blood; his eyes burned bitter. He started off, into the patio, and they followed.

Saunders thought, My God, he heard all that. He thinks we crucified her. He felt shriveled with awkwardness. At the same time, a mixture of other emotions boiled in him—envy among them, because Chuck Myles possessed a woman who, crippled or not, was one of the most beautiful Saunders had ever seen.

Myles stopped by the fountain, turned to face them. "When you fellows come back," he said in an ominously subdued tone, "you'd better have the local law with you. We won't let you in, we won't talk to you, unless we're forced to."

Farrel rubbed his chin with his thumb. "You could help us out if you wanted to."

"I think she said it all. In there." Myles had the piece of harness—it was a bridle and bit, Saunders noted—in his hand like a quirt, and from his expression he wouldn't mind using it like one.

"She doesn't remember much. But you ought to," Farrel persisted.

"I told my story at the inquiry," Myles said, "but now I'll tell it one more time. It doesn't amount to anything. Sonya and I were in the lounge car and we argued because I'd been drinking a bit and she thought I ought to stop until we got to L.A. We argued on the way back to the compartment, and we were standing there facing each other when the train hit. If you've ever been in a train wreck you know what that was like and if you haven't you don't: We got out somehow. I think I carried her. Parmenter was around. He found blankets, drinking water, some sort of mild pain-killing drug, aspirin I guess. And that's all." Anger glittered in the gaze he swiveled from Farrel to Saunders. He hated them, hated their guts; and he was letting them see it. Saunders's skin prickled with heat; he wanted to swallow and couldn't. Why the devil hadn't they gone on to other claimants? Why had they come back here so soon?

A dry wind rushed from the hills above the house. Leaves scattered, a plume of smoke exploded from the chimney. "There's murder in it now," Farrel said, as if he didn't even see that Myles was on the verge of giving them the bum's rush.

"Good-bye, gentlemen." Myles drew his lips back in a caricature of a smile, showing the edges of his teeth.

Farrel shrugged. "Good-bye, then."

They walked out to the car and got in. Farrel put the key in the switch, pressed the ignition button; his motions were mechanical, as though he were thinking about something else.

The car lurched away, down the road to the big gate and the browsing cattle. "That was as embarrassing as hell," Saunders blurted. "All that stuff about their marriage. I thought there for a minute she was on the verge of telling us ..." He didn't finish; didn't quite know how to finish.

"So did I," Farrel said dryly. He coughed hoarsely, a rasping noise. His voice had been harsh and gravelly all day. "I'd sure like to know what was in the corner. The thing she couldn't quite see."

"What would it matter?"

"Damned if I know. I just wish she might have seen it."

Saunders glanced at him. "You keep digging at her about

what she might have lost in the wreck. Is that your angle?"

"I don't care what she lost," Farrel said. "I want her to remember. Most of all I want her to remember where she saw Parmenter."

18.

The long miles peeled off under the spinning tires. They didn't talk much. Farrel admitted to himself that he felt tough. It wasn't all hangover. His throat hurt, his chest felt heavy. He should have let Saunders drive. When they turned into the basement garage it was the end of grinding concentration. Farrel stepped out of the car and thought longingly of a drink; but first they had to check out in the office upstairs.

The big outer room was empty except for Pete, who was smoking a last cigarette and looking at the girls in the office across the way. The girls were primping and putting on coats. The air smelled stale, end-of-day. Farrel glanced over at Ryerson's door. The door was open and Ryerson was in there at his desk, something brisk and waiting in his attitude.

Farrel thought incredulously, Oh Lord, he's got it all set up already.

His stomach crawled and phlegm rushed into his throat. I could tell him I've caught a cold, Farrel thought, knowing he wouldn't really do it. He followed Saunders into the inner sanctum and they sat down.

Ryerson nodded briefly. "Been checking on Snowden. He's conscious, he's going to live. He admitted taking the sleeping pills, so that lets the wife out. I gathered they had some notion she might have managed it."

"They've been separated recently," Saunders offered.

"Uh-huh. Seems that's why he wanted to kill himself—he says. It could be the truth."

Farrel knew that Ryerson would rather it wasn't the truth; Ryerson would like it if Snowden was Parmenter's victim, had been driven to murder and now was losing his nerve and wanting to die before they caught him.

"Now, this other thing." Ryerson picked up some trip passes and a couple of work slips from his desk. A funny startled look came over Saunders and Farrel knew that the kid hadn't guessed till now what Ryerson had managed to do so quickly. "The jobs were arranged through the Division Engineer's Office, so nobody up there can get wise. Here are your tickets." He separated the four pieces of paper, gave Farrel and Saunders each a job order and a pass. "The train leaves Union Depot at ten minutes of seven. The outfit cars are on a siding a little this side of Sagebloom. Around milepost seven thirty-five. Keep your eyes peeled. You can spot them as you go by. You'll walk back from Sagebloom."

Saunders seemed too flabbergasted to grasp what was happening. He looked at the two slips of paper as if he didn't believe they were real. Finally he managed to say, "What'll we take with us?"

A dry smile touched Ryerson's mouth. "Got a duffel bag? Stick about three pairs of jeans and some old shirts in it, plus an extra pair of shoes. Don't take your good stuff. You're not going on a picnic."

That seemed to take care of everything. They pocketed the slips of paper and rose to go.

Ryerson shot a look at them. "You both know what Versprelle looks like?"

"I know what he looked like six years ago," Farrel growled.

They nodded and went out into the other room. Pete was covering his typewriter, humming a tune. Saunders went over to his own desk and just stood there slackly. He appeared to be plagued by a terrible worry and indecision, as if there were too many things to do all at once and he wasn't going to finish any of them.

Farrel didn't feel too spry himself. He didn't exactly feel like rushing home and gulping a snack and ramming some clothes into his battered suitcase and then taking a train for the desert. He wondered how much of a hike they'd have from Sagebloom. Miles, probably. Then his attention was caught by Saunders's harried and woebegone air.

It was obvious that Ryerson's move, in spite of the warning, had somehow caught Saunders unprepared. Farrel thought back briefly through the days they'd spent together. Saunders obviously hadn't thought at the beginning that they could solve the Lobo Tunnel wreck at this late date—and he could still be right. On top of that, he'd given indications of wanting to make like a ball of fire on the job. Farrel wondered if there could be some trouble in Saunders's private life, some recent change, some problem he couldn't handle. Farrel said to himself, I ought to stroke my long white beard and start giving advice.

Me give advice! It's a laugh.

He didn't feel playful, but in passing Saunders he gave him a quick light punch on the arm. "Cheer up, pal. We just joined the Foreign Legion."

Saunders gave him a dazed smile.

Across the room, Pete took in the exchange with a waggle of eyebrows.

Farrel walked quickly over to Main Street and ducked into a bar. He downed a couple of double whiskies and the croupy exhaustion gave way to a feeling of hot energy. Thus braced, he picked up a pint at a liquor store and caught a bus home. There, while he stuffed the suitcase, he added to his strength. Mrs. Bellows came tapping, a tray on her hand. He let her in; she put the tray on his dresser and went out discreetly. Farrel lifted the snowy napkin and examined the food. Hot beef sandwich. Big cup of coffee. A piece of green-apple pie with melted cheese.

Filling—and killing to the glow. Farrel took a piece of newspaper off the heap on the table, wrapped up the sandwich and the pie and put them in with the packed clothes. The coffee he disposed of carefully in the basin in the bathroom.

He didn't feel at all bad now. The prospect of the trip, and working tomorrow on the track, had taken on the aspect of a lark.

Saunders also hurried over to Main Street, where he found a store which sold secondhand clothes and luggage. When his mother had gone on her tour she had taken all of the suitcases, though none would have been suitable even had they been at home. He had once owned a duffel bag but now had no idea what had become of it. Probably his mother had long ago given it to the Salvation Army.

The store stocked used duffel bags. He bought one, along with several pairs of work pants and some T shirts. At the last minute on an impulse he added a disreputable-looking sweater he noticed on a heap of odds and ends. The very frightfulness of its appearance attracted him, seemed to match his mood. The proprietor of the store explained that the sweater was new, had never been worn, and that its shocking state was due to its having been in a shop fire.

Only a tramp would be caught in a sweater like this one. It was a bulky garment and though probably of wool, had more the look of raveled burlap. Originally it had been some bright purplish shade, but the smoke or the water used in putting out the fire had splotched it here and there. It looked as if something had bled thinly on it. Nasty. Saunders paid for the clothes and went out almost jauntily.

At home he showered and dressed in a pair of the jeans, a knitted white shirt, put on his oldest shoes and hat, and then shrugged his way into the purple sweater and buttoned it up the front. Then he went down the hall to Betsy's door.

She came at once. She looked him over and then put a hand to her mouth as if to stifle a scream. "No! No!"

"I'm going to be away for a while," he said. "I want to talk to you."

She glanced over her shoulder. "I'm not sure that I—"

He shoved her aside and went into the room, then slammed the door. Then he grabbed her. He held her close and kissed her lingeringly and possessively.

She got her head down finally, her cheek against the awful sweater. "What's got into you? Are you berserk or whatever it is?"

"I'm going away and I won't be seeing you." He tried to pry her chin up and after a moment she let him. It got very quiet in Betsy's place.

They were sitting on the couch, and Betsy said, "Why do you have on those dreadful things?"

"I'm going to work on a chain gang. I mean a track gang." He wasn't even conscious of the significant slip. "It's about drugs. Somebody's been peddling hop to the men."

Her eyes grew wider and she said timidly, "Is it dangerous?"

"Shouldn't be." He shrugged it off.

She stroked the horrible wool that looked like burlap; she was in the crook of his arm, quite close. "Is this a disguise?"

"How do you like it?"

"It's fine."

He'd never before noticed how soft and little and slender her hands were. Here she was, working all day at whatever people did in libraries—medical libraries—and her hands were as soft as if she kept them in butter. Her chin was awfully cute, too. He loved her terribly.

"I've got to go. I shouldn't have come here," he said, "only there was something I had to tell you."

"Tell me!" cried Betsy breathlessly.

He told her, as well as could be expected.

"I love you, too," she said. "Couldn't you see how I was chasing you?"

He hadn't noticed. And he didn't believe it now.

When the sheer press of time tore him from her, he went back to his room, put the duffel bag on the bed and began to stuff things into it. When he was about through, his gaze fell on the bed itself, the bed in which he had expected to spend that night. A sudden intuitive suspicion crossed his mind.

He hurried to the phone, got the night sergeant at the office. From the night sergeant he obtained Farrel's phone number at home.

Farrel said, "Hello."

"This is Saunders. Say, I just happened to think—what about bedding in those places?"

Farrel swore. "My God, we'd have frozen. He didn't say a word. We'll need a couple of blankets apiece. Old ones."

"Anything else you can think of?"

"I'm damned glad you happened to think of bedding."

There wasn't anything else that occurred to Farrel, so they rang off. Saunders turned back the spread on his bed, and it was what he had expected, a woolen blanket that looked too new and a handmade pieced quilt. He knew what his mother would say if he took either of them with him.

On the chance that his mother had given him the best of things, he looked at her bed, too. Electric blanket. How could he have forgotten? He'd bought it for her last year.

He went back to Betsy's, desperate, and Betsy produced what he needed, two worn army blankets which she said had belonged to her dad. He jammed them into the duffel bag on top of the small bundle of clothes.

Betsy was at the elevator when he went out. She put up her fresh lips to be kissed. She looked little and lonely, as if already she missed him. Saunders was enormously touched and pleased. He had a sense of ownership about Betsy now, as if she were somehow part of himself.

When he walked up to Farrel in Union Depot, Farrel did a double take and then seemed to suppress an inward convulsion of laughter. Saunders noted that Farrel looked much more cheerful, even before sight of the sweater; not physically improved, but as if his tiredness and some inward ache had been relieved. Saunders could judge what had happened. In his own turn, he cast quite a cynical glance at Farrel's suitcase.

They got off the train at Sagebloom. Saunders had spotted the lights of the outfit cars back at least three miles. They had a hike in front of them.

The moon was rising at the rim of the black horizon. The sky above was picked by a million stars. The air smelled of sage, of windy miles of desert, of scored rock and empty passes that led nowhere. Saunders had slung the duffel bag by its drawstrings over his shoulder. Farrel's suitcase hung solidly at the end of his arm. They started down the track. Pretty soon the little huddle of lights that marked Sagebloom were lightning-bug-sized in the distance. It got very quiet except for the sound of their footsteps.

"I never could walk ties even as a kid," Saunders said. "I wonder why they put them such an aggravating distance apart?"

"I have a hunch we'll find out." Behind the uplift, the cheer left by the booze, Farrel entertained a vague uneasiness. He decided that it was because he missed the gun. For many a year he'd packed the equalizer on his hip. Not having it now when he was walking into something he couldn't plan in advance gave him a feeling of nakedness.

Saunders said, "I can't get over the way Ryerson had it all arranged when we got back tonight."

"Nothing he could do would surprise me." Farrel seemed to speak from long acquaintance. But to himself, he made a correction: he *was* surprised that the Chief hadn't tossed him out on his can because of Rule G violations—a long time ago. Ryerson was no fool and neither was he paid by the company to coddle drunks. His tolerance in this case must spring from some other source. He must figure, for instance, that Farrel had one more good job left in him. A necessary bit of work.

Lobo Tunnel, of course. It had to be. Farrel found himself smiling a little in the dark.

Tucked away in Farrel's brain were all of the details of six years' work on the tunnel wreck. Ryerson hated to toss *that* out. Now here was Saunders, put to the task of picking his brain, of carrying on if the drinking reached a point where even Ryerson couldn't ignore it.

The kid was pretty good, but he wasn't that good. He couldn't step in and learn the million and one items that so far had added up to nothing and tomorrow might give the answer to all of it.

They needed Farrel. But God help him if he ever cleaned up that wreck.

He scuffed gravel under his shoes, looking at the thin

shine of the moonlight on the rails ahead, listening to the silence that spread around them like a sea. He was mostly aware, as was usual these last few years, of his condition in regard to the supply of liquor at hand. He felt good now, not dying out yet; and there was almost a half of a pint, plus an unopened new fifth in the suitcase. He'd bought the fifth on the way to the depot, making room for it by abandoning Mrs. Bellows's sandwich and pie. He had offered the food to a stray dog, who had growled at him, had waited until he had walked away before gobbling voraciously.

The suitcase touched his knee, satisfactorily and liquidly heavy. The blanket, rolled and strapped to its other side, made a bulk that didn't interfere. Thus walking, with Saunders quiet, Farrel brought his mind around to Versprelle. He had always been thoroughly satisfied that the ex-section hand had caused the wreck. Though he had never met Versprelle, he had after a while gained a definite impression of the sort of creature he was: a wild animal inadequately disguised as a human being. The dog near the depot, showing his teeth at the hand offering food, was higher on the scale of ethics than Versprelle. Versprelle had exploited his fellow man by peddling drugs; and when this wretched game was ended, had involved many innocent people in a ferocious revenge.

And he could be up there ahead in the outfit cars, under another name, waiting like a snake under a rock.

The wind felt cooler. I wish I had the gun, Farrel thought.

"My feet are killing me," Saunders grumbled. "I've got some of this damned gravel in my shoes."

"It shouldn't be much farther now."

They rounded a curve, plodding, and in the distant night lights showed in yellow squares.

As they came closer, Farrel sized it up. The outfit cars were spotted on a siding to the right of the main track.

The bunk cars, converted boxcars, were small and square; against the dimness Farrel made out the higher rounded roof of an old passenger coach. This should be the foreman's place. With Saunders following, picking his way over the ballast, Farrel walked over and pounded on the door. A voice yelled, "Come in."

Farrel opened the door and they climbed steps to the vestibule, where the foreman met them. On the work orders his name had been given as G. Amatisto. He was a stocky, pleasant-faced man with black hair and deep brown eyes. He had on clean denim pants, a blue shirt, carpet slippers on his feet. Saunders shot a quick glance into the car beyond and was surprised—it was fixed up quite comfortably, with overstuffed furniture, a radio, bookcase, and lamps. A woman sat knitting on a chair by the radio; she smiled at Saunders as their eyes met.

They handed over the work orders and Amatisto examined them, then nodded gravely. "Okay." He walked to a table where some papers lay spread out, time sheets and so on, and put the work orders down there. "I'll be right back, Mama."

"Sure, go ahead," the woman said, not dropping a stitch.

Amatisto changed his shoes and then all three men went out into the dark. Saunders said, "Where do you get your electricity?"

"Drop a line from a power pole," Amatisto answered. "You fellows want to bunk in the same car?"

"Don't mind if we do." Farrel tried to make it sound casual, as if they might have become acquainted on the way here.

"Let's see." Amatisto appeared to think it over as he walked. He stopped all at once by the door of a bunk car. "Uh-huh. In here, then."

The windows spilled light towards them. From inside the car came the murmur of men's voices. They were a

long way from town but here was warmth and a place to
sleep and human companionship.

And perhaps Versprelle.

19.

The layout inside was quite simple. In each corner of
the car was a double bunk, one above the other. In the
wall opposite the door was a washbasin with running
water, some shelves, some wooden lockers. Out in the
middle of the floor sat a small cast-iron pot-bellied stove,
crackling now with warmth.

It was clean, but nothing fancy.

In a bunk in the left corner a poker game was going.
Two men were on the bunk and two others were pulled
up on stools. They were using the foot of the bunk for a
card table. All four looked around as Amatisto came in,
followed by Farrel and Saunders.

Farrel's glance skipped from face to face.

One had bright red hair and a red beard about two
weeks old; a big guy with heavy arms, enormous hands, a
chest like a barrel. He was on a stool. The other guy on a
stool was slim and wiry, with a brown wind-toughened
face and a high forehead verging to baldness. The two in
the bunk might have been brothers. They looked somewhat alike, both in their twenties, fairly husky; pale, too,
as if they hadn't been on the job long and had been shut
up somewhere before coming out here.

They were the only men in the car, and none of them
was Versprelle. Farrel set down his suitcase with a sense
of sudden relief.

"Who's winning?" Amatisto asked, inspecting the cards
on the blanket.

"Does it matter?" said Red Beard. "We're playing for

matches."

"Practice, huh?"

"Could be." Red Beard scooped up the cards and began to shuffle. He looked from Farrel to Saunders. "Who's this, a couple of new suckers?"

"Ha, ha," Amatisto laughed agreeably. "No, they've come here to get rich. No use you fellows corralling all the jack."

The men playing cards exchanged glances as though Amatisto's humor were painful to them.

Red Beard began to deal. "They'll find out how rich they'll get."

Amatisto took Farrel and Saunders into the other end of the car. "These, up here—nobody's using them." He pointed to the upper bunk on either side.

"Nobody's using that bottom one there, either," said the half-bald man. "Cheesy took off tonight and he's not coming back. He said to tell you."

Amatisto wrinkled his brow. "He's got time coming."

"He said he'd pick it up in L.A."

Amatisto shrugged. "Okay, a bottom bunk here, then, if one of you wants it."

Saunders threw his duffel bag into the upper bunk and Farrel laid his suitcase on the lower. The mattresses were bare. Farrel put out a tentative hand, patted the rough ticking. "What the hell's inside these things?"

"You expect innersprings?" Amatisto asked incredulously.

Saunders stood with his toes on the rim of the lower bunk. He gave his own mattress a punch. "Sounds like corn shucks or straw."

"Good clean straw," Amatisto agreed, as if he were a landlord displaying the furnishings. "No bedbugs. D.D.T. takes care of that."

"What more could we want?" Farrel muttered.

Amatisto went over to the door. "Breakfast at six-thirty. In the dining car—down that way." He jerked his thumb in the direction opposite his own car. "Good night, fellows." He grinned at the card players and went out, shutting the door behind him.

The players went on with their game, not paying any attention to Farrel and Saunders; but Farrel noted that when he and Saunders exchanged any remarks there was sudden quiet among the others as if they were listening. They want a line on us before they get friendly, Farrel thought. And he added to himself, They're damned stand-offy for section hands.

Anything to do with the marijuana peddling? Probably.

After a while Farrel stood up from his bunk and said to Saunders, who was sitting in the upper with his legs hanging, inspecting the blisters on his feet left by the gravel, "I'm going outside. Want to come along?" He winked, shook his head almost imperceptibly.

Saunders said, "Not right now. Don't fall into that thing. It's dark out there."

"I wouldn't fall into that."

He went out and shut the door, and went around the car to the back. The latrine sat off a short distance. Amatisto had pointed it out in passing. It was painted bright yellow and was not hard to see in the moonlight. Farrel walked over there, then beyond, to a slight rise studded with ocotillo and scrubby sage. He squatted down and stayed there for a few minutes, looking the outfit over.

There were six of the bunk cars, then a tank car for water, beyond that two more cars, dark now, which were probably used for cooking and for feeding the section hands. He couldn't see anyone stirring. There were lights in all of the bunk cars, and once in a while he could see movement inside. But no one came out. Farrel thought about the marijuana. I'll bet they score at night, he told himself. Too risky pushing reefers by daylight. Saunders and I are going to have to keep a watch out here—somehow. One of us will have to have a bowel complaint.

But not tonight. On this first night they'd have to keep their heads down, allay suspicion if there was any.

He lit a cigarette and smoked it, sheltering the glowing end in his hand. He heard a door creak open and then close; and in a moment a figure passed from the next car towards the one he and Saunders were in. He waited, thinking that the walking man might go on to the foreman's car; but he didn't. Another door creaked on its hinges. He was inside their car now, someone who had been visiting elsewhere when they arrived. Farrel decided he'd better go have a look.

When he went inside he found that the poker game had come to an end. One of the young fellows was playing solitaire on the blanket; his brother—as Farrel thought of him—was lying in the upper bunk looking at a comic book. The new arrival sat on the upper bunk opposite, shedding his pants and yawning. He was a slight skinny man with grayish skin and twitching, watery eyes. Farrel took a good look; he wasn't Versprelle.

Saunders was sitting on Farrel's bunk and Red Beard sat opposite. They were talking. Farrel looked around for the other man, the near-bald man with the leathery face. He wasn't here. Farrel was careful to show no curiosity. He wondered if the man had followed him out, watched him. If he had left the car after Farrel had settled himself on the knoll, Farrel would have seen him. It must mean that he had gone out while Farrel was still walking towards the latrine.

This job is going to take some careful doing, Farrel thought. He walked to his bunk and sat down beside Saunders and accepted a cigarette from the pack Saunders offered. Red Beard was smoking the same brand, and

Farrel had a hunch that Red Beard had come over to bum
a cigarette.

Red Beard was looking into Farrel's eyes. "My name's
Graham. Bud to my friends." He jerked a head towards
the door. "Brownie went outside. The kids over yonder
are the Henty brothers. Marko's the one in the top bunk—
came back while you were gone."

"I'm Farrel." They shook hands. Bud Graham had a
paw like a bear's. In spite of what seemed to be a friendly
attitude, Farrel thought, there was something about him
which implied he had charge of the car and passed judgment on newcomers before the others took them in.

"You guys come up from L.A.?" Graham wondered.

"Yeah."

"Amatisto's not a bad guy," Graham said. "He'll let
you take it easy a day or so until you get the hang of
things." Under this was the implication, or question perhaps, as to their experience or lack of it.

Saunders muttered, "I'm a little out of practice."

"Oh, you'll do all right," Graham assured him. "The
other cars are full of Mexes. You know—*mañana*." He
grinned above the cigarette in his fingers. "Work, *mañana*.
Get the lead out, manna. Today, *nada*."

Farrel had seen the section gangs at work, and Mex or
not, they'd been doing the job. He thought Graham was
sounding them out, or getting around to something else.
"What's your job?" he asked abruptly.

"I use a hammer."

Farrel said, "You've been here awhile, then."

Graham drew hard on the cigarette. "Sure."

"They'll put us to shoveling gravel."

"Probably." Graham wasn't watching them now. Farrel's
comments had shown a certain knowledge of the routine
of section work; and this seemed to cause a lessening in
Graham's attention.

"I wish I had something to put on these damned blisters," Saunders said, glancing down at his bare feet.

Graham nodded, went over to one of the lockers, took out a first aid kit and tossed it to him. "Ought to be something in that." He strolled to the other end of the car and watched one of the Hentys play solitaire. Nobody else approached, or showed any signs of friendliness; but neither was there a sign of suspicion. Farrel decided that Graham had put him and Saunders on probation. So far, so good.

Pretty soon everyone began settling down in the bunks, stripping to his underwear, rolling up in the blankets. The man Graham had called Brownie came in, grunted a greeting, rolled himself into the lower bunk across from Farrel. When everybody was settled down, Graham, a giant in patched knitted underpants, snapped off the light hanging from the ceiling.

Farrel lay there intending to get up after a while and sample the pint now stowed in a locker. But in spite of the scratchiness of the straw beneath him and the snores of the Henty brothers—who must share a mutual deformity of the adenoids—he drifted off to sleep. It was dawn when he awoke with the usual thirst. He slid into his clothes, went to the locker and stuck the pint under his coat, and went out to the latrine. Alone there, he slugged down what he needed before breakfast.

When he came back in, the others were beginning to stir.

Presently he and Saunders trudged with the others down the track to the dining car. Here were benches and tables, the smell of coffee, the rattle of crockery. As he eased himself into a place on a bench, Farrel examined those already eating. He was still expecting to run into Versprelle at any moment; he imagined that Saunders felt the same.

There was chatter in Spanish, dark faces bent over plates,

a couple of shuffling bull cooks in white aprons waiting on the tables—but no Versprelle.

He didn't come in later, either, with the stragglers.

His appearance here would have shortened things. Now there was the day to get through.

The men collected outside, pulled the motorized hand-cars onto the tracks and loaded them with their tools and themselves, then took off down the rails. Farrel rode, arms circling his legs, and looked at the scenery. The country was big and dry and empty. Saltbush and desert holly straggled in the washes. Farrel thought, The desert always wakes up, with a bang—the sun hot and blinding, no mist, no morning haze, and right away everything is as sharp as midday.

Far in the distance, across the sweep of a valley, he saw a huddle of buildings against a mountain, and remembered that there were supposed to be mines in the vicinity.

They came to the section of track being repaired. Here ties were being replaced. The old ties were splintery, chewed by the wheelmarks of derails. Also, the ballast had lost its springiness and needed working over. The men hopped off the cars, lifted the cars off the tracks, and after some chatter and stirring around, gradually fell to work. Amatisto put Saunders on a wheelbarrow, gave Farrel a shovel. Farrel found Amatisto's eye on him now and then during the morning. Farrel made no pretense of expertness with the shovel or of wanting to be a ball of fire on the job; he fell in with the routine of the others, followed their lead.

The process of renewal involved pulling the spikes and removing the tie plates, then jacking up the rails, working the ballast and refilling low spots with new gravel, setting new ties, lowering the rails into place and driving the spikes home again in the fresh wood. Afterwards more fresh ballast was tamped in around the new ties, leveling the spaces between. Farrel knew that this process kept the roadbed "alive." Without it the ballast packed down, lost its springiness, and the trains rode hard.

He began to feel pretty stiff and tired during the latter part of the morning. He propped himself on the shovel and looked around to see how Saunders was doing. Saunders was down the track a way. He had just dumped a load from the wheel-barrow, had started back to the long hummock of ballast put there previously from a supply train. Farrel could see sweat on his bare back. He'd shed the shirt and the sweater long ago, tossed them onto one of the little cars they'd ridden here.

Farrel listened to the conversation around him. Most of it was in Spanish. He caught words here and there. He turned around, and found Graham's eyes on him. Graham had a sledge hammer across his knee, resting, while another hand put some tie plates in place. His face was flushed, sparkled with sweat; but he didn't look tired. He grinned at Farrel briefly. Checking further, Farrel noted that the Henty boys were doing what he was, shoveling. They could be beginners, then, too. The leathery-faced man whom Graham had called Brownie operated one of the jacks.

He looked for Marko's wizened gray face and watery eyes.

Marko was taking a break, too; he was over beside one of the handcars shuffling through the shirts and sweaters and old coats tossed there in a heap. Farrel watched him, wondering what he was after. It looked as if he were hunting for something, trying to keep his skinny body between the men on the tracks and what he was doing. His attitude was one of nervous haste. All at once Farrel realized that his close attention and curiosity might be noticed. He deliberately turned sway, wiped sweat from his face, and got busy with the shovel.

At noon they put the cars back on the tracks and took off for lunch. At the bunk cars they washed, and some had a smoke before going into the diner. Lunch was hearty and filling, without frills. The bull cooks kept the tables supplied with hot refills, plenty of coffee. Farrel found that he was hungry. The bottle in his locker had less appeal than the food. The heavy work, the sweat, the fresh air had given him an appetite.

Outside, he ran into Saunders. They'd been careful not to seem too friendly. Now Farrel nodded and said, "How's it going?"

"This is hell," Saunders said quietly, with conviction.

"Amatisto gave you a tough job."

"No, I can't see how I got so soft." Saunders was looking now at his swollen, blistered hands. "Hell, I didn't have this much trouble in the Army, and there they really gave us the business."

"How long ago?"

Saunders smiled slightly. "Four years."

"Well, you know the old saying. Some people retire and others just get jobs as railroad bulls."

"When I get back to town, I'm going to join a gym."

"Not a bad idea," Farrel agreed. He was looking over the rest of the men. Some of the Mexicans had squatted in the shade of the cars, were chattering together in Spanish, laughing a lot, their white teeth flashing through the smoke of their cigarettes. Three Negroes were shooting craps in a doorway. The men who shared the bunk car where Farrel and Saunders had slept were sitting on one of the handcars—the Henty brothers a little apart from Bud Graham and Brownie and Marko. Studying the group, Farrel decided that Graham and Brownie and Marko weren't exactly making the Hentys welcome, and the younger men were uncomfortable about it. They wanted in, wanted all the way in, and the three old hands were turning their backs and carrying on a private talk.

Farrel would have liked very much to have questioned Amatisto about these three; but of course there was no way to do this without showing his hand.

He said to Saunders, "Maybe you could chum up to those two, the Hentys."

Saunders didn't look around. "I don't know. There's something cagey about them. I think they've got wind of something, they're trying to wedge their way in."

"At least get around them, look dumb, and listen."

"I don't have to look dumb," Saunders said. "I *am* dumb, or I wouldn't be here on a wheelbarrow."

Amatisto came walking up the siding from his private car, and as this seemed to be the signal, the men got the cars back on the rails and took off. There were some changes during the afternoon. Amatisto switched jobs on Saunders and Farrel, giving Farrel the wheelbarrow. Farrel thought for a while he was going to drop. The sun was hot now, the desert wind blew fine dust into their eyes, the load he had to wheel from the gravel supply to the tracks seemed enormous.

Some passenger trains went by under slow orders, the engineer waving at them and people staring at them from the windows. When the freights showed up there was banter between their crews and the extra gang, most of it profane in nature.

Getting a drink from the water can on one of the handcars, Farrel found himself next to Brownie. He thought Brownie was giving him the once-over quietly, pretended not to notice. Brownie said, "I thought I saw you out by the latrine last night, kind of wandering around."

In that instant Farrel knew that Brownie had followed him out to see what he was going to do. Brownie was a spy, so he must have something to spy about. Farrel said grouchily, "I goddamn nearly took off right then. Just tried to make up my mind to light out and go. Didn't want to come up here on this cruddy job anyhow. I got a race system, any time I want to start taking it easy."

"I've met guys before with race systems," Brownie said. "Standing just about where you are now, and looking like you look—a busted gut from toting a wheelbarrow. You know what I think about the horses? I think they're the craps."

"Ah, you don't know what you're talking about."

"You think I don't?" Brownie asked. "You think I've been out here on this damned desert all my life?"

From his looks, the wind-toughened skin, the eyes buried in wrinkles against the sun, Farrel would have said yes, practically. He tried to see whether Brownie believed the yarn that he'd been wandering outside trying to make up his mind to go back to L.A. But Brownie's glance flickered away, his face was a mask that betrayed nothing.

"I still haven't made up my mind to stay," Farrel grunted.

"Ah, you'll stay," Brownie said. If there was meaning in this beyond plain cynical jeering, Farrel was unable to place it.

20.

The hours of that day had dragged unendurably for Peg Parmenter.

She had dutifully helped Mrs. Crown to cook and mend and clean, she had assisted Mr. Crown in the trimming of the wild shrubbery around her own home, and she had kept her mouth shut on her thoughts. But Peg was young and restless, and now rebellion was growing.

At first Mrs. Crown had taken the line that Peg was staying with them because it was what her remaining guardian, her father, would wish. But late in the day the tune had changed. Mrs. Crown had begun to ask questions and to throw out hints, and Peg saw that the Crowns believed what they had been told by her aunt. They must know all about her father, his desertion of her and her mother and the scandal in Mexico, the dark suspicions of Aunt Libby that he was all sorts of a crook. She tried to remember back when the Crowns had moved here, but it had been so long ago that she couldn't place the date. Perhaps they had been here always, she thought, ever since Mother was at home and Dad working for the railroad.

Now Mrs. Crown was trying to pump her.

Peg kept close as a clam, eyes innocent. She was in the kitchen. It was growing dark outdoors. Mrs. Crown had given her some potatoes to peel.

"Of course I expect you to be loyal to your father," Mrs. Crown was saying, "but if there is information about him that you haven't—"

"Listen!" Peg cried.

Mrs. Crown, cutting biscuits on a floured board, lifted her head sharply.

"Next door. It's the phone." Peg jammed the bowl of peeled potatoes into the sink and ran for the door. She had the key to her house in her skirt pocket. She rushed out into the twilight, around the house to the gate, then in through the front door. The phone was still ringing in the darkened living room.

She lifted the receiver. "Hello."

There was silence, and this drew out until she began to fear that no one was going to answer.

"Hello again."

"Peggy?"

It was her father's voice, her father's name for her. She gripped the phone hard in an upsurge of relief. "Oh, Dad, why didn't you call before? Are you all right?" Her thoughts mocked: *all right—looking as he does?*

"Sure, sure. Peggy, are you alone there?"

"Yes. Well, for now anyway. I just ran in. I've been staying next door, the neighbors, Mr. and Mrs. Crown—"

"Did you get the money?"

"N-no."

"Why not?"

"Oh—"

He didn't wait for her explanation. "Hey, did anybody come around?"

"The police. And two men from the railroad. They had badges, too. That was night before last, after I got back from Sagebloom. Oh, Dad, Aunt Libby was there too and she's dead!"

"I know that." He didn't seem to attach much importance or any emotion to it, a fact that settled on Peg with a touch of shock. "Anybody else?"

She debated about telling him; but the truth rushed out willy-nilly. "Somebody tried to get in at the back door! That was much later ... I got terribly scared! I was all alone, and they were trying the knob, and I knew they were going to get in, and I panicked and screamed. That roused the neighbors." Her heart thudded at the sudden memory of terror, all too vivid. She cried into the phone, "I'm scared, I'm scared! Who is this person?"

"Hmmm." He was stalling. Or waiting for her to collect herself.

As if an icy command had reached her over the wire she straightened her face, ironing the fright from it, brushed at her blown hair and drew a deep, calming breath. She took a moment to look around. Across the room the open door showed the front yard, the twilit sky and the street. The mown lawn looked bare. The thicket that had lined the windows was gone, pruned away; a gray light seeped in. "Do you know who it was?" she asked calmly.

He waited another moment and then said, "You imagined it. Have you done any poking around in the house?"

"Why should I? What is there I haven't seen a million times before?" She pretended bewilderment, still knowing what he meant: he wanted to know if she had found the stuff under the panel in the bedroom closet floor. A sense of danger stole over her; but now she was sharper, braced for it. "Of course I took some personal things over to the neighbors. I need them there. Is there something you want? Something I could bring you?"

"No. No, just wondering." Relief lightened his tone. He went on then in a different vein: "They giving you a hard time about Libby?"

"Who? The neighbors? They know—"

"The cops."

"Oh. They were here just once. Night before last. Four of them. Two L.A. City detectives and two from the railroad."

"Listen, tell me what those railroad dicks looked like." She told him as well as she could about Farrel and Saunders.

"Yeah, I know one of them. The young one. What did they ask?"

"Oh ... was I there when Aunt Libby was killed, did I know she'd gone to Sagebloom on an early train, all that stuff."

"And what did you tell them?"

"That I caught a ride out of that town—I guess about the time Aunt Libby was killed."

"Is that the truth?"

"Yes."

"Didn't anybody show?" he demanded sharply.

"In Sagebloom? Why, of course! That's why Aunt Libby was murdered, she must have seen whoever it was and when they—"

"Shut up!" His voice was savage. "You hear this now, Peggy, and remember it. Don't mix my business with this thing about Libby. There's no connection between them."

"No connection—"

"None at all. Tell that to the cops. Libby's dead and probably she got that way from poking in where nobody wanted her. She was like that. I knew her from years before, and she was always a goddamn snoop and a prying bitch. But I won't have my affairs dirtied with her dying."

Peg gasped, "But why would she have—"

"I don't know." He seemed to be shouting at her over the phone, though actually his voice wasn't raised much. "You get this straight and keep it straight. My business in Sagebloom had nothing to do with murder."

"But, Dad, listen. Down there—"

"You chickened out on me, goddamn you!"

"Down there in San Diego, the first errand I did for you, someone shot at me. It was dark, I had to crawl, I wasn't imagining things...." She paused to listen. The line was dead. He'd hung up.

She was trembling with frustrated anger. She put the phone into its cradle and waited, hoping he would call back. She yearned to tell him a few facts, how it felt to be a patsy, a sucker. He wouldn't have listened, though, if she had reached him. She sensed that she had been telling him things he didn't want to hear when he had hung up. Whatever had happened down there near San Diego, and whatever had happened in Sagebloom, he wanted her to keep under her hat. No, more than that, he wanted her to think there was no danger.

Calming a little, Peg decided that her father was a fool.

He was trying to pry money from someone who would rather kill than barter, and this in itself was insane enough; but to top it he wanted to ignore the risk.

She went over to the door and looked out at the street.

Her face was pensive. The pale light brought out the outline of her splendid figure and shone in her hair. Peg thought, I don't see how I can stand another day with the Crowns. And even if I liked it there, they'll want me to stir myself sooner or later, they'll expect me to get a job and settle down. Maybe sell this place and board with them.

She made a gruesome face at the twilight sky.

I need money. I need money terribly. Not the dinky dough you work for in a factory or an office. I want big dough for good clothes and good times. I'd like to buy a lot of duds and go over to Las Vegas, for instance, and meet somebody there, a guy with plenty of jack, knows how to have fun. She licked her lips. In her mind's eye she saw them together, she and the flashy gambler; her breast swelled inside the cotton blouse.

It isn't as if I didn't have the looks.

She stroked her hands down over her thighs.

Need money. Need money. Need money.

The future seemed to spread before her as gray and barren as the street. She stood looking out for a moment or so longer, then turned, shut the door and locked it, and walked cat-footed to the rear of the house. She turned in at the door of her mother's bedroom.

Parmenter came out of the phone booth. He was sweating. He felt sick. There was a fluttering around his heart.

The flophouse lobby was in shadow, which was a good thing, since the grimy floor and the broken furniture looked better that way. A single bulb burned above the desk, where the clerk sat on a stool looking at a comic book. The clerk was a fat man with a lot of broken veins in his face. He wore a dirty T shirt, jeans, and carpet slippers. He smelled oddly of mouthwash. He glanced up as Parmenter shuffled towards him. "Want the room again?"

"Yeah."

Parmenter put down a single dollar bill. The clerk tossed him a key. Parmenter started for the stairs, then turned back. "I feel pretty tough. Guess I'd better get a bottle."

The clerk sucked his teeth. "Huh."

"Where's the nearest liquor store?" Parmenter asked, knowing the answer.

"Well ..." The clerk examined him shrewdly, "What're you drinkin'?"

Parmenter said boldly, "What've you got?"

The clerk grinned as if Parmenter had cracked a joke. "You kiddin'? The liquor store's three doors down, on your right. Can't miss." He pretended a renewed interest in the comics.

Parmenter went to the lobby door and put a hand on the worn knob.

"Hey!" the clerk said.

Parmenter thought, I ought to pretend I don't hear the bastard. But instead he looked back over his shoulder. "Yes?"

"Come 'ere."

Parmenter went back to the desk.

The clerk said, as if taking Parmenter into his confidence, "You want wine, go on to the store. You want somethin' with juice in it, I might save you some money."

Parmenter shook his head. "What do you make it out of? Paint thinner?"

"Ha, ha, ha. No, I save the laundry water off'n them sheets upstairs."

"You're out of business, then," Parmenter pointed out. "Those sheets haven't been washed since they were brought in here."

The clerk pretended to be rebuffed. "You want some hotshot, or not?"

"Is that your brand name?"

"I might think of prettier."

"Don't go poetical. What are you asking?"

"Fifty."

Parmenter felt in his pocket, brought out two quarters and put them down. The clerk put down a toe behind the desk, pulled out a box, rummaged in it. A solid shape in a brown paper sack slid up, across the linoleum and into Parmenter's hands. The quarters disappeared. Parmenter noticed in passing what extraordinarily dirty nails the clerk had.

He went upstairs, down the hall, opened his door with the key. The room was barely big enough for the three-quarter-sized bed and a scuffy bureau. He snapped on the light, then turned it off again. He lay down on the bed and took a drag from the half-pint bottle. The stuff was horrible; it went down like liquid fire.

He thought, I've got to plan things.

Mostly, right now, I need money. Not a lot, but quick. What Peggy gave me is gone. I can panhandle a little.

When I feel better, I'll hit the street.

He drank again, and choked, then kept it down. The fluttering around his heart stilled to a burning pressure. He slipped into drowsiness and dreamed of the days in Mexico, the fabulous bank roll at the beginning, the roistering and the women and the high living, and then that damned Mex in the sights of his gun, and afterwards the long drabness of Islas Marías. He remembered the wind off the beach and the brilliant sun; and how crazy wrong it had always seemed, a jail set down like a green jewel in a purple sea.

Parmenter rolled on his face and slept.

When he woke he sat up groggily. He could hear a juke-box in the distance; a neon glow blinked off and on against the framing of the window. He went to the window and raised the blind and looked out. It was dark now.

He shivered, and ran his hands over his chest, coughed tentatively. He searched for the bottle, found it under the pillow, drank again.

He didn't feel any better for the booze or the nap. He felt awful.

He shook his head over his predicament. Got to keep going till I can pry something loose. Goddamn bastards, standing the kid up like that. Need money. Need money bad, enough to keep going until I can pry something loose. The flittering thoughts circled in his brain. Need money. Pry something loose. Pry … loose. Money….

He stumbled downstairs and out upon the pavement. A man in a gray overcoat and a snap-brim felt hat, very prosperous, kind of fat, looked into Parmenter's outstretched palm and shied away. The second pedestrian was tall and thin, glasses pinched to a bony nose; and he seemed not to see Parmenter's hand at all.

"God sakes, just a quarter for a bowl of soup!" Parmenter whined after him.

The tall thin man paused and looked back. "Why don't you go to the Mission, poor fellow?"

"Go to hell."

The door of the flophouse was still less than fifteen feet away. Parmenter went back to the lobby and rested in one of the broken chairs. The clerk, deferring to the increasing dark, had lit a bulb above the alcove where the stairs stood. In Parmenter's gaze, the bulb expanded, then shattered into splinters of light. The pain in his chest increased.

God's sakes, I can't sit here and pass out, Parmenter thought. His glance settled on the phone booth. With an effort, a conscious tightening of will, he got out of the chair and into the booth with the door closed. He dialed for the long-distance operator, asked to place a call collect. Then he waited.

"Your number does not answer, sir. Shall I try again in fifteen minutes? I'll call you when the call is completed."

"Yeah, yeah."

The stuffiness of the booth seemed to congeal around him. The air was thick, stifling; he couldn't get the door open fast enough. The clerk glanced at him over the comic book and frowned.

Parmenter went back into the street. The open air seemed to relieve somewhat the panic he felt about breathing. He leaned against the wall beside the big pane, the flophouse letting out a dim glow, shadow lettering in reverse on the pavement, *Hotel Winfield*, a smell of frying onions and the hammer of the jukebox; a mass of impressions he didn't try to sort or assimilate. Breathe, just breathe, he told himself. To hell with the money. But when a figure materialized out of shadows, when shoes crossed the Hotel Winfield on the pavement, his hands shot out automatically—both of them.

The man paused. "Well ..." Neatly manicured fingers dropped a dime. The steps went on, slowed, came back. "I say there ... are you sick or something?"

"Fine. Fine." Parmenter stood with his arms hanging, mouth open, leaning forward slightly; he tried to focus on the man's face and got a bleared impression of clean skin and heavy brows. "Thanks," he remembered to say, "thanks for the dime."

"Wait a minute." The man took out a dollar bill and tucked it into Parmenter's lifeless fingers. "Get a good meal under your belt."

He walked away then, quickly.

Parmenter put the bill and dime into his sock. If he was going to be taken sick, he didn't want anything in his pockets.

In about fifteen minutes the phone began to ring in the booth in the lobby. The clerk took the call, then went to look for Parmenter. He found Parmenter outside, a few feet from the door, sitting on the sidewalk with his back against the wall of the building. Parmenter's eyes were shut and his breathing had a ragged hoarseness; there was something wrong with his color, too. A couple of women walked past, chippies in red coats and patent leather slippers, and they giggled at sight of what they thought was a passed-out drunk.

The clerk was worried. He went into the lobby and first of all disposed of the bottled stock under the linoleum-covered desk. Then he hung up the phone in the booth and used a dime of his own money to call the cops.

All the way to Georgia Street Emergency Hospital, Parmenter was mumbling about the injustice of putting a prison on an island in the tropic sea.

21.

Farrel crawled into his bunk and shut his eyes. He ached in every bone, the tendons in his hands quivered, he had the feeling of being permanently stooped, and the whiskey he'd drunk after dinner had had no effect except to collect into a heated lump in his belly. Nothing could counteract the effects of the day spent at unaccustomed hard labor. Right now he should be outdoors, scouting around, looking for somebody in the act of buying or selling marijuana—and all he could do was lie and twitch.

His job wasn't simply to become a section hand; but as far as he could tell now, that was about all he was up to.

Saunders wasn't feeling too bad, apparently. He was over at the washbasin now, shaving. He'd had a shower previously, in one of the other cars. Some were so equipped. He looked kind of sunburned, his face a little tighter, more alert, was all.

After he'd finished shaving, had combed his hair and put on his shirt, he came over to Farrel's bunk and sat down. The poker game was in progress at the other end of the car. Saunders spoke softly. "I've written my girl a letter. I'm going into Sagebloom to mail it."

Farrel lifted his head. "You're going to *walk* to town?"

"Sure." Saunders jerked his head almost imperceptibly towards the poker game. "Notice if anybody leaves right after, will you?"

Farrel propped himself on an elbow. "I guess I ought to get out, too."

"Stay here and seem to take a nap and listen. I don't think we'll get anything, unless it just falls our way. Somebody's pretty cute here."

"Uh-huh." Farrel lay down again. Saunders put on the horrible sweater, lit a cigarette, and went out. In less than a minute Brownie tossed in his hand and strolled out, too; but he came back pretty quick. He'd seen where Saunders was going, and the direction was somehow reassuring. Farrel thought that over.

There's something around here they don't want meddled with, he thought. The town, Sagebloom, hadn't anything to do with it. If there was weed stored in the vicinity, it could be buried in any direction from the outfit cars and finding it would be almost impossible.

I'll bet there's a tea party going on right now, somewhere. He rubbed his jumpy fingers and tried to stretch the kinks from his spine.

Brownie's the watchdog but that doesn't mean he's boss. Judging by looks and temperament, Graham ought to be it; but, hell, it could be anybody. Farrel shut his eyes and breathed deeply. Goddamn you, Versprelle, he said in his mind; I want you so bad I can taste you. And you taste awful.

Versprelle wasn't here in this extra gang. If he was peddling, he was doing it as an invisible man.

Farrel remembered two little items then. One, that a man had quit and walked off yesterday before their arrival. No warning. Had time coming. Pick it up in L.A. Dammit, that had to be checked on. Here I am lying on his bunk and I forget all about him.

The second item was much more vague and there was no way of checking on it now. It was the memory of a sound. While Farrel had waited in the dark of the desert night beside Libby Walker's body, he'd heard the noise of a motor. Probably a plane.

Possibly one of the little motorized cars used by the extra gang.

One of the Henty boys said, "You sure play 'em close to the vest."

And Bud Graham rumbled, "My pappy taught me that. You got a complaint?"

The Hentys chimed together, laughing cheerfully, "Hell, no. You ain't even winning. You could play 'em face up and do as good."

"So I'm lucky in love!" Graham boomed.

Cards snapped, the mumble of talk diminished; time passed peacefully. Then somebody yawned.

"Haven't had a decent hand all evening." This was Marko's reedy whine, with sniffles. Farrel had him pegged as an old addict. A mule, too, maybe, an addict who sells weed to keep himself in H. That had been a funny business with the piled coats.

Brownie said, "Oh, the hell with it!" He got up and went back to the door, opened it and stood there as if looking out at the night. Farrel watched him through half-shut lids. He decided that Brownie was checking up, in case Saunders had doubled back.

Brownie turned slowly, surveyed Farrel in his bunk. "Pooped out, huh?"

Farrel grunted wordlessly, as if almost asleep.

"That race system look pretty good?"

Farrel shook his head without opening his eyes.

"Who's got a race system?" Graham demanded.

"Feller here." Brownie went to the bunk across from Farrel's, began to shuck his clothes. "Funny the importance people put on money. You'd think the stuff had something to do with staying alive." He laughed a little, dropped his shoes one at a time, shuffled the straw in his mattress.

"Speaking of money," said one of the Henty boys, "when do we get paid?" He waited a moment; no one answered; and then in a quieter tone he asked, "And how does a guy score around here, anyway?"

It got very quiet in the car. The only noise was that made by Graham, shuffling the cards against the blanket.

"Did I say something?"

"Not that I heard," Graham answered. "Who's in this game? Marko?"

"Going to bed," Marko said in almost a whisper.

Farrel couldn't see the faces. Brownie was rolling himself into his blankets. The others were out of his line of sight. But Farrel guessed that there were some pretty blank looks being passed.

"How do they pay us?" the other Henty demanded. "Bring the cash out here?"

"You'll get checks," said Graham.

"Checks? Huh, where'll we cash them? Who'll give us dough for the paper?"

Marko erupted in a burst of wheezing mirth. Graham said grouchily, "Oh, dry up, Marko." He pushed back his stool and rose, stretched with his arms over his head, staring in Farrel's direction.

"We have to go to town to cash them?" the Henty boy persisted.

"Ah, you'll catch on." Graham scratched his belly

through his undershirt, belched, headed for the door.
Marko still rocked with muffled laughter.

Big joke, Farrel thought.

He was asleep when Saunders came in. Saunders stood
on the edge of the bunk to crawl upstairs, and that woke
him. It was dark and the two Hentys were emitting ade-
noidal snores. "Hey," he said softly.

"Yeah," Saunders answered, letting him know who it
was.

The next morning they managed a minute alone in the
car after breakfast. "Listen," Saunders said, "I learned a
few things. The town, little as it is, is in an uproar over
the murder. Must be six of the inhabitants think now they
saw the murderer. Second-guessing, I think. They describe
the character as everything from a bum in dungarees to a
mine super type in a Cad. The ones who had contact with
Libby Walker—the station agent, the bartender, and the
old guy in the general store have set up shop as ex-
perts."

"The usual pattern," Farrel growled.

"Well, now, there's this. There have been a few strangers
now and then. You know, you asked the bartender about
Versprelle and it occurred to me afterwards that he might
have had the good sense to stay out of a place like that.
Either he'd get through town quick, or if he had to wait,
he'd do it out of sight. If anyone noticed him he'd be
quick to identify himself as a section hand on a day off,
or as somebody from one of the mines. And as a matter
of fact, the old boy in the general store remembers somebody like that. Stories didn't quite jibe, either, as if he
might have forgotten between times."

"Description checks?"

Saunders shrugged. "Not too well. Little guy, though.
Turning gray. Soft-spoken. Seems to know the country."

"He knows it. What about a car?"

"Hasn't shown one. Hikes or hitchhikes."

Farrel chewed his lip. Outdoors, they were boosting the cars onto the rails; there was the clang of shovels and other tools.

"Another thing," Saunders went on hastily. "This bird who checked out in such a hurry before we showed up. I called up Burns in L.A. last night from the public phone in the bar, asked him to take a look; I'm to call back tonight."

"You be careful on that phone," Farrel warned.

"Oh, sure. What surprised me, though, was that the bartender didn't show any signs of recognizing me from the other day."

"It's the sweater," Farrel gibed. Inwardly, however, he was uneasy. Using the phone was a risk. Even if no one had overheard the conversation, someone might wonder why a section hand had to make a call after the first day on a job. The usual thing, he knew, was to arrive broke and to save contacts for later, when you had some money in your jeans. "About this guy clearing out. There couldn't have been a leak."

"I don't see how, the way Ryerson handled it."

"Some of these cookies have a sixth sense when time's about up," Farrel said slowly. "Or it could be nothing."

"If Burns finds out anything, I'll know tonight."

Thinking it over, Farrel quieted his uneasiness with the thought that Saunders's trips to Sagebloom might rouse less suspicion than any prowling done around the outfit cars.

The morning went by like the other, in hard work and monotony. Farrel got so that he shuffled along in a perpetually bowed position, as if something had broken in his spine. It was easier than trying to straighten up now and then. Amatisto kept him on the wheelbarrow, and Saunders graduated to placing ties. In the middle of the afternoon a new wrinkle developed. The extra gang stood aside while a hopper car crept along slowly, dribbling ballast directly onto the tracks. Farrel had some relief then from the wheelbarrow.

At noon he was too tired to eat. He nipped on the whiskey. During the afternoon he developed a horrible thirst and a headache. This was a hell of a place, he decided, to keep a glow on.

He began to worry about whether he could hold out.

When they finally knocked off and went back to the outfit cars, Farrel flopped on his bunk without thinking of dinner. Some time passed; he was alone; and then Saunders came in carrying a plate of food and a cup of coffee. He set these on the edge of the bunk, took a spoon and fork out of his shirt pocket.

Farrel was dumfounded. Of course he was used to Mrs. Bellows and her calculated offerings; but this gesture on Saunders's part was beyond comprehension. He stared at the food and the cup of coffee. As for Saunders, he seemed half embarrassed by his own actions. He sat down on Brownie's cot opposite; a match flared in his fingers, he touched it to a cigarette.

Farrel picked up a piece of meat on the fork, began to chew. The rubbery exhaustion extended from the crown of his head to his toes, but the act of eating was in itself revivifying.

Saunders blew smoke, a thoughtful look in his eye. "Something's cooking. Everybody's pretty cheerful tonight. I think payday's coming but it's more than that. There's fun brewing. I wish to hell I knew Spanish."

I've got to get off my back, Farrel thought; at least I do know a few words in that lingo.

"Now there's nothing being said between Marko and Graham and Brownie," Saunders went on. "They're quiet, keeping their traps shut. The Hentys are puzzled."

"One of the Henty boys tried to score last night after you were gone," Farrel said. "They froze him out."

"Uh-huh. I heard one of the Hentys ask Graham at dinner what the chattering was all about, and Graham pretended he didn't know. I don't think it has anything to do with marijuana; the chatter's too open and too giggly."

Farrel shook his head. "I'll go to one of the other cars later on, take a shower. Maybe I can pick up what it's all about." He finished the food and downed the last of the coffee. "That brought me back from the grave. Thanks a lot."

"Oh ... it wasn't anything."

They smoked for a while and then Farrel said, "I've got Marko pegged for a mule. Stand over in the door, will you, and make like a lookout while I run through his locker. He's got a hype and some horse someplace."

Farrel got off the bunk, his bones protesting. Saunders walked to the open door and leaned there, pulling on the cigarette as if taking down the end of a butt before tossing it out. The desert lay flat for miles, paper-white under the dying light, the thin ocotillo and the squatty saltbush etched in smoke, and far off in the distance lights glittered against the wrinkled hills.

"That business of Marko's with the coats yesterday," Saunders said softly. "I couldn't get a good look but it might have been the delivery service."

"Uh-huh."

"You think he's peddling marijuana to keep himself in heroin?"

"He didn't get those watery eyes and those sniffles playing leapfrog," Farrel growled.

Marko's locker had no padlock on it; the wooden door swung open and a smell of dirty clothes rushed out. Farrel explored. Wadded down solidly in the bottom of the locker were three dirty shirts, some socks, a garment that seemed to be the remains of one of Graham's unionsuits, and a mildewed felt hat. Pushed to one side was a cigar box. In this was Marko's shaving stuff, a tattered washcloth, toothbrush, three pencils, some snuff, a couple of old letters and two scarred tablespoons. Farrel flipped the spoons over and inspected their burned backsides. "Like I thought." He put it all back and shut the locker.

From the door, Saunders said, "Nothing else?"

"He wouldn't keep it here. My guess, he's got it buried somewhere around the latrine, makes his fixes inside there."

Farrel was feeling better now. He borrowed one of Saunders's towels and went to the next car for a shower.

He came back by and by, his face knowing and somewhat astonished, but now there was no opportunity to talk to Saunders. Graham and Marko and Brownie were playing cut throat, a new location, Brownie's bunk opposite Farrel's. They were quiet but seemed in a good humor. Graham waved a bear's paw at Farrel, the red hairs on its back gleaming. The Henty boys lay in their bunks in the other end of the car, silently and offendedly looking at old magazines.

Saunders was mopping soap off his chin, obviously preparing for the trip to town.

Passing, Farrel said, "Man, you stepping out again?" Only mildly curious, as if they were practically strangers.

Saunders said, "When night comes, I got to go. Somewheres."

"Young punks," Graham grinned. "You ought to be saving it up, boy. You're going to need it."

"Yeah?" Saunders studied him across the towel. "For what?"

"Surprise coming." Graham and Marko and Brownie exchanged wise looks. One of the Henty brothers put down the magazine and lay still, listening. But nothing further was said.

Saunders put on his shirt and the sweater and went out. Brownie didn't bother to watch at the doorway; apparently he had made up his mind about Saunders's errand.

After about ten minutes, on a chance, Farrel went out and walked down the track a way. It was pretty dark and he didn't think anyone could see just where he was going. The hunch paid off. Saunders was waiting for him.

"What was that all about?"

"Oh, it has something to do with payday all right. Something to do with cashing the checks, too. Somebody's going to show up out here with a house trailer. It must be a pretty big trailer, and the roads are nothing much, so I guess it'll be pulled by a jeep or truck. These people will cash checks and they also ... uh ... sell merchandise."

"They sell stuff?"

"Do you know what the word *puta* means in Spanish?"

"No."

"It means whore."

"You mean—"

"Yeah. Three of them. A blonde and a brunette and somebody they call Bombo, whom I take to be the madam. 'Bombo' you can translate freely as 'rump.' This all happens come payday, day after tomorrow. Hence the anticipation and excitement."

"Oh, for Pete's sake," Saunders said, as if bewildered. "Now, I'm kind of mulling over another idea along this line. Marko and Brownie seem sort of keyed up, too, so maybe payday means something more, something special for them. Maybe under cover of all the hooraw over the girls, they do a bit of business on their own."

"Yeah," said Saunders, thinking about it. "That sounds good."

For some reason it occurred to Farrel at that moment that now there was no irritation, no disapproval or enmity between him and Saunders. He actually liked the kid. When you got right down to it, Saunders was a solid guy. He and Saunders were a pair, a team, after all. The life of either could well depend on the quickness, the courage and honesty of the other. And he had no doubts about how Saunders would stack up.

22.

Two nights later, sure enough, when they rolled in from work there were a jeep and a big silver trailer parked discreetly off in the middle distance among the sage. No sign of life about it; all venetian blinds at the trailer windows were drawn tight and the door was closed.

Amatisto had taken off early, driven to Sagebloom and collected the checks from the agent. Now he stood beside the diner, all dressed up, ready to pay off. Farrel knew from the gossip that Mr. and Mrs. Amatisto always took this night to go to town for dinner and a show. A tactful maneuver, Farrel thought.

Everybody scrubbed up and most of the men shaved. There was a regular traffic jam in the showers and around the washbasins. Clean shirts appeared. The smell of hair pomade was noticeable. Dinner, however, wasn't too well patronized. Some bottles were broken out, passed among friends, and by twilight things were pretty cheerful.

Farrel strolled around, taking it all in. As in any bunch of men, there were cliques. Men of like temperament and background naturally gravitated to each other. However, it was noticeable that the Hentys were left out, were strictly alone, and that Graham and Marko and Brownie constituted a group which no one else tried to join.

There was a gradual stir, a drifting away, and now Farrel noticed that lights shone in the big trailer, the blinds were up and the door open. A big redheaded woman in a green satin dress leaned in the doorway, smoking a cigarette in a long holder. A faint clink of glassware and the music from a radio wafted on the desert breeze. One of the more uncouth among the extra gang gave forth a wild, Comanche-type screech. The woman in the open doorway tipped ashes from her cigarette in an elaborately refined manner. The radio music grew louder.

Farrel found Saunders standing by one of the cars, watching the trailer as if he could hardly believe his eyes. Farrel thought, Hell, he was in the Army. He was in the Army but it didn't take, it didn't change him. Mama must have a pretty tight grip. He recalled then Saunders's saying that his mother was gone on an extended trip. Perhaps there had been nothing calculated in the relationship; it had simply happened; and now Mama was as eager to shake her son as son was unconsciously to be free. Yes, it could have come about that way. He wondered briefly about Saunders's girl, what kind of girl she was.

Saunders nodded towards the trailer. "Are you going over there?"

"It'll look funny if we don't." Saunders glanced at him sidewise and Farrel went on, "I never did hanker for commercial fun, especially with the traffic what it is here. But we could buy the madam a drink. I've got a bottle with some left in it."

"What about Graham's outfit? They're inside now, all spruced up, just waiting for something—not the girls, either."

"They're waiting till it gets dark and late, and safe," Farrel said. "Then I think we'll hear some offhand talk about maybe going into Sagebloom."

"You think they're set up to buy tonight?"

"They'll never have a better opportunity."

Farrel went in for the bottle in his locker, and it was the

way Saunders had said: Graham and Brownie and Marko
had cleaned themselves up. Marko had turned his shirt
inside out, not much improvement, and Graham was
manicuring his nails. Farrel pretended a great joy over the
arrival of the trailer. "Ain't that something? Right at your
door!"

The three gave him cool stares. Graham clipped a nail
precisely.

"How about it?" Farrel persisted jovially, addressing
the remark directly to Graham.

"Mama, hand me down the benzedrine," Graham muttered.

"Like that, huh?" Farrel pretended to be put out.
"What's the matter? Weren't you guys invited?"

"We're nerving ourselves," Brownie said dryly.

On his way back to Saunders, Farrel thought about it.
There was definitely an air of covering up; Graham and
Brownie were making a great show of boredom and indecision. Marko, less under control, couldn't stop sniffling
and jerking and blinking.

Farrel and Saunders strolled out to the trailer. It was
pretty crowded, men thick inside, moving back and forth
in the narrow passageway from one end of the trailer to
the other. The blonde and the brunette were apparently
holding court in the rear section; beyond a half-shut dividing door came laughter and squeals. The big woman
in green satin had pressed herself into a niche beside a
counter, was pouring drinks there. Farrel popped the bottle
down beside her and she glanced up at him. She took a
long interested look. Farrel had the funny impression that
he didn't look quite right to her, that she sensed something
in him that alerted her.

Finally she said, "Well, hello. I'm Bonnie. Who're you?"

"Hi, Bonnie. I'm Johnnie." She smiled slightly, her gaze
on the mixture she was stirring in a glass pitcher. He fore-

bore to mention her nickname in Spanish; wondered if she knew it. If she knew it she didn't care anyway.

He and Saunders had a drink. Pretty soon a businesslike look settled on Bonnie and Farrel knew that they were expected to begin other arrangements. They excused themselves and drifted out, trying to leave the impression that they'd be back soon.

Farrel led the way off down a shallow wash. It was almost completely dark now, there was just a smoky green light on the farthest edge of the horizon. A screen of sage and scattered Joshua trees hid them from the outfit cars. "We're going to have to take a chance," Farrel said.

"Do you think there's a possibility the delivery will be made here?"

"The least, and if we depend on it we can be crossed up, have to wait till next payday—and damned if I think I could hold out. We're going to have to guess, and jump first."

"Sagebloom?"

"One of us. I'd like to be around that culvert by the water tower. I've got a crazy idea that's where it might be."

A few days past Saunders would have argued with him. In Saunders's eyes he had read the pity for a broken-witted slob on a treadmill; Saunders had wanted to come up with something sharp and new on every point of the investigation. Now he was willing to listen, to give a little.

"I'll go to Sagebloom," he said.

"Keep out of sight as much as possible."

"It could happen anywhere between here and town, or on any of a dozen other miles of track," Saunders went on. "Or even away from the rails altogether, on some desert road we'd never think of."

"That's one of the chances we're taking," Farrel growled.

"The other one is that they'll show up where we are, alone, and that we'll have a rough time. Maybe very rough."

"It's one or the other," said Saunders thoughtfully.

"It sure is." Farrel found himself rubbing his hip, automatically checking the gun that now wasn't there. He was in a rut. "Well, let's get going."

They picked a way down the wash, then angled back towards the tracks, hitting the rails on a curve, almost out of sight of the lights from the outfit cars. They walked quickly, not talking much. Farrel was aware of a dragging tiredness, the aftermath of the long day's work. His energy was running out swiftly. He had a longer walk ahead than Saunders, too; the thought crossed his mind to change places, let Saunders stake out beside the water tower; but he dropped it. The water tower was his baby, his responsibility; he wanted to be there when the payoff came ... if it came.

He thought longingly of "borrowing" one of Amatisto's little motor cars, but this was out of the question. Too much chance of being seen, of warning the quarry.

They finally got to Sagebloom. The two bars seemed to be pretty busy. Some of the men had come into town already from the outfit, Farrel knew, perhaps ten or twelve out of the forty-odd.

Saunders said, "I'm going to wait here on this dark side of the station for a while."

"Okay. I'll be seeing you."

As he walked on towards the water tower, Farrel thought back through the past few days. He couldn't see where he or Saunders had passed up any bets. Saunders had gotten the dope on the man who had checked out the day they'd arrived; Burns had looked him up, and he was clean, an old hand with a habit of unexpected and apparently reasonless moves. The one thing that had been promising was Marko's business with the pile of coats; and if he or Saunders had jumped Marko then, probably there would have been weed on him. But catching Marko wouldn't lead them to the source of supply, wouldn't turn up any possible link with the man Farrel hoped to find, Versprelle.

Tonight was their chance and their one hope, and for his part Farrel promised himself that if the night's work came to nothing, he was through here. He wanted nothing more to do with Lobo Tunnel. To hell with the wreck, Versprelle, Parmenter, Parmenter's blackmail victim and whoever had murdered Libby Walker. A job was a job and of course Ryerson was boss and had the right to send him where he wanted him; but as far as Lobo Tunnel went, he was worn threadbare. Maybe Ryerson had expected him to fail, an idea Farrel had entertained more than once before, and so wouldn't be too disappointed.

Saunders had proved himself; at least that much had emerged. He was able to wait, to observe, to adapt himself, to work as half of a team. He could go on with Lobo Tunnel with someone else and no doubt in time he'd clear it up.

The miles plodded away under Farrel's aching legs. Suddenly he found himself looking up at the ruined water tower, a dim skeleton against the night sky, a cockeyed beacon of rotting staves, a scarecrow beckoning with broken knuckles. It stood there sharp against the starry sky, somehow unfamiliar, not as he recalled it, and he had an ominous sense of its meaning. It made a damned good landmark for a rendezvous amid the monotonously duplicated miles of desert.

He stood quiet and listened, and there was nothing. Even the breeze was still. He stooped and put a hand on the rails, found no hint of vibration. He walked down to the entrance to the culvert and stood there for a moment, and heard nothing but the silence.

Behind the framework of the water tower he sat down to rest his legs. He took off his shoes and rubbed his feet. He wished for a drink. But then after all, he didn't have long to wait. A pair of headlights twinkled from the distance like unexpected jewels. For just a moment the ragged timbers above shone with light. Then, while the car was still at a good distance, the lights vanished and the sound of the motor died. Farrel put his shoes on.

In about ten minutes he heard somebody walking.

He couldn't see much of the figure in the dark, just a shifting blob of shadow. He listened to the footsteps, trying to gain an impression there, got the idea that it was a man, not a heavy man, and that he was easy in his mind, strolling without worry, waiting for someone or something.

After a while the figure disappeared, Farrel couldn't see where; and then like the slow opening of a mouth, the shape of the culvert was outlined with a growing light; and Farrel realized that the man had gone into the culvert and started a tiny fire there.

"Now, that's something!" Talk about confidence, brass, and gall. So sure of not being interrupted he made a fire to see by. Farrel grinned sourly to himself.

Pretty soon he heard the sound of the little motorized car on the rails. It didn't make much noise. It didn't come all the way to the culvert. A few minutes after the sound of the motor stopped, three figures came stooping and hurrying into the light from the culvert. Farrel was too far to be sure, but he had a very good idea this was Graham and Co.

In Sagebloom, in the dark beside the station, Saunders had seen a flitting ghost—three of them in fact, scooting past on the grade which led to the hills, motor cut, the car coasting silently.

Three faces had stared towards the lights of town. As the speed of the little car had died, Brownie had jumped off to push. Saunders had watched spellbound. Then, safely past town, the motor had sputtered back to life.

He thought, stunned, Why, Farrel had been right all along. The instincts of the old railroad bull had been as dependable as day following night. Only, now Farrel's spot was unenviable. He had Graham and Brownie and Marko headed his way, plus their contacts from the opposite direction. Saunders cursed, jumped up to run after them.

No, wait a minute. There had to be a better way.

He hurried into the station. The agent looked up from a stack of waybills, no curiosity at first, taking in the sweater and the work pants, the dusty hat. Then his eyes, skipping past Saunders's face, returned. A look of uncertain surprise came over him.

"Remember me?" Saunders said crisply.

"Uh ... you were out here a day or so ago. Yeah, you're one of the investigators from L.A."

"We've been working on a case not far from here. Look, I need a car bad. Do you have one here I could borrow?"

"My car's parked down the block."

"May I use it?"

"I guess so." The agent was taking some keys from his pants pocket. He took his green eye shade and laid it on his desk. "What's up?"

"We may have some action. I don't suppose you have a gun?"

"Sorry, no, I don't."

The agent led the way, Saunders on his heels, a short distance to a parking area beside a shed. There were whoops now from one of the bars, someone came out scuffling, a voice yelled in anger. The agent looked over there. "Here are the keys. I'd better get back. Sometimes things get pretty rough, nights after payday."

Saunders crawled into the driver's seat. It was a middle-aged Ford, nicely kept; he started the motor, checked the gas—there was plenty— and backed out into the street. In another minute he was headed down the highway, already starting to worry for fear that he wouldn't recognize the turnoff to Lobo Tunnel and the water tower beyond.

Farrel rose to his feet, tiredness and stiffness gone, all of his attention on the faintly glowing mouth of the culvert. He took out his wallet, opened it to his ID card. It was all he had, that and guts, and he was wondering if he had enough of the latter.

He walked towards the culvert, trying to go silently. Inevitably there were crunching noises, scatterings of gravel, and when he reached a point where he could look inside, the four men squatted in the culvert were turned to face him.

A little fire, not more than a few sticks and twigs, burned against the cement wall; it threw a flickering glow over Marko and Brownie and Graham, and against the side of the fourth man's face: nostril and lip and chin were carved, pale against shadow, and two eyes looked out like glimmering coals.

"Come on out, all of you, with your hands up," said Farrel confidently, displaying the ID.

"Who says," Graham growled.

"I do."

Marko whined, "Now lookie here ... whoever you are ..."

"Come out and read who I am," Farrel invited.

"Hell, I know who you are," Brownie put in. "I smelled you, and you stunk."

"Out," said Farrel. It seemed to him that the fourth

man, bundled in an overcoat, hat pulled down, was with-drawing towards the fire. He had a bundle in his hands, brown paper tied with twine, perhaps half the size of a shoe box or a little bigger. He inched crabwise, sheltering himself behind the others. "Out," Farrel said, louder than ever.

By some unseen agreement Marko was elected; he crawled forward, stooped under the curved ceiling, his hands quivering. He came out and without raising himself, circled around as if trying to gain the shadows. "Stand right there," Farrel commanded.

"I ain't done nothing! You got me all wrong!" Marko quavered, but Farrel wasn't listening, knew that Marko had been sacrificed to draw his attention. He kept his eyes on the three remaining in the culvert. At the same time an uneasy warning flashed in his mind: what was wrong? Why hadn't the fourth man quenched the fire, smothered it in the instant Farrel had appeared to give them all the protection of the dark? Farrel thought, He's got a use for the fire, that's why. He was beginning to guess what it might be. He went close to the opening of the culvert, stooped to watch them, ignoring any danger from Marko.

"Come on out!"

"Sure." Graham made a pretense of moving; his big hands were knotted into fists. Brownie hung back; his eyes were sly. Farrel inched into the culvert, his head bent; he smelled the cold given off by the thick cement, stirred dust, the acrid tang of smoke. Behind Graham and Brownie the fourth man was tearing open the paper par-cel.

He peered quickly at Farrel, then threw a handful of stuff on the fire; and this was Farrel's break, because he threw too much all at once and the small flame started to die under the avalanche. It shook, flickered blue, almost went out.

Farrel had no choice now; he needed that evidence. As the flame wavered and recovered and began to feed on the fresh supply, as Graham and Brownie waited, Farrel launched himself. He tried to dive between them directly at the fire. He felt Brownie brush aside with the force of impact; he grabbed with both hands at the stuff now spilling and falling from the torn brown paper. There was an animal noise from the fourth man, a chopping cry.

The fire flared, renewed; and for just a moment before Graham and Brownie turned on him to try to tear him to pieces, Farrel found himself looking full into the illuminated face beneath the hat. It was a face he would never forget. Though his memory of it was gray-and-white, the colors of the photograph in the old file, in flesh it was not much different.

Versprelle. Lipless mouth, mean eyes, and all. Farrel felt like shouting with joy even as Graham began to punch him into unconsciousness.

23.

Farrel tried to jerk himself into a ball, protecting his stomach, his chin, out of the reach of the jumping fire and Graham's hammering blows; but at the same time, he managed to grab a handful of the stuff from the sack and throw it out the other end of the culvert into the dark. By God, there'd be something left when this fracas was over.

He almost wriggled free, got out that other way too, until Versprelle connected with a kick that caught him at the base of the throat. Farrel collapsed strangling and Graham fell on him, greedy for punishment, grabbing his head—his hat was gone now—and then pounding his face into the dust-and-cement floor of the culvert.

It seemed to Farrel that the bones of his nose, his jaw, exploded into splinters. His eyes seemed driven back into his skull, the crowding figures and the leaping fire far away. He was disconnected wraithlike from his body, floating in a red muck, his hands at the end of octopus arms, tingling. He wanted suddenly to sleep.

But it takes a lot to flatten a man like Farrel. He is like an old range bull who has weathered many winters, out-stared a lot of wildcats and kicked the stuffings out of countless stray wolves. He's half leather; his heart is iron. Farrel was an old cop and he too had kicked the stuffings out of wolves, the human variety; and he had no intention of letting this winter be his last. When Graham made the mistake of crawling half erect, Farrel rolled over.

He found that his knee was in an interesting position and brought it up sharply. Graham grunted, his back bowed, the fists spread into hands and clawed at his pants. Farrel lurched then, jerked Graham aside and into Brownie's baffled arms; and while they writhed, fighting to be free of each other, by some miracle of timing Farrel found Versprelle's outstretched leg and pulled it under him and lay on it and tore off the shoe and pushed the foot towards the fire. Versprelle was grabbing at spilled reefers and loose weed and didn't know for a moment or two what was going on.

Then the sock began to burn and Versprelle screamed.

Brownie or Graham, one of them, began to beat on the back of Farrel's head, a sharp fast tattoo, *put put put*, like a jackhammer. Farrel ignored it. All he could see from his swelling eyes was that burning sock, and then Versprelle's curling toes against the brightness of the flames.

Versprelle had built the fire, renewed it with the weed, and so let him enjoy it now by toasting his toes at it—lit-erally. So Farrel decided.

But Versprelle had other resources. He forgot the goods he had come to peddle; he ripped at his coat and it flopped open and his hands were jerking at the gun in the soft leather armpit holster. The gun came out smoothly, and in spite of his jumping around and the agony in his foot he got it pointed straight at Farrel. Farrel stared into the barrel. It was right in his face. Farrel put up a hand and twisted the gun around towards Versprelle and Versprelle was so outraged by pain and hate that he couldn't stop pulling the trigger. Bullets erupted into his flesh.

Farrel got to his knees, the gun in his hand. It felt good. It wasn't the familiar heft of his own gun, but it was solid and satisfying. He pointed it towards Graham and Brownie and they took their stunned gaze off Versprelle, sprawling in his own blood, and at Farrel's motion they backed off out of the culvert.

Saunders was out there with Marko. He had a lug wrench in his hand. He said, "Are you okay?"

"Fine." Farrel rubbed moisture from his upper lip, looked at it; by the light of the headlamps a few feet away he saw that it was blood. He mopped at himself during the rest of the evening, using his own handkerchief, then Saunders's, then a box of cleansing tissues supplied by the station agent.

They first took Graham and Brownie and Marko back to Sagebloom, kept them in the depot until the Sheriff's men got there. Then there was a further wait until reinforcements arrived. Farrel got on the phone meanwhile to L.A., called Burns at the office and told him what had happened here so he could relay it to Ryerson.

Farrel went back to the culvert with some of the Sheriff's men to gather up Versprelle's cigarettes and loose marijuana, and to explain just how Versprelle had been killed.

Saunders stayed with Graham and his friends and participated in the questioning that followed. It was thus, in one of the interrogation rooms at the desert headquarters, that he learned from Graham that Versprelle had often boasted that he was the man responsible for the Lobo Tunnel wreck.

Parmenter stared at the ceiling of the hospital room; he made clucking sounds in his throat. The nurse bent over him, wiped spittle from his lips, smiled into his unseeing gaze. "Would you care for a drink of water?"

The oxygen tent was on its way.

Parmenter went on clucking to himself, his thoughts distant, dimming now, all the memories stirring and lifting together like a flock of leaves in a wind. There had been a little girl, a very little girl; her face flew by, was gone, in the gusty rising, and then Parmenter seemed to hear the pounding of surf and to smell the odors of the sea.

"They shouldn't have put it there—" He wanted to tell the little girl about the incongruity of it, the prison on an island you'd dream about, the mossy jungle creeping down to the surf and the Pacific out beyond, a green blaze under the sun, the real jailer at Islas Marías. Then other faces, brown faces, swam by on the flying tide and he found Spanish on his lips, quick and liquid.

All that emerged, however, was the clucking noise. He was still doing this when they adjusted the plastic tent above his head.

When the first faint light of dawn came into the sky, Peg Parmenter awoke and lay with her eyes on the window; beyond the pane she could see the sky, a few dim clouds, a few stars still shining. This is the beginning, she thought, the wonderful beginning of a most important day.

Over and over she had slipped away from the Crowns to the house next door, where she had read and studied

the stuff she had found under the closet floor. Since her
father was angry at her, no longer called her, she sensed
that it was up to her alone to get what she could. She did
not consider it blackmail; the word never entered her
head. She needed money, and the printed and typewritten
pages were somehow worth money, and it was as simple
as that, just a trade.

It had taken a long time to make sense out of it. The
typescript was unbearably drawn out and boring, most
of it meant nothing, questions and answers, the names of
people she'd never heard of. At times she had almost de-
spaired, but need had kept her at it, and finally some of it
began to make sense. There were faint underlinings here
and there. When you looked all through the newspaper
clippings, and studied the underlined portions of the typescript, and some of the old moldy newsprint photographs,
a pattern glimmered. Then near the end she had noticed
the one clipping which did not concern the wreck; she
had made note of the New York City date line, and things
had begun to hum.

Realization of the truth flooded her. Why, these people
had cheated the railroad! They'd robbed the railroad of a
terrific lot of money!

She wondered how much her father had made them
pay in the beginning. Fifty, a hundred thousand? Half of
what they had? No, she thought shrewdly, not that much;
he must have had plans for them to continue to support
him and to do that he must have left enough to be in-
vested.

By now, if the money had been handled wisely, there
should have been a magnificent increase. Money made
money. Her father had been stupid to waste his share, to
throw it away. But then, admittedly now, her father wasn't
very smart. Look at the way he had attempted to collect
from these people—sending her out, a cat's paw, to meet

someone in the dark, in an out-of-the-way place where danger was obvious.

She had made all new plans. Daylight, dozens of witnesses, a crowded and busy spot. The Union Depot, in fact.

The real difficulty had been in locating these people again. But then, knowing from the New York newspaper clipping what the man's occupation had been, she had taken a chance that he might have contacts among those of like employment, old acquaintances who could supply an address. A call to the Los Angeles City Library downtown had given her names of various associations; checking these, she had found the man listed in one as a member and the secretary had had no hesitation about giving out the name of the town in which he lived. From then on there was nothing to it.

Now in the early dawn she lay happily satisfied, knowing that all was arranged, the hour and the place was set, the amount of money mutually agreed upon. Peg couldn't see how anything could go wrong up until the time the money was handed to her. Her danger afterward would be acute and she would need all her wits to get away. In Las Vegas she would get a bleach job, new clothes, jewels. She'd meet men. There were always a lot of men around the gambling tables. Peg had never been to Las Vegas, of course, since Aunt Libby's skimpy wages did well to cover rayon hose and two-bit lipsticks—but she knew all about it from the movies. And it was gorgeous!

She got dreamily out of bed and inspected the clothes she would wear that day. She frowned over the cotton blouse, the plaid skirt made over from an outsize coat Aunt Libby had bought at the Salvation Army and worn for two years, the baggy stockings and the old shoes. Horrible stuff to have to wear today, when things were so close to changing ... She lifted her head sharply. There had been a scratchy noise at the window. She waited, and a branch of rose bush tipped against the pane, the thorns rubbing, and Peg let out her held breath on a long sigh.

Downstairs, Mrs. Crown was sitting at the kitchen table, sipping a cup of leftover coffee and looking at the morning paper.

"Look," she said. "Up there where your aunt was killed ... the railroad police caught some drug peddlers."

Peg glanced at the headlines indifferently.

"One of the men, one who got shot, is supposed to have caused a wreck there years ago."

Peg's interest perked up. She took the paper and read the article through, but it was pretty short. There didn't seem to be a lot of information as yet. A man named Versprelle was dead. He'd shot himself by accident when one of the railroad dicks had tackled him. He was suspected of having caused the Lobo Tunnel wreck. An explanatory sentence was added to the effect that the railroad police had never given up working on the wreck, had been searching through the intervening years for Versprelle, to question him. He had been a section hand in the district six years ago, had been discharged from the job because he was believed to be supplying the gangs with marijuana. Peg put the paper down and glanced at Mrs. Crown, saw the curiosity in her eyes, the silly pretense at disinterest.

"An unsavory affair, isn't it?" Mrs. Crown said. "Wasn't the tunnel, Lobo Tunnel, the place where the wreck occurred that your father was in?"

"The same," Peg said briefly, going over to the coffeepot on the stove.

She expected further quizzing, but instead Mrs. Crown changed the subject. "Your poor aunt! I can't get over the funeral. It was lovely. Not many folks there, but it was nice."

Yesterday afternoon. Peg had already forgotten about it. She drank coffee standing by the sink, and meditated.

At nine-thirty she was to walk into Union Depot carrying a small overnight case. Into that case she was to stack twenty-five thousand dollars.

Dad was scared, she thought, and broke and desperate. He let the man choose the place, the time; and they weren't any good. He almost got me killed. She tensed with anger, and then heard the chair creak as Mrs. Crown got up from it.

"Eggs, dear? Boiled or scrambled?" There was not quite the warmth of invitation that there had been at the beginning. Under the tone was a hint: Your poor aunt is dead, and your father disappeared and your mother in a mental institution, and so it is time for you, darling, to rustle your young bones and get yourself a job. Something nice and respectable. They'll teach you to type and to do book-keeping almost anywhere these days. The market for young girls with big beautifully shaped breasts was never better. The bosses will dote on you. And you can bring home fifty or more dollars a week without half trying.

Peg's young mouth was bitter. "One egg is plenty. Scrambled, if you want."

Just so Dad doesn't queer it, just so he doesn't get a wild-haired notion to do something himself, she thought fiercely.

I'd split with him, she mused, if I knew where he was. I'd give him a little to keep him quiet, because this business is like having a private mint, money coming in in lovely big chunks, and he's got to stay out of it. It doesn't belong to him anymore. It's mine.

Remembering the dreadful way he'd looked, the horrible color, the draggingly ill way he had walked, she was momentarily concerned. He might get pretty desperate if he felt bad enough. Of course, if he really conked out and was too bad, she was safe. He'd just have to stay in bed and be a bother to nobody.

Lay low, Dad, she warned in her mind. Keep your hands off until I get hold of that twenty-five thousand dollars!

She ate the egg and toast Mrs. Crown set out for her. Tomorrow morning she should be eating breakfast in bed in some swanky hotel in Las Vegas. That dream world swam before her eyes and she smiled secretly at its glories.

The big waiting room had quite a few people in it. Still, there were a good many vacant chairs. Peg walked around, close to the wall, past the information booth, the ticket sellers, and paused by a shop selling candy and magazines. She was not as composed as she looked. A nerve in her wrist, the hand holding the case, quivered now and then with a feeling like a mild electric shock. Her mouth was dry. She felt conspicuous.

She saw a man coming towards her and a warning flared; she wanted to shrink back, avoid him. He had on dark glasses and he looked as if he spent a lot of time outdoors, getting a tan. "Miss Parmenter?"

She faced him, trying to summon her voice. The dark glasses made a mask, hiding his eyes, hiding the expression with which he gazed at her. His mouth was enigmatical, neither kind nor cruel. The planes of his face were lean and well modeled.

"Yes, I'm Miss Parmenter." She forced her tone lower. "Did you bring the money?"

"No, Miss Parmenter, I did not."

She didn't know how to answer this. The beginnings of anger stirred in her at his impudence.

"Don't you want to know why?" He waited, a slight smile curving his lips. "You must want to know, so I'll tell you. To start with, the money isn't mine. It's my wife's. You see that, don't you? I couldn't give away something that belonged to her."

Her words burst forth, much too loudly. The woman selling magazines glanced over at her. "You got it through a trick!"

"We won't go into that now. Trick or no, it was all settled long ago. Your father was a witness. At the investigation. At the trial afterwards, when we were awarded damages. We might be afraid of your father, Miss Parmenter, where we wouldn't be afraid of you."

"My father's with me in this. Why, you know it! You know he sends someone else—"

"He sent your mother the other time," said the masked face, nodding. "But you see, things have changed. Your father is dead. He died at about four o'clock this morning." He seemed to be spelling things out to her through a thickening fog of horror. "He was the witness who might have confessed to perjury. He might have changed the verdict. But not now."

"Died?" Her voice was a croak in her own ears, and behind the word she seemed to hear toppling noises, her dreams crashing in disaster. She wanted to lift her hands to cover her ears, an instinctive defense, but couldn't; she carried the overnight case which was supposed to be full of money now, and her heavy purse packed with stuff she wanted to take with her to Las Vegas.

"I'm almost sorry for you," the man went on mockingly. "You're young and pretty. You're of an age to love pretty clothes and good times. I don't suppose—"

"How do you *know* he's dead?"

He shrugged as if the matter were of no importance. "There's no mistake about it. Your father put through a call to us several nights ago from a certain telephone. The long-distance operator kindly tried to renew the connection, but your father meanwhile had been taken ill. Or so she informed us, apparently having talked to someone at that address. It was simple from then on to trace your father from the emergency hospital to General and to keep track of his condition."

The whispering noises of the crowded room seemed far away. And Peg was scared.

"I think that concludes our contact," the man said. "I advise you to stay away from me. It isn't just the money, big as the money must seem in your mind. There are other matters that must not be disturbed." He waited for some sort of promise, perhaps. "Do you want me at your back door again some night?"

She shook her head frantically.

"And you won't have any foolish thoughts of going to the people at the railroad ... or to the police?"

She nodded jerkily, puppet-like.

"Good-bye, Miss Parmenter. And good luck."

She felt sick, dirty and crushed. She sensed that some horrible evil had crept close, had held up a mirror so that she could see herself. So that she could see the infection in herself, the criminal desires, the filth.

His vanishing figure swam in her sudden tears.

24.

The morning light made even the office cheerful, almost got up close to the ceiling to dissipate the eternal shadows there. Behind his desk, Ryerson exuded wolfish satisfaction. He was fresh-shaven, his eyes were bright, his teeth shone. "No confession, but with what the others swear to, we'll say Versprelle and close the file. Lobo Tunnel is finished. Pete can take the whole shebang to storage." He swung a little in his chair, eying Farrel and Saunders. "You both look pretty good. Working for a change must have agreed with you. Except—" His glance sharpened on Farrel. "What the hell happened to your nose?"

"The floor of the culvert. With Graham on my back."

"Too bad. Is it broken?"

"Not broken. Just bled all night. I'm supposed to keep an icebag on it."

"Hmm."

"There's another thing, sir," Saunders said. "This character named Marko claims to have witnessed the murder of Libby Walker. He was out on a borrowed handcar, digging up some weed he'd cached after buying from Versprelle the week before. In the distance he says he saw a car turn off the highway and a few minutes later, by the car's lights, he saw Miss Walker carried to the tracks and laid there. Then some pounding went on. The murderer was a man. Marko isn't sure he can identify. He's waiting to make a deal, of course. When he needs a shot of H his memory is going to improve remarkably."

"He's an addict?"

"Arms full of puncture marks."

"I heard the motor of that handcar the night I waited beside her body," Farrel said. "It was a long way off, though. Unless he pushed for a while before starting the motor, he was too far away to see much." He glanced from Saunders to the Chief, hating to throw water on Saunders's hopes. "I wouldn't bet on him."

There was a short space of thoughtful silence. Then Saunders asked, "Well, what's this about Parmenter?"

A shade of regret clouded Ryerson's satisfaction. "He died this morning. Couldn't talk, didn't say a word to the nurse or anyone else. If he'd wanted to."

"How did you hear so soon?"

Ryerson said, "All he had on him besides a few cents in change was a scrap of paper with Wall's name and address in Chula Vista. Trying to get an identification, the hospital people called Wall, and when Wall was through talking to them he telephoned us. Collins went out there—you know, Collins recognized Parmenter in Union Depot—Collins went to the hospital morgue and it was Parmenter, all right. We'll never get anything out of him now."

There was more silence. To Farrel there didn't seem to be anything to say. This was a dead end. Parmenter knew who had lied, who had rooked the railroad; probably knew who had killed Libby Walker, too. And now he was dead and what he knew had gone with him.

Ryerson roused himself. "Oh, we're not through yet." He said it as if reassuring himself perhaps more than the two investigators. "Couple of things we can check before we admit we're licked. I want one of you to go to see the flophouse clerk who called the ambulance. Collins got his name off the hospital records. The address, too. Parmenter might not have been staying there, of course. He could have gone in there when he got sick to ask for help. But it's a chance."

Saunders said, "I'll go."

Ryerson went on, "Then there's Parmenter's daughter. Someone ought to see her."

Farrel said, "Why don't you go see the girl instead? I'll talk to the clerk."

Saunders seemed surprised.

Farrel said, "You're young and from the way she eyed you I think she believes you're kind of good-looking."

Saunders was obviously embarrassed. He thought about Betsy at 6 A.M., hair in curlers and face cream around her eyes. She was beautiful and warm, melting in his arms; and he wished to hell his mother would come home so they could plan the wedding.

"We won't squeal to your girl," Farrel said, "in case you're called to make the supreme sacrifice."

Saunders grew red. "Oh, shut up." Then he grinned. "I'll go see Miss Parmenter. Why not?"

"Sure. What's she got?" Farrel jeered.

Ryerson said, "All right. I'll see both of you in a couple of hours." When they went out his gaze followed. Now, there's a pair, he thought, pursing his lips. Then, surprisingly it occurred to him: By God, they *were* a pair!

They were still the same two individuals he'd sent out on this hopeless case, but something prickly and stand-offish had rubbed off. They liked each other. They thought as a team, dividing the job as it seemed best, no suspicion or jealousy between them.

Ryerson saw Pete peeking in at him through the glass, and shook his head. Pete answered with a wink.

At eleven o'clock Farrel and Saunders were back.

Farrel said, "Parmenter had been staying at the flophouse for the last couple of nights before he got sick. He was registered under his real name. It's a real rough dive. I don't think Parmenter had made a collection; he'd have been living better."

"Figures."

"Now, just before he became sick Parmenter tried to put through a long-distance telephone call. The line was busy, or something; the operator called back while Parmenter was sick and the clerk hung up on her. But afterwards, when the ambulance had taken Parmenter away, the operator called back a second time. She and the clerk had a confab. He told her the man she was trying to reach was sick, had been taken to the hospital; and then, thinking that there might be a relative on the other end of the wire, the clerk asked for the number and wrote it down, promising to relay it to Parmenter when and if he returned."

"You've got that number?"

Farrel tossed a slip of paper to the desk. Ryerson picked it up and looked at it and a twitch of surprise crossed his mouth.

"You checked this?"

"It's the Myles place."

Now Saunders, too, had something to offer. A newspaper clipping. "I went out to Parmenter's house. The girl wasn't there. I asked next door and the woman said she'd been staying with them since the aunt died. She thought the girl might be out looking for a job. At least, that's what she said at first, and then she began to let down the bars a little and admit that she was worried. She was afraid the girl was up to something."

"Parmenter's business?"

"Well, she didn't think the girl had been hearing from her father at all. This Mrs. Crown just had a hunch the girl might be doing something unwise. You know what she thought? She thought Peg Parmenter might be planning to sell some scandalous story to the newspapers. And this is why." He put the clipping down in front of Ryerson. "It's from a New York paper, as you can see ... over six years ago."

"Myles was arrested for wife beating," Ryerson said, his eyes busy.

"Very few papers would bother with it, but this had an angle: Myles claimed that he'd been shot up in a plane during the war and that he had periods when he blacked out and wasn't aware of what he was doing. The paper gave it a play along that line. Aftermath of the war, and so on."

"Where did this neighbor get this?"

"From the room where Peg had been staying."

"Anything more?"

"Yes. She asked me to go with her, and we went next door and looked through the house. In a back bedroom closet was a hoard of stuff. Must have been Parmenter's—newspapers, a lot of typescript of the investigation, pictures, and so on. Nothing new in it. Parmenter must have kept it with the idea of refreshing his memory if necessary. I think this Mrs. Crown had been over there before I

came and didn't know what to make of it all, and was
scared, and wanted advice. I told her not to worry, that I
didn't think it meant Peg Parmenter was having dealings
with a scandal sheet."

"What do you think it means?" Ryerson snapped.

"I think the girl was trying to get a line on Daddy's pro-
spective sucker."

Ryerson's gaze was as bleak as stone. "There's nothing
here that will convict Myles of lying about his wife's injuries. Or of killing Libby Walker."

Farrel said, "Don't you want us to go and lean on Mr.
Myles a little?"

"Warn him?" Ryerson said sharply.

"Hell, he's been ready to jump for years," Farrel argued.

"All right, then," Ryerson agreed. "Go breathe down
his neck and see how much jumping he can do."

They ate lunch on the way, in Elsinore. Farrel tanked
up on beer and barely nibbled a ham sandwich; but Saunders didn't even raise an eyebrow. He didn't care, didn't
wonder if Ryerson knew. He had a lot of new ideas about
Farrel since that affair in the culvert.

They drove on. The day was sunny. The hills were rusty
against the autumn sky. Some birds flew along the horizon,
a long V, headed south. The fat cattle looked at the passing
car. Haystacks were golden, spilling over in the stubbled
fields.

"I like this country," Farrel said. "There's a feeling to it.
You get a feeling of fall out here, you can see the weather
changing."

Saunders thought about Sonya Myles. "What do you
think happened in that compartment just before the
wreck?"

"Maybe Myles will tell us."

"Six years is a hell of a long time. Do you really think

she never has remembered?"

"I think she's afraid to remember," Farrel said. "Just like she's afraid to get out of that wheelchair. She's safe as long as she doesn't remember and as long as he thinks she's still a cripple."

"You think she can walk?"

"I wouldn't be a damned bit surprised," Farrel said.

"Maybe we could catch her off base."

"Now, that'd be something!"

"What're you going to do when we get there?"

"Take a good look at Mr. Myles."

Saunders grinned a little. "He told us to come with the local law if we wanted to get in again."

Farrel shook his head. "I don't think Myles wants to see the local law as bad as all that."

They came to the big white-timbered gate, and Saunders got out to open it, waited to close it when the car had passed. Leaves from the sycamores rattled on the car roof; the tires crunched them in passing; and then they were at the big archway leading to the patio, and there was Mrs. Myles in her chair, just as they had seen her the first day they had come.

Farrel and Saunders got out of the car and walked in under the arch, between the open wings of the iron Spanish gate. She waited for them.

"Yes, gentlemen?"

Irony, Saunders thought; she knows we aren't here on a gentlemanly errand; we're here as cops to pin something on her and her husband. He said, "Hello, Mrs. Myles." She was as beautiful as ever, but she was tired. Exhaustion and tension had burned her fine.

Farrel said, "Is your husband at home, ma'am?"

"I think so." She blinked as if the sun bothered her. "He went into Los Angeles earlier, but I believe he has returned. Is it about this man Parmenter, have we seen him, and so forth?"

"Yes, it is, Mrs. Myles."

She began to speak rapidly. "Well, I have some news, then. A couple of days ago someone called in the evening ... or rather the operator called and said someone wanted to reach us, someone in Los Angeles. Chuck was out doing something in the barns and I took the call, or tried to take it; but the connection was broken after a moment. Still later, the operator called again and said that a man named Parmenter had wanted to talk to someone here, but that he had been taken sick and was unable to answer the phone at this time." She broke off as if out of breath. "That's it, gentlemen, and it's a weird bit, isn't it?"

"Well, we knew about the call, Mrs. Myles."

"Did he intend to ask us for money? Is that the meaning of the call?"

"I think so," Farrel answered.

"We wouldn't have paid him a cent," she said. "Why would we? He was nothing to us."

"His testimony helped get you your settlement," Farrel pointed out.

"His among others," she agreed. "But all that they did was to tell the truth."

Farrel nodded. He was sweating in the sunlight, the effect of the beer, the warm drive, and a kind of pressure emanating from Mrs. Myles, perhaps. He said then, stumbling a little, "Do you know what is in the corner of the kind of compartment you had on the train?"

"The corner? What do you mean?"

"The last time we were here, Mrs. Myles—"

"Oh, that!" she cried, as if remembering the former conversation suddenly. "I know what you mean. I said that I could visualize the whole thing, the luggage, the window—"

"It was a washbasin," Farrel said.

Saunders stared at him, thinking, Now when in the hell did he figure that out?

"In that particular compartment, at that time," Farrel went on slowly, "there was a basin which let down from the wall and jutted quite a way into the room."

"Well, if so ..."

"You and your husband came hurrying in. You'd had a fight in the lounge car and you wanted to get him out of sight of other people before he grew violent and disgraced himself as he had in New York."

All the color swept from her face. She tucked her hands together in her lap. She seemed to shrivel inside the fluffy white robe.

"Inside the compartment you tried to soothe him. You let down the basin and wet a towel and turned to him, wanting to dab his brow or some such thing, anything to cool him down. He must have grabbed you instantly and thrown you against the basin. He bent you there, beating at you. He cracked your spine."

There was no wind, no sound—Mrs. Myles seemed breathless, frozen there in the sunlight like a lovely statue.

"When you screamed, when your legs wouldn't work, when you fell to the floor in agony, he was stunned; but he must have rung almost at once for the porter. The porter came and looked, and went out to search for a doctor, and on the way he spoke briefly to Parmenter. And then the train ran into Lobo Tunnel and the world crashed." He waited, wondering how long the tension could hold her keyed like that until she cracked. "Isn't that what happened, Mrs. Myles?"

She tried to answer. Her lips moved.

"Wasn't it like that?" Farrel persisted.

"I ... I suppose it was." Her hands gripped the arms of the chair and she pushed herself erect. She stood on her two legs, looking down at them. "I can walk a little. I've been walking ... just a few steps now and then ... for almost a year."

She looked at them with wounded, hurting eyes. She tottered over to the fountain and leaned on its rim and began to scream, "Lotti! Lotti!" Her voice made a ragged squawk in all that stillness, full of lonely fear and desperation. "Lotti!"

Saunders tried to think of something to do. He sensed that if he approached her or touched her she'd go to pieces. There wouldn't be words to the screaming, just an animal noise with years of hatred and fright behind it.

Mrs. Myles began to cry between screams, long harsh sobs that shook her from head to foot. She screamed and cried, and then Lotti came running, doing some yelling of her own. She spat some words at Farrel and Saunders and tried to lead Mrs. Myles towards the house.

Sonya Myles fought her. Words tumbled into the still air, a high shriek—she wouldn't go to the house again, not so long as she lived. She wanted some clothes flung into a bag so that she could leave. She had to get away. She had to escape the madman who would kill her if he saw her on her feet.

Saunders saw movement in the shadowed veranda. Chuck Myles stood there, watching the scene in the patio. He listened to his wife's cries and he looked around, here and there, as if sizing up the place, wondering if it had been worth the trouble. Then, seeing Saunders's gaze on him, he beckoned.

Saunders walked back, watchful, on guard.

"What's that all about?" Myles asked in a drab tone.

"I think she has some idea of leaving this place, Mr. Myles."

Myles looked at some stuff growing by one of the pillars, potted cactus in Spanish ollas. "I don't want her to leave. This is her home. I'll go." He lifted his eyes and stared directly at Saunders. "I never wanted her to know. More than the money ... more than anything ... I wanted her to believe she really had been hurt in that wreck."

"Do you want to make a statement?" Saunders said formally.

Myles thought it over. "I guess I might as well. What does it matter? Shall I begin by telling about the murder of Libby Walker? She saw me pointing a gun at her niece in that desert town ... not that I knew of the relationship at the time. I simply saw that she was a nosy and dangerous woman." In spite of the hearty tan, a good physique, Myles looked sick.

He looked as if those screams out in the patio were tearing into him, drawing blood from hidden wounds deep inside.

"Come into the house," Myles said in his sick voice, "where you can write this down while I tell it to you."

Saunders followed him in, leaving Lotti and Farrel to cope with Mrs. Myles and her hysterics. Myles indicated some chairs, went to a desk for paper and pen. It was a big, homelike room, Saunders thought; he thought of the beautiful new barns and the fat cattle and the kind of life you could live here, alone in your castle in the hills like a Spanish don in a play. A nice life but not worth what Myles had chosen to pay for it.

Mrs. Bellows filled the icebag from the refrigerator and Farrel carried it upstairs to his room. He began to shuck his clothes. It was just a little past six, there was still a little daylight left, but he was going to bed. He was half dead.

He shut his mind to thoughts of the broken woman by the fountain, or that fathead Myles, or Parmenter with his schemes, or poor old Libby Walker. He was indifferent to the fact that the Snowdens were reconciled. He didn't even feel like congratulating himself for having solved the Lobo Tunnel wreck after six years of stalemate. He did, though, feel a little proud for having lasted as long as he had as a section hand.

Now, that was something!

He lay down on his back, stripped, and put the cold icebag on his swollen, aching nose. There was a shock at first, but then it felt good. He should have tried this on that black eye he'd had a while back.

The coldness spread from his nose down into the bones of his face; and then he felt cold all over and started to shiver. He took the icebag off his nose and sat up, rubbed his head.

He stretched out and tried again; but after the initial moments of relief there was a sensation as if his brains were freezing.

He sat on the side of the bed and looked at the icebag in aggrieved disgust. The doctor had promised that the ice would help the pain, remove the swelling and promote healing. He needed comfort desperately because he craved to sleep.

After some thought Farrel went into the bathroom and brought out a drinking glass. He dropped some of the ice from the rubber bag into the glass, added liquor from a bottle in the bottom dresser drawer, and sampled the mixture. He decided that the ice had possibilities after all.

After a while he stretched out and closed his eyes. For just a moment, in a flicker of memory, he recalled Lobo Tunnel as it had been years ago, a black mouth in the side of the hill.

On the floor within reach of his hand was the glass. Wrapped around it, keeping it cool, was Mrs. Bellows's icebag.

THE END

Dolores Hitchens Bibliography
(1907-1973)

Novels:

As by Dolores Hitchens

Jim Sader mysteries
Sleep with Strangers
   (1955)
Sleep with Slander (1960)

Standalone books:
Stairway to an Empty
   Room (1951)
Nets to Catch the Wind
   (1952; reprinted as
   Widows Won't Wait,
   1954)
Terror Lurks in Darkness
   (1953)
Beat Back the Tide (1954;
   abridged as The Fatal
   Flirt, 1954)
Fool's Gold (1958)
The Watcher (1959)
Footsteps in the Night
   (1961)
The Abductor (1962)
The Bank with the
   Bamboo Door (1965)
The Man Who Cried All
   the Way Home (1966)

Postscript to Nightmare
   (1967; UK as Cabin of
   Fear, 1968)
A Collection of Strangers
   (1969; UK as Collection
   of Strangers, 1970)
The Baxter Letters (1971)
In a House Unknown
   (1973)

Plays:
A Cookie for Henry: one-
   act play for six women
   (1941, as Dolores Birk
   Hitchens)

As by Bert and Dolores
   Hitchens

F.O.B. Murder (1955)
One-Way Ticket (1956)
End of the Line (1957)
The Man Who Followed
   Women (1959)
The Grudge (1963)

As by D. B. Olsen

Rachel Murdock mysteries
Cat Saw Murder (1939)
Alarm of Black Cat (1942)

Catspaw for Murder
(1943; reprinted as Cat's
Claw, 1943)
The Cat Wears a Noose
(1944)
Cats Don't Smile (1945)
Cats Don't Need Coffins
(1946)
Cats Have Tall Shadows
(1948)
The Cat Wears a Mask
(1949)
Death Wears Cat's Eyes
(1950)
Cat and Capricorn (1951)
The Cat Walk (1953)
Death Walks on Cat Feet
(1956)

*Prof. A. Pennyfeather
mysteries*
Shroud for the Bride
(1945; reprinted as Bring
the Bride a Shroud,
1945)
Gallows for the Groom
(1947)
Devious Design (1948)
Something About
Midnight (1950)
Love Me in Death (1951)
Enrollment Cancelled
(1952; reprinted as Dead
Babes in the Wood,
1954)

*Lt. Stephen Mayhew
mysteries*
The Clue in the Clay
(1938)
Death Cuts a Silhouette
(1939)

As by Dolan Birkley

Blue Geranium (1944)
The Unloved (1965)

As by Noel Burke
Shivering Bough (1942)

Short Stories/
Magazine Novels:

Stairway to an Empty
Room (*Collier's*, Mar
31, Apr 7, Apr 14, Apr
21, Apr 28 1951)
Strip for Murder (*Mercury
Mystery Magazine*, Oct
1958)
The Watcher
(*Cosmopolitan*, May
1959)
Footsteps in the Dark
(*Cosmopolitan*, Feb
1961)
Abductor! Abductor!
Abductor!
(*Cosmopolitan*, July
1961)

The Unloved (*Redbook,*
   Oct 1965)
If You See This Woman
   (*Ellery Queen's Mystery
   Magazine,* Jan 1966)
Postscript to Nightmare
   (*Cosmopolitan,* June
   1967)

A Collection of Strangers
   (*Redbook*, Sept 1969)
The Baxter Letters (*Star
   Weekly,* June 26 1971)
Blueprint for Murder
   (*Ellery Queen's Mystery
   Magazine*, Aug 1973)

Julia Clara Catherine Maria Dolores Robins Norton Birk Olsen Hitchens, better known to mystery fans as Dolores Hitchens, was born December 25, 1907 in San Antonio, Texas. She married Beverley S. Olsen, a radio operator on a merchant vessel, around 1934. Beginning in 1938, Dolores wrote a series of mysteries as

D. B. Olsen. It is not known whether she divorced Olsen or was widowed, but she was re-married to Hubert A. Hitchens by the early 1940s. After her marriage to Bert—who was a railway detective—they collaborated on a series of five railroad mysteries from 1957 to 1964. Dolores also wrote an excellent group of standalone mysteries, including *Fool's Gold* which was filmed by Jean-Luc Godard as *Band of Outsiders* in 1964, as well as the critically applauded *Sleep With Strangers* and *Sleep With Slander*. She passed away on August 1, 1973 in Orange County, California, followed by Hubert in Riverside County in 1979.

Black Gat Books

Black Gat Books is a new line of mass market paperbacks introduced in 2015 by Stark House Press. New titles appear every three months, featuring the best in crime fiction reprints. Each book is sized to 4.25" x 7", just like they used to be. Collect them all!

1 Haven for the Damned
by Harry Whittington
978-1-933586-75-5, $9.99

2 Eddie's World
by Charlie Stella
978-1-933586-76-2, $9.99

3 Stranger at Home
by Leigh Brackett writing as
George Sanders
978-1-933586-78-6, $9.99

4 The Persian Cat
by John Flagg
978-1933586-90-8, $9.99

5 Only the Wicked
by Gary Phillips
978-1-933586-93-9, $9.99

6 Felony Tank
by Malcolm Braly
978-1-933586-91-5, $9.99

7 The Girl on the Bestseller List
by Vin Packer
978-1-933586-98-4, $9.99

8 She Got What She Wanted
by Orrie Hitt
978-1-944520-04-5, $9.99

9 The Woman on the Roof
by Helen Nielsen
978-1-944520-13-7, $9.99

10 Angel's Flight
by Lou Cameron
978-1-944520-18-2, $9.99

11 The Affair of Lady
Westcott's Lost Ruby /
The Case of the Unseen Assassin
by Gary Lovisi
978-1-944520-22-9, $9.99

12 The Last Notch
by Arnold Hano
978-1-944520-31-1, $9.99

13 Never Say No to a Killer
by Clifton Adams
978-1-944520-36-6, $9.99

14 The Men from the Boys
by Ed Lacy
978-1-944520-46-5 $9.99

15 Frenzy of Evil
by Henry Kane
978-1-944520-53-3 $9.99

16 You'll Get Yours
by William Ard
978-1-944520-54-0 $9.99

Stark House Press

1315 H Street, Eureka, CA 95501   707-498-3135
griffinskye3@sbcglobal.net   www.starkhousepress.com

Available from your local bookstore or direct from the publisher.

Manufactured by Amazon.ca
Bolton, ON